midnight sun

a McKenna chronicle

elizabeth miller

midnight sun

a McKenna chronicle

Midnight Sun, a McKenna Chronicle

Cover Art by Najla Qamber Designs

Editing by Lauren McKellar

Synopsis: When sheltered journalist Charlise "Charlie" Carter first met the brooding and enigmatic presidential hopeful Colin McKenna, it ignited a passionate affair that set both their lives racing in a new, yet terrifying direction. Hunted by her past, Charlie was forced to face her fears and the stalker who could have ruined the future she barely hoped to have. Determined to lay history to rest, she overcame those obstacles to claim her spot next to the influential man she loves.

Now, with the presidential campaign behind them, Colin and Charlie have it all. Power, passion and a love so true nothing could come between them. With the grandeur of the wedding approaching, Charlie is swallowed by the enormity of becoming American royalty. She knows living in the White House, with all its scrutiny, won't be easy, but she's more secure with herself and with Colin.

Just when everything settles into a new normal, and it appears nothing can eclipse their bond, the unthinkable happens. Colin's worst nightmare is brought to life. He must race to save the one woman who brought order to his world and a happiness he never thought possible. With history seeming to repeat itself, Colin fights to hold them together and prepare for a new life that could possibly be the end of Charlie's. Midnight Sun is a story of redemption and a bond so strong, it rises above pure evil.

ACKNOWLEDGEMENTS

Some big THANK YOUs I have to shout out as the McKenna Chronicles come to a close. When Midnight was first released, I knew nothing about publishing. I was so lost and a few people took the time to help a fledgling author find her way. Lauren McKellar – you make me a better writer, you're an amazing editor and a bright star on a dark night. Najla Qamber – such an incredible talent, it's been so fun working with you on all things Midnight. Kate Stewart – your kindness and guidance during a time when I was drowning in a churning sea remains with me every day. Hugs to you all, and I hope one day I'll get to give it in person. To my blogger friends, thank you, thank you, thank you for every kind word, your encouragement, and for your voice. Lovely readers, I feel the love for Charlie and Colin, I feel it and I thank you for adoring them as much as I do. Truly, every post 'like', every comment, every review is so important to me and I don't take them for granted. Without you, these stories would stay in my head. Big hugs, and so many thanks!!! Bryan, Jackson and Sean, who have sacrificed their wife and mother during evenings and weekends so that I may live my dream and see it to fruition—with love and thanks and hugs and sloppy kisses. Everyone who has played a part in this series, shared their thoughts, critiques and encouragement, I love you to pieces.

Xoxo -EM

PROLOUGE

November—Election Day

Colin

TWENTY YEARS.

Half of my life spent in preparation for this day.

Tension tightens my shoulders. Working non-stop for the last month, maybe even the last twelve, has pushed me to the breaking point. Nerves I rarely feel simmer below the surface of my skin on the verge of erupting.

Charlie manages to tame them.

And she knows inherently that I need her to.

She taunts me, even as the bright lights of a television crew document each minute we wait. It's in the exaggerated sway of her hips as she walks away from me. Round, luscious hips—accentuated by the belt cinching her waist—beg for my hands. I know she's provoking me when she turns to look over her shoulder with lowered lashes and parted lips, lips that spread into the same lazy smile she dons after I make her come. It pulls me out of the polls, out of my head, and into the suite where we're sequestered until the outcome is announced.

I rub my chest as my heart constricts. I love this woman. And I adore her even more as she stops at the buffet table to pick through the fruit tray. I've become surprisingly enamored with strawberries and bananas, especially when they're in her mouth.

A smile finally tugs at the corner of my lips, and I look around. Surrounded by integral staffers that have worked their fingers raw, I wait. My sister and Brett and my parents are here, proud and full of hope. Evan with his arms crossed and lips moving as if counting the votes himself. Fitz and Kyle: this is either the end of the road or the beginning of a new one. Parker and his wife: he'll stand beside me either way. We'll lead together or not at all. Win or lose. Everything has led to this moment—one that will decide if we are good enough—if *I* am good enough.

All eyes spring to the door, and most divert quickly when Ella walks in. Her back is straight with an air of superiority that hasn't endeared her to many. Following close behind are her parents. John nods, but doesn't stop until he's at the bar in the corner, pouring three inches of bourbon in a tumbler. Joan makes her way to the other side of the room with a long white box tucked under her arm. Stopping next to Charlie, she draws her from her fruit and into a one-sided conversation. Charlie tips her head as a blush blossoms on her chest, and she accepts Joan's offering.

Removing the lid has her eyes go wide. She pales, and tension returns to my shoulders tenfold. My pulse takes off and my feet act on automatic start, but I'm halfway to her when she recovers. A *thank you* is mimed from her mouth, before she steps back and slips into the bedroom. I'm right behind her, but Joan catches me on the fly.

"Colin, dear." Taking my cheeks in hand, she pouts. "This day has been a long time coming. I'll forever wish my daughter was here to see you take this next step, but I'm thrilled you've found someone . . ." she smiles and winks, ". . . so similar. It warms my heart."

And she chills mine into a frosted acknowledgement. Nodding, I swallow past her trip down memory lane. "Excuse me."

Two seconds later, I'm closing the door on her nonsense and struck speechless by the woman before me. Charlie. My breath lodges in my throat. Her beauty is not only in her stature as she stands tall, shoulders back, red hair flaming in waves halfway to the delicious curve of her ass. But in her voice and how she induces a smile with kind words or her wit, it's in her honesty and compassion. An instinctive, almost predatory need to protect her lives within me, and it surges forward now. I'll crush anyone who even thinks about hurting her.

"Baby?" She turns, arms wrapped around her midsection. "What's wrong?"

Shaking her head, she says, "Nothing you need to worry about."

I approach and stop only when we're hip to hip. The feel of her under my fingers is enough to ease the tight ache across my chest. She tips her head back and eases her hands around my neck.

"What'd Joan say?" I ask, and watch her for any signs of distress.

"A very kind congratulations on my impending move into the White House."

I raise my eyebrow. "And?"

Charlie sighs, her posture slumping so more of her weight is held in my palms. "I didn't care for the gesture that went with it. Roses." She shudders. "They remind me of Shane and I hate it."

"Come here," I murmur, but she's already snuggling against me. "I'll take care of everything. You won't have to see them or him. He'll never hurt you again."

Flashes of a hot July night in Texas bombard my already overloaded mind. Roberts with a gun, crashing into Charlie, and the burn of the bullet as it entered and punctured my lung. But it's the repeated abuse she endured that's never far from my thoughts. He stole her innocence at fourteen, and then returned years later to take her life. My arms tighten around her. Too many questions remain unanswered to cross Shane Roberts off of my list of things to do when the campaign is over.

"My hero." She licks and sucks her way up my neck and chin, and suddenly I'm not thinking about flowers or lunatics. Charlie's doing her damnedest to keep me in the present. She tugs my hair until our mouths touch, and then her teeth take hold of my bottom lip. *Christ.*

I growl and stick my tongue in her mouth. She giggles and humors me with a soul-searching kiss. I'm hungry for more than her whimper; I want to own every cell of her being, every breath, every plea, and offer the same in return. My fingers run through her silk curls and then I grab a handful, tugging until her neck is exposed. I love her response. A throaty moan, tightening grip, and my mind blurs into a lifetime of Charlie. I grind into her until she won't remember anything but me. Then she pushes away, more beautiful now than when we walked in—swollen lips and the devil in her eyes.

"You'll be the death of me, woman. Don't look at me like that or I'll forget the thirty people in the other room and take you against the wall."

Her damn answer is to turn, look over her shoulder, and bat her black lashes. I stalk after her, smiling through her laugh as we open the door to Election Day anxiety.

Twenty years.

Televisions play on high volume, red and blue waging war on screen. Numbers volley, electoral votes assigned, and with each one my pulse races. Energy hums beneath my skin as I repeat both speeches, one a consignment that Bryce did it better than me. The other will see us to the steps of the Capitol on Inauguration Day.

I sit and then stand, and pace in between. Charlie watches from the sidelines, always with a reassuring smile that takes mine from plastic to real. I feel the weight of her eyes on me wherever I am, with whomever I'm speaking to. Sometimes it's her hand on my lower back, and the rigid line of my spine relaxes against her.

"No regrets," she whispers, when California goes blue.

I swallow a lump, but when I turn to her I'm immediately centered. One look and I know—I've done everything right. Because it was my way, my truth, and I stood with integrity in front of this country. "No regrets," I murmur into her temple, and then press my lips there to take her in. She smells like me, with a hint of vanilla and the kind of comfort found in the most cherished possessions. *Mine*.

Twenty years.

And so it goes for hours until the instant it's over.

The room falls to silence, yet my breath rushes into the space where thoughts should be made. I'm numb. CCNB's Carlyle Anderson calls it, and everyone spins in my direction as I sink into incredulity.

I fold over, hands on knees and heart pounding in my throat.

Twenty years.

So much time to work toward one goal, one finish line that would determine the course of my life when it ended.

"Baby." Charlie falls to the floor to cradle my face. Eye to eye, I watch my future play out in her beauty. She's everything I need.

But I have more than I ever thought possible.

I bury my head in her neck as I pick her up until her feet dangle above the floor. It's possible my grip is too hard, but I need her. I need this silent moment to make way for the many loud ones to follow. The tight hold she has on my hair grounds me to a new reality.

It's over.

She tugs hard enough that I peel away to place us forehead to forehead. Her breath, cooled by a mint, meets mine in heavy puffs. I find her eyes, so green I get lost in the forest.

Twenty years. The grueling pace and tough decisions are drilled into clarity with three words. Words made all the sweeter by her sultry voice.

"Congratulations, Mr. President."

ONE

Colin - December

SHANE ROBERTS. THERE IS no one I despise more. Not because the wound in my shoulder aches each night, a reminder of the ill-fated Fourth of July celebration that narrowed my world to a bullet. But because what he did to Charlie when she was fourteen is heinous.

Traveling the eleven hundred miles to confront her attacker was easy. Waiting for the truth was not. The authorities have been held at an arm's length away due to Roberts's mental health issue. An apparent psychiatric break and suicide attempt just prior to his arraignment landed him in the Texas State Institution for the Criminally Insane. Answers have been slow to come—until now.

Today brings me to the face of evil. Roberts' eyes are pitched to black in the poorly lit room. The singular lamp hanging from the ceiling casts a grim shadow along his hollowed out cheeks. A small smirk lifts the corner of his mouth as he tips the chair back on its hind legs. Palms, laid flat on the table, hold him steady, along with the chains shackling his wrists and ankles together. *Insane my ass*. This man is calculating. I'd bet my left arm he's planning a plea deal for freedom in ten years or less.

The legal system may be slow to find retribution, but I am not. Hatred such as I have never felt before simmers in the pit of my stomach, begging for release. The possessive love I have for Charlie demands nothing less.

Fitz's whisper is meant only for me. The two other Secret Service agents stand behind us, flanking the door. "Don't get your hands dirty with this filth," he says. I nod, but promise nothing.

"Man, I feel like a celebrity. Got the new Pres-e-dent coming to visit little ol' me," Roberts says in a guttural drawl. "How's my girl? Charlie's hot, ain't she?"

A growl rips from my throat. "Watch your mouth. You don't have the right to speak of her, ever."

He laughs, and Fitz takes a step forward.

Raising my hand stops them both. "You're walking a fine line, Roberts. I'll ask the questions, and as long as you answer them we won't have a problem. Do you understand me?"

The smirk is back. "I ain't afraid. I know who you are. You're the white knight—the face of justice. You can't make me talk. You can't do anything or it'll bring down your fancy house of cards."

In a second I stand over him. His chair loses its precarious perch at my insistence, and the resounding thud of his skull as it hits the cement wall bolsters my resolve. Wrenching my fist in his shirt, I pull him close. "Let me be clear. I am Colin McKenna, elected as the forty-sixth president of the United States of America—the most powerful man in the world," I ground out between my teeth. "I can make you talk."

The force of my release is punctuated by the bounce of his head for a second time. I'm not playing. Not where Charlie is concerned. Not with him.

"Are we on the same page, Roberts?"

He rolls his shoulders and neck. That damnable lift of his lip has yet to be erased, and for a minute I see what Charlie did all those years ago. Fury clenches my fist.

"Her tight little cunt loved my co—"

There is little time between the movement of his mouth and my hand making contact with it. I hit him with so much force blood paints the once white wall. All of the anger living inside of me since I read Charlie's health records is released—freed upon the bastard who stole her innocence and so much more. A resounding roar escapes my throat when I connect again, this time splitting my knuckles on his cheek bone. His scream is driven into a grunt as I light into him. One side and then the other, until Fitz pulls me away, holding my upper arms back in a vice grip.

"Anymore and he won't be able to talk," he says loud enough so I can hear him above my jagged breath.

Jerking out of his hands, I straighten my jacket but never take my eyes off of Roberts. I've made a mess of his face, a cracked lip and cheek, but it's a sight better than what I walked into five minutes ago. "You feel me now? Know where I'm coming from, you slimy bastard?" I drag in a lungful of air, not expecting more than the moan he returns. "Good. Tell me what I need, and I'll walk out the door. But so help me . . ." I lunge forward to grab his collar, "if you so much as think her name again I will fucking end you."

Roberts puffs out a breath, sputtering through blood-tinged saliva. "You're crazy . . ."

I smile and perch my hip on the table in front of him. The hanging lamp swaying above my head drives him from manic shadow into raw truth—he can't hide from me. "I'm protecting what's mine. Let's get started so I can get on with my life." Staring at his swelling eye for any signs of a lie, I ask the one question that's been burning a hole in my gut for the last five months. "Who helped you?"

There's no way he could have learned the minute details of my schedule without insider knowledge. This is a hard truth that gripped me after Arkansas and the bloodied room he created. With the election behind me, it's time to make good on the vow I made to end this once and for all.

Because I know it's not over.

Someone used Roberts as a means to an end.

And I won't let it happen again. Not to my Charlie.

He coughs and then moans, "No one, man. It was just me . . ."

My fingers circle his throat and squeeze. "Wrong answer. Try again."

Fumbling against his chains, he tries to grip my wrist. "I can't . . ." I loosen my hold, and he takes a gulp of air. "I don't know. You have to believe me. I don't know who it was. They called or left stuff for me at hotels."

"What stuff?" I press my thumb against his windpipe, and his mouth falls open as if seeking oxygen. "Tell me."

"Money. Details. You know, like where you'd be, or instructions to take pictures. It had everything I needed to know. Where you were staying, when you would arrive, if Char . . . if she would be with you."

"Go on."

"That's it. I don't know anything else."

"I think you do."

A cry breaks from his broken mouth. "I swear. They didn't tell me anything. Just what to do."

"Who's *they*?"

"I don't know! No names were exchanged. She always told . . ."

Anger tightens my hold. "She?"

"Fuck," he blusters as his face turns purple.

"Sir?" Fitz calls, but I wave him off.

"Who is *she*?" I demand.

"I don't know. Sometimes a dude would call, or the lady. She was a real bitch, but I never met her. None of them. I have no clue who they are."

My gaze is torn from his to the blood-splattered wall. Awareness claws through my chest, instincts shouting that it's someone close. Close to the campaign.

Close to me.

John? *Ella?* Goddamn it! Anger, so much unadulterated fury rolls up my spine and into my hand that clenches until the whites of Shane's eyes bulge through.

"Why'd you do it?" It's not possible to believe he thought he'd get away with this.

I loosen enough for him to sputter, "What else was I doing? She offered me money. A lot of it. Said I could plead out. I'd spend a few years in the cell, but when I got let go I'd have more money than I could make in my whole life. Why not?"

"You make me sick," I say, and let the rage take over. I squeeze. For Charlie, for her tears and the nightmares, for the innocence she lost because of this monster, and for all of the other girls he ruined. I squeeze until he's red and then purple, and his fingers dig into my skin as if they're begging for mercy. Mercy I don't have. Not for him.

"Enough, sir," Fitz says in my ear. "He's not worth it."

I want my own monster to let loose and take him out of this world, but Fitz is right. As deplorable as he is, Roberts will pay for his crimes against us by spending the rest of his life in prison.

Slowly, my grip loosens, and the tension seeps from my limbs. "You're not worth the fire they'll burn your dead carcass with."

As soon as I take my hand from his throat he slumps in the chair, gasping. On my way out, I pause by the door and nod to the nameless agents who will make this meeting disappear, a perk of my new position. "Gentlemen."

To Roberts, I turn and throw a similar smirk to the one he started this conversation with. "Oh, and I forgot to share some of the better news I've learned today." I relish the fear peeking from his barely-there pupils. "These men are here to assist in your transportation to the State Penitentiary. It seems my newfound job may have more benefits than I'd anticipated." I chuckle over his groaned *that's not fair.* "Expediting the outcome of your psychiatric review is one. Imagine my joy when I learned it said you're completely sound to stand trial. Another?" My grin reaches in and pulls out all the animosity I have toward this animal. "Your new roommate is BoBo Dennies, arrested for his overly expressive nature toward young men."

Roberts's sputtered cry follows me out. Shadows breach the waning evening light, casting streaks of hope against walls that see very little of it, and I'm struck by just how gone I am. I'm a made man, and not in the sense most would understand. Passing through a nursing station protected by bullet-proof-glass, my feelings are there for everyone to see on the cover of *News Today*. Tucked into a magazine rack is Charlie and me, my thumb tipping her chin up. She's doe-eyed and smiling. But it's the softened expression blurring my features that give me away. More often than not, when photographed I have the hard lines befitting a president burrowed in my brow and strengthening my jaw. Not in this picture, and never with Charlie. My besotted grin clearly shouts a stronger headline than the one type-faced in blue.

Everything I worked to gain during the last twenty years rests in the balance of her hands. I want to sink into her drowning softness and never recover. With Charlie, strong-willed and fierce by my side, I'm invincible.

Along with that comes terror. If I know it, others see it. They see it in print around the world: I'm careful with a treasure I have only recently discovered. Charlie is my weak link, and someone has already used it against me.

As I wrap Fitz's proffered bandage around my knuckles, I contemplate life before her and then after. My world was methodical and quiet. I was driven to one end, and I used people to get there—men for their power and women for sex. And then she came with an innocence that belied her trouble-filled childhood. She's pure and good and everything I need to be a better man. Now, amidst the order I've created is a swirl of perfect red-haired chaos. I prefer the after—definitely the after.

The ammonia-drenched hospital sanitation cannot erase Charlie's sweet scent that remains buried within me. I can conjure her smile, and her embrace beckons me home. Slipping my phone from my breast pocket, I send her a quick text.

I'm coming to you now, love.

My heart rate rushes forward, and I wish the next four hours would lapse without time. Her reply is almost immediate.

I'll be waiting, hot pants.

It triggers a genuine smile and is almost enough to relax my shoulders. Almost.

She's in D.C., sheltered as much as I can make happen, given her propensity for freedom and my need to protect her. Sommerton and Sawyer are with her during every waking moment. Someone is out to ruin us, but I won't stop until they're sitting side-by-side with Roberts. I can't let this reach her again. The only chance I have is to prove who the hell *they* are.

We're down to ground zero.

It's us or them.

Two

Charlie

"FOXTAIL IS SECURE. REPEAT, Foxtail is secure."

I hide a giggle behind my hand. Kyle smiles and releases his hold on the small microphone hidden in his sleeve. "Something funny, boss-lady?" he asks, while falling in line behind me, a place he's been more often than not during the last six months.

After the election I accused him of creating my code name, but he assures me the government's communication agency is to blame. I'll go down in history as Foxtail to Colin's Firestorm. I laugh again. Our world turned spy movie.

"Just the direction of my life," I say, and then stop talking and walking, because I'm overcome by lace and tulle and silk. So much silk. I'd groan if I wasn't sure that Therese "The Bulldog" Wainright would have my hide, and then she'd have me in exactly thirty-two yards of luxury. How one person is expected to carry around so much material for more than eight hours is beyond me. But it's what America wants.

What *they* want. My heart stutters as I stare at the beautiful yet over-the-top creation—made just for me. It's on display in the center of the suite, surrounded by twelve-foot red brick walls and curtained windows spanning from floor to ceiling. A Dupont Circle loft rented for the top-secret design and each subsequent fitting of my wedding dress. *Talk about a spy game.*

On more than one occasion I've considered eloping. Running away to the private Florida Island we visited just after the election gets more appealing as the big day draws near. Colin and I retreated there with friends to celebrate his win, my thirtieth birthday, and to relax before he dove back into work. Now, he's busy with his transition team, designating government personnel, agency heads, and selecting new cabinet positions.

His schedule has become so demanding it drew him away to California and Texas during the last forty-eight hours. I tremble and wrap my arms around my stomach. These nerves have nothing to do with lace and tulle, but Shane Roberts. I don't like Colin being in the same state as that bastard.

Kyle misunderstands my sudden reserve and nudges me forward. "Don't be afraid. I'll save you if it attacks."

I glance at the beast before me. "You'll shoot it?"

"Promise." He grins. "I'm good with a gun."

"Wish me luck," I say, just as Ali pops out from the kitchen, the door hidden behind the silk-laden mannequin.

"Hey, gorgeous. Ready to get married?" She leaps around the piles of fabric and grabs me for a hug.

I sink into her embrace and squeeze. "You made it." My relief that the hospital accommodated a midday break from her shift is evident when I won't let her go.

She laughs. "No time for freaking out, Charlie-girl." Peeling out of my embrace, she smiles, and her beauty blinds me.

"I'm not, really."

Grabbing my shoulders, she gives me a onceover. "You are. I can see it in your ginormous bug eyes."

I roll them for her benefit. "Thanks. You're so reassuring."

"Glad I could put you at ease. What maid-of-honor duties do I have but to look fabulous in my dress and to calm your nerves?"

I point to the silk concoction. "Your job might be harder than you think."

"You don't like it?"

"It's beautiful."

"But?"

I shake my head. "Nothing . . ."

Taking my hand, she pulls me around the faux Charlie, a dummy the designer had made exactly to my specifications for wedding-dress alterations. "Don't *nothing* me. Just because everyone, and I do mean every man, woman, child, and their grandmother's sister's brother, has an opinion about this day, more importantly, you do too. You only get one crack at it, *foxy*." Yanking at my high ponytail, Ali laughs, really laughs and I can't help but join in. In seconds we're doubled over with tears streaming from our eyes in the best stress-relief known to man.

"Excuse me, ladies." We bolt upright. "Save the hysterics for another time," Therese barks, while rounding on us with her steely stare. "Shoulders back, Ms. Carter." In a second, we're both ramrod straight. I catch Kyle's eye; his telltale smirk lifts a corner of his mouth.

Therese is most definitely running the show. Just as she transformed me into Charlise, she has taken the wedding into the next millennium—with a dash of nostalgia, because my style lends to vintage chic. She glides over to brush a kiss on each of Ali's cheeks. Turning to me, she does the same.

"You both look lovely." But she hesitates when her gaze narrows in on the dark circles under my eyes. "What have you done?" Therese clicks her tongue and tips my chin down for closer inspection.

"I haven't slept well the last couple of nights."

"The President won't have time to coddle a lonely wife. You need to get used to an empty bed." I catch her puckered lips the moment my eyes roll, and her tart retort is just as sour. "Perfection is expected, Ms. Carter. This wedding is more than you. The public is very connected with this administration because of your fancy blogs and open conversation on live television. You and the President have allowed them in and with that, you risk disappointing those that brought him to the pinnacle of his career."

Tugging on her Pepto-Bismol pink jacket, she ensures I sense her distaste for my course of action. Asking for public participation in wedding planning through social media was a huge coup during the campaign, but now it's as if Colin and I are lost in the Grand Canyon.

Nodding, I say, "I understand."

"I hope you do."

Her sigh is lost in a rush of wind when Mom, Gram, Colleen, and Ryanne hurry through the door. Gram gets to me first. I love her wink when she uses her hip to push Therese away.

"Hi, beautiful girl." She beams. Rosy cheeks from the stiff December air have never looked better on anyone. Fully recovered from her cardiac scare last summer, she's healthy and vibrant. "I just bought out every shop on Connecticut Street. Your grandfather may need oxygen when he gets the bill."

I squeeze her close once more, but my chuckle is muffled by the next round of hugs, first Mom and then down the line to everyone in the family who wants a preview of my dress.

"Ready for the wedding of the century?" Ryanne asks, and then glances at the show-stopper in the middle of the loft.

The flush crawling up my chest is interrupted when Victoria Wu, the most sought after designer in America, bursts in from her work station in the back bedroom.

"My schedule is tight today. Let's get Charlie into the gown for a final fitting."

There goes my heart, tripping into a new beat. *I'm getting married.* I'm three days away from marrying the soon-to-be leader of the free world. Colin McKenna, Mr. President. *Holy cow. Mrs. First Lady, Foxtail, Charlise*. The room starts to spin.

"Breathe." Ali nudges my ribs.

I gasp. "Yes. The dress. Sure. Can you help me?"

In actuality it takes everyone, sans Kyle, who steps outside for privacy purposes, to get me buttoned into a dream. Cinderella couldn't have done better. Taking my hand, Victoria leads me to a podium in the center of the makeshift fitting room and everyone moves behind my silhouette. As I lift my head and take in the mirrored vision before me, I feel worthy of Colin and America's desire for a princess on his arm.

Excited chatter falls to silence as everyone stares. Tears rush to my eyes. For the first time amongst all the chaos called wedding planning, I feel like a bride. Delicate lace covers the strapless ball-gown and comes up high on my chest, only to transition into the lightest wrist-length sleeves. Tulle billows out the skirt, the poof accentuated by my nipped-in waist belted and held tight with a vintage blue and white diamond broach to match my engagement ring. Laid out behind me, the train seems miles long. Sparks of light glitter from gems as if it were a field of snow on a sunny winter day.

Emotion clogs my throat. I try to hold it back with one hand over my mouth, while the other sweeps to my stomach and the pit of emptiness that will always be in my womb. I squeeze back the waterworks threatening to flow.

Mom rushes up and clenches my fingers between hers. "Hey, what are you thinking?"

I stare at her hands, lined from living. Years spent in the sun, gardening and with her children, playing, laughing, *loving*. My chest rises with a deep breath, constricted by the enormity of the next few days and the rest of my life.

My whisper is meant only for her. "I want to give Colin everything he ever hoped for, more than he could dream of, and to be enough to keep him satisfied every day of his life."

Mom shakes her head. "Oh, Charlie-girl. You are all of these things to him already. Saying vows will only strengthen the bond that has formed between you."

I nod. Yet one shadow falls over my beautiful life. "I know," I say, instead of going down that darkened path. Now is not the time. "I do know this." I smile, and she helps me wipe away a lone tear streaking down my cheek.

Mom tilts her head and looks at me, really looks at me. It's as if she can read my mind and all of my fears. "You are his everything,

Charlie. There isn't anything you can't give him. You *will* have a family one day. The two of you will be the most loving, generous parents. I won't have you believe anything less."

I cough out a cry and grab her into a fierce hug. "I want to be just like you: the perfect mother and the best teacher." Ali and Gram squeeze in, wrapping their arms around us, and we rock together for a long moment. The Carter women—strong and resilient.

"I hate to interrupt, but we're on a timeline." Victoria taps her watch and breaks up the love fest just in time for Therese to run through a list of final wedding day preparations.

My family, which in my mind already includes Colleen and Ryanne, stands to the side as Victoria and her assistant smooth, pin, and tuck. I'm overwhelmed by the length of my to-do list, and none of it is earth-shattering. Therese snaps off makeup, hair, programs, rehearsal, seating, menu, rings. *Rings!*

Amongst all of the other mundane tasks, I almost forgot the most important. Colin's wedding band. My appointment at Carys Jewelers immediately follows this fitting. Everything else swims around in my head until I'm whisked away, stripped, and redressed in my designer jeans. Sooner than I think is reasonable, Ali heads back to the hospital to complete her shift, and I've said goodbye to everyone clearly labeled Charlie's team. I'm exhausted ten minutes later when I meet Kyle at the door to the building.

"Too much Therese for one day?" he asks.

"You could say that." The cold air bites at my lungs, but it also clears my head. "Do you mind if we walk the few blocks to the jeweler?"

"Whatever you need."

Opposite of Kyle, dark where he is light, silent where he is brash, Sawyer takes up the rear. Kyle ensures the path ahead is unobstructed. I hate that he either walks before or after me. Sometimes I just need him to be a friend, not my bodyguard, but I've come to terms with the safety measures put in place. I'd never deny Colin that reassurance. Not ever again.

Washington during the holidays is magical. The cold concrete is warmed by the subtle glow of white lights, strung from trees along the sidewalks. Lit day and night, there is no escaping their good cheer. The atmosphere is charged with a subtle vibrancy as people prepare for New Year celebrations that will overtake us in just a few days.

I'd like to tuck my chin into my scarf to steer clear of the wind howling down the street, but that would be bad press. As Colin is so good at relating to people, it's something I've come to master as well. For those knowing smiles, or half-waves, the I-know-her-but-I'm-not-sure-if-I-should-say-something nods, I always respond in kind. I can no longer hide in the back of a room, listening for the truth. I'm the center of attention, and I've learned to enjoy the connection it brings.

"What's got that brain of yours on a countdown to explosion today?" Kyle asks, falling in line next to my shoulder.

I can't help but smile. "Hey, at least I'm not running. You're not dressed for it," I say, glancing at his shiny black shoes.

"There is that miracle. But I'll save my thanks until you're behind a closed door."

"Ha! You love a challenge. Before we get into that, let's talk about you for a while, shall we?"

"What?" A grin pops out, deepening his dimple.

"Have you spoken with Faith about the wedding and your plus-one?"

The smile gets even bigger and he tips his head down as he kicks a stick. "I have . . ."

"And?" I adore the color as it rises on his cheeks. I'm not the only one who blushes over love. This strong, calculating, tough-as-nails yet sweet-as-pie Secret Service agent fell head over heels for a girl while we were in Florida.

"I'm in for two."

His color darkens at my squeal of delight. "This is one adjustment to the seating chart I'll be happy to approve."

I glance both ways to get my bearings at the corner of R and Connecticut, and then my heart stumbles. I was not expecting this.

THREE

KYLE CLOSES THE DISTANCE between us when my gasp breaches the din of post-holiday shoppers.

"What's up, Charlie?" I sense he's scanning the crowd from behind his sunglasses. I know he finds his target as he tears them off.

Wide-eyed and staring, I can't look away from Alex Miller. He stands just outside of a coffee house twenty yards away, a petite blonde woman leaning up to whisper in his ear. Her long hair is loose and moves in time with the whipping wind. I don't need to see her face to know who she is. *Ella Montgomery.*

Months ago, seeing the two of them not twenty-feet away would have brought fear knocking at my door. Not anymore. I won't let them wreak havoc on my psyche. With my lip lifted in a snarl as the vile couple hovers close to the doorway, I mumble, "I didn't realize how dirty the streets are this time of year."

The bitter tang of brewing coffee scented in the air morphs into bad blood the instant Alex spots me. From relaxed reticence, he shifts his shoulders and draws up to full height. The subtle move to his posture sharpens his eyes. They narrow in and pin me to the sidewalk. Sawyer rushes forward, and Kyle calls my name at the same time as Alex begins to speak. I'm struck by the movement of his mouth as he says, "Abby."

Holy shit. An urgent chill rolls down my spine and I freeze.

"Come with me." Kyle's command is lost as Alex plays on repeat. The word falls off his tongue once more as Ella drags him into the coffee house. His eyes never leave mine.

"Charlie!" Kyle steps up his game and propels me into the hub of lunchtime pedestrian traffic, in the opposite direction from the latest turn of events. The blast of a car horn breaks my trance, and it is then I feel the heavy rise and fall of my chest.

"Move it, Carter." Kyle's all business, his hand on my shoulder urging me to pick up the pace.

Glancing behind to the coffee shop, I catch Sawyer stepping inside the door to confine the couple. The sharp tap of his head as it bobs up and down speaks of a good tit-for-tat.

"What the hell was that about?" I mumble, more to myself than anyone else, but Kyle responds.

"Stay away from that maniac, Charlie. He's not stable."

I slip from his grip and yank on his arm to slow him down. "How do you know?"

He stops and shakes his head. Face to face, I find the crisp calculation that borders his pupils when he's in stealth mode. "Don't ask me that. Just trust me."

"Kyle, that's not fair."

"Fuck," he snaps. "Keep walking." A hand to my back prompts my surge forward, and with a sigh, he begins. "I did some digging. When I heard that Alex started popping up where you were, I took a deeper dive into his past."

I stop again, wide-eyed. "What did you find?"

He swings around and we're confronted by a truth only a few people know. The rigid set of his jaw tells me everything. His nod only confirms it. "I pieced together the affair and the kid—none of which screams insane to me—cruel, but not crazy. The part that does, Charlie?" His tone grabs my attention when my gaze blurs into the distance. "The thing that tells me Alex is over the edge of reason is his obsession with a ghost."

"Abby . . ." Needles of knowledge prick my skin. *Alex Miller is dangerous*. The places I've bumped into him, unintended on my part but maybe more premeditated on his, erupt from memory: Blake's party, the hotel pool, the debate, the store last summer when he approached from behind. But more frightening than all of those is that he may have been following me elsewhere and I'd have had no idea. My pulse hammers in my throat.

"Yeah, Abby." Kyle sighs again and looks around the street. "Alex's predatory stare when he sees you, and the fact that *you look like her* . . ." Shaking his head, he pulls me closer so I can't help but close out everything but him. "Charlie, all of this tells me he isn't playing with a full deck. So do me a favor? When we see him on a street corner, let's move the other way. Fast. And if I'm not with you? Run."

"You're scaring me," I whisper, trying to keep my ragged breath under control. The heated puffs of it breach the bitter cold around us.

"Maybe I'm trying to. At least until I figure the whole thing out." Tipping his head down and leveling me with his piercing stare is enough to drive home his point.

Wrapping my arms across my midsection, I shiver with relief when Sawyer pulls up behind us, tucking something into his pocket. Without anymore hesitation on my part, I get back in line with the moving crowd, Kyle on my tail once more. I glance back at the shrinking coffee shop. "I got it. I won't take any chances if I spot him again."

"That's what I like to hear, foxy."

THE SOFT SOUNDS OF Mozart float around the kitchen and mute the brutal pounding of the hammer. Poor chicken. It's on the receiving end of my angst and a meat mallet. Spread out on one side of the huge kitchen island is the remaining ingredients for Cordon Bleu. The other I eye with hostility.

They're cute, sweet even, if I think about it. But when I do, I'm lost in a sea of sorrow so thick it's hard to find the surface. Two hours into unwrapping the mounds of gifts from well-wishers and foreign nationals all over the world, I happened on one from State Representative Someone-Or-Other.

I wail on the chicken harder, working up a sweat. The white card embossed with my soon to be initial bounces with each strike. And then her *I hope next Christmas these will have a place on your tree* greeting falls to the floor and lies open—staring back at me in silent censure of the truth hiding in my womb. Glancing up, tears blur the outline of the silver baby booties, an ornament that will stay packed away for all of time.

"Whoa, what do you have against that poor animal?"

I gasp as the words register, and at the muscled arm snaking around my waist. At the same time, I'm disarmed of my weapon before it can rain down on its victim once more.

Colin. I sink into his chest, turning and lifting my head so his beauty can erase my ugly thoughts. One of my hands winds through his on my stomach, and the other finds purchase in his hair to pull him down for a kiss. Even with the room cast in shadow, his eyes twinkle as if the wick of a candle has burst into flame behind them. Our mumbled greeting is lost in the first pass of his lips against mine, but it's light and too short to count. The next is just as soft, yet longer, and I open for him to deepen the intensity. "I missed you so much," I say when he doesn't heed my invitation. "Please."

His groan hits me in all the right places when he lets it loose and smashes his mouth to mine. In a second, I'm turned by his hands and then they're all over me, holding me close one moment, roaming along the line of my spine and down to my ass in another. With a firm grip, he lifts me from the ground and I wrap my legs around his hips. Testing my self-imposed abstinence-before-the-wedding rule, I grind into the thickening bulge just below his belt buckle.

"Christ, you better mean it, baby," he grounds out, and tips my head back to splay me open for his savage teeth. A new beat starts in my groin when he sucks my nipple through the fabric of his cotton dress shirt I put on to keep him close to me—the only barrier between the wet heat of his mouth and my sensitive flesh.

"I love that you're wearing this. But, Charlie . . ." He bites down, and then releases me when my moan melts into the concerto.

Our eyes lock and his features sharpen in the light thrown from overhead. Dipping to nudge apart the fabric hiding me from his gaze, his cheekbones appear in sharp relief, as if they were etched from stone. Lips, plump and pink from my mouth, suckle my bared skin. "I'm living on my last thread of restraint."

Gripping my neck, he takes me into a possessive hold, as if I belong to him and he has the power to breathe life into me. Because that's what he's done. Brought me from the mundane and painted my world with his vibrant color. I've given myself to him, my almost husband, and the thrill lighting up my spine and along my arms is not from fear. Never do I fear Colin, the man who taught my body to beg for his touch.

"I've played your game for almost two weeks. Nine days that tested my strength more than the goddamn presidential campaign." Leaning in, he whispers in my ear, "I can smell your arousal. And, God, I want you. I have wanted you every minute of every day. So keep grinding your pussy against my cock and I will lay you down on this table and have you for dinner. So help me, I won't stop. Not until you're begging for a reprieve, and then I'll give you my tongue." Finding my eyes, he makes sure I understand his tolerance level—by the urgency lurking behind his, it's estimated at zero.

Oh, my.

We're at melting point.

My body responds on autopilot, and I squeeze him in a vice-grip with my legs. "To hell with your fucking rule," he says, and then takes in my whimper with his mouth. Licking and biting into mine with such intensity, he leaves little room for an argument. Holy hell, how have I denied us this connection? The all-consuming race to fulfillment that's not satisfied until he's inside me, pushing, pulling, driving, *demanding* that I give him all of me. It's been too long since I felt his raw need to take me with a wild abandon that drives all thought from my over-thinking brain.

I give up and strip him. Tongue lashing against tongue, we groan together as our limbs fight with fabric until we're chest to chest.

The minute my beaded nipples scrape against his skin, he sweeps the dreaded present from the far end of the island and lays me down.

I hiss "yes" when he snuggles between my thighs and then reach for him. "No," I cry at the shrill pitch of his phone and his hesitation. I sigh with relief when it goes to voicemail, and at his renewed attention to my breasts. He's got them in a firm grip, held tight together so he can torment them with the tip of his wicked tongue, one and then the other.

The ringing is back. It becomes relentless and something screams urgent by its incessant wail. Colin must agree. Burying his head in my cleavage, he heaves out a long sigh. I hold him with hands woven through his hair. *Don't leave*, I chant to myself, overcome by his smell, his skin, his breath rushing against me—*him*. But the moment is broken. Kissing my breasts and then my mouth, he stands.

"Saved by the bell," I mutter. His smile is wry, and maybe a little desperate. I giggle, but have to rub my thighs together to displace the ache his attack started between them. The move doesn't go unnoticed. Colin's gaze scorches over every inch of my quivering stomach and sticks on my peaked nipples. If the red flush blazing up his neck is any indication, I think he might explode.

"Easy, tiger." I try to soothe him as he helps me up and off the counter.

Tipping his head back, he looks to the ceiling as if praying for divine intervention—which goes unheard, unless God uses cell phones. "I better get that. I've been waiting for a call from Phil."

What? "Phil?" I ask, and the tension that knotted my shoulders earlier in the day is back.

Rubbing a kiss into my temple, he murmurs, "Give me a minute and I'll explain."

What can I do but slip into his shirt and worry as he grabs his cell, and steps into the living room? For so many months, I had nothing to do but work on Colin's campaign and our wedding. The long weekend in the Florida Keys was a welcome respite from the pace of our life. The days filled with friends and the nights overflowing with Colin left little time to think of anything else, so I didn't. When we came home, my focus was lent to the holidays and prepping for our families coming in for an extended stay. Any extra time is spread thin between final preparation to become Mrs. McKenna and moving into the White House shortly thereafter.

Long gone is the anxiety that held me captive when Shane Roberts was loose and in the weeks following his attack. I've kept in contact with Sylvia, my counselor. With her help, our now weekly discussions are more about current events than fears creeping out in my dreams. I don't shelve my feelings; I deal with them.

I've been so good, felt better than I have in my whole life. The world accepted Charlie Carter with open arms. The girl from Michigan with a sordid past and a bright future is America's sweetheart. No longer forced into a shell I was never comfortable with, I can be me wherever we go. Leopard print is my friend again and so is my favorite leather jacket. I've learned daring mini-skirts and risqué tanks are better suited for behind closed doors than on the front of a thousand magazine covers. And I'm okay with that. I love my life.

What I don't want to interfere with it is the creeping threat of Alex and Ella. The mere mention of Phil's name has me thinking Colin is not the only one at melting point.

FOUR

WITH HAMMER IN HAND, I pound out my chicken and then layer on the prosciutto and cheese. Ten minutes later I bend over the oven to ensure the placement of the pan is perfect when a familiar rumble has me shaking my ass in response. Thankfully, I have on a pair of plain, white panties—a failed attempt on my part to keep the temperature at a livable level between us. I should have known nothing could squelch the heat.

I turn to the delectable sight of Colin McKenna leaning over the counter. Swirling Chardonnay in my now almost-empty glass, he can't stop staring at the line where his dress shirt meets my bare legs.

"See something you like, Mr. President?"

Never taking his eyes off me, he knocks back the remaining wine. "Do you think you're safe?"

The hair on my arms bristles to attention. I'm never safe from Colin and I like that. I really, really do. "Mmm, I hope not. But my moment of weakness has passed. Three more nights, baby, and I'm all yours."

His answer is to huff and pour another glass of wine. And that's when it hits me—a ragged edge torn along his knuckles is red and blares *this is painful*. I'm on him in a flash, his right hand held in mine. "What did you do?"

He tips my chin and then smooths out my crinkled brow. "Everything is fine."

"You always say that before telling me something that's going to raise my blood pressure."

"I do, yes. Because I want you to know there's nothing to worry about. Keep your blood pressure right where it is."

"Too late." I place his hand between my breasts where he's sure to feel my heart pound out of control.

"What happened?"

"I saw Shane Roberts."

"You did what?" It squeaks out of my mouth in a pitch that could shatter glass. The earth falls away from my feet in a nanosecond and I bend over, clutching my stomach to stave off hyperventilation. This day has gone from bad to worse.

"Baby, come and sit with me." Colin gathers me under one arm, the wine bottle and glass held in his other hand as he maneuvers us into the living room to snuggle on the couch. No amount of alcohol can numb me for this story. My nerves are shot more than once as he recants it in his calm there's-nothing-to-worry-about-I'm-better-than-apple-pie-with-whipped-cream-on-top voice, which is meant to soothe. But I clutch his fingers so tight that on more than one occasion he cringes and reminds me that everything is fine. Shane Roberts met his fist and then went off to prison. End of story.

He shakes his head. "I have always suspected he didn't act alone, and now we know for sure. That's why I went to see him. I had to find out for myself."

"God, Colin." I sigh and steal our shared glass from the hand on his thigh to take a long drag. "Why didn't you say something before you left?"

"Because I knew you would worry and there was no need."

I roll my eyes to the ceiling and blink away tears. "You're damn right I would have," I choke out as my voice cracks. His muttered *everything's okay* is lost in my hair when he buries his nose there and hugs me tight. I was not ready for a Shane Roberts confrontation. Now that it's happened, I'm torn between horror that Colin would put himself in that situation and a burst of giddiness that he defended my honor. Everything about our relationship is new for me. I've never been treasured like this—lost with him in a love so deep neither one of us would survive without the other. And that's why his safety is at the top of my priority list. Brushing my fingers over his injured knuckles, I whisper, "Don't do it again, okay?"

"I'm done with Roberts. Phil has everything I learned today, as little as it is. I've asked him to step up the investigation, dig into the campaign and those who've worked closely on it. That's all."

"Who? What member of your team would want to hurt me?" I think back to the few connections I made for the short period of time I was in Indiana. Molly, but she's my friend. Tim—the IT guy with a crush? Doubtful. More glaringly apparent is Ella. But would she go so far as to sabotage Colin's campaign because the Montgomery's hate me? I never thought it possible.

When my gaze meets my fiancée's, I think we're on the same page. Worry lines creep out around his eyes.

"Why would Ella and Alex go to such an extreme?"

His brow falls into three lines. "Alex? No, he's a follower, but I can't imagine him capable of being led into this. Hell, he couldn't even confront me when he lost Abby and I've always thought he blamed me for the accident. Her phone records proved she called him just before the truck collided with her car and I'm sure she gave him a rundown of our fight. But this would take his passive-aggressiveness to the far end of extreme." The lines get deeper, and he shakes his head as if to expel the thought.

"My hunch is John. He did it for power. He's been clear on his desire to be my Chief of Staff. If I were married to Ella, he would be in one of my ears steering the direction of my ship, and she would be in the other. It would be as if he were president and I the manifested puppet to serve his bidding. He's always assumed the position was his, but that was never my intention. Evan accepted the role a week ago." Running a hand down his face and then up through his hair, he lets out a sigh. "I think Ella bought into his quest because it served her desire to drive you away. When that didn't happen easily, they stepped up the game and involved Roberts. It backfired in Texas when I took the bullet meant for you." His fist clenches against my thigh in the same fashion that his jaw is, rigid and ready for a fight. "All this time, I've struggled to change the duplicity built so soundly within political platforms, yet it was raging at full force under my blind eye."

"Are you sure they did it?"

"There are few people I have fully trusted; this family is one of them. I was bound to them through marriage as well as politics, but I've gone through every other possibility. It has to be true, yet I still can't believe John would do this."

"What are you going to do?"

Tilting his head, he stares through me for a minute, and his features relax as he does. Leaning into my cheek, he mumbles, "I'm going to marry you" while nibbling a path to my ear. "Because I can't wait to call you wife."

"Mmm, that's my favorite thing you've said all day. But really, this is huge, Colin. They've been a part of your life for a long time."

He nods. "Phil will call in as soon as he knows something and I'll make decisions then. In the meantime, I'm all yours from now until the wedding. Feel free to tie me to the bed post . . ."

I laugh. "I was thinking more along the line of thank you notes and picking up your tux from the cleaners . . ."

"That too." I can feel his smile against me, and we just sit wrapped together with his fingers sneaking under the hem of my shirt. When they hit the edge of my panties I sigh and he says, "So, now that I've confessed my sins, it's your turn."

I pull away to study him, and I'm met by an inquisitive, arched eyebrow. "What do you mean?

"Why were you beating the shit out of dinner when I walked in?"

I giggle. Flexing my hand into a fist, I blow on it like a smoking gun. "You have Shane Roberts and I have a chicken."

"Funny, but you're not distracting me."

After the slightest hesitation, I hop up to retrieve the gift and card that brought my mood to a low simmer. After all, Colin and I have vowed to communicate, and this topic had burned a hole in my chest for weeks now. On my way back, I slow down and let my heart race ahead of me. Mr. McPerfect sprawls out on the couch with no shirt, the wide brim of his muscles firm and outlined to perfection as he sits with both arms on the back of the cushions in wait. His legs are parted just enough to let me know something's stirred to life. Something that's hard for him to control because I've held him at bay for nine days. Now this is enough to distract a girl from her woes.

His smile takes on a feral glint. I can see it in his eyes as they snake over every inch of my flesh but then cool when he spies the baby booties in my hand. His brow falls as I settle into my spot on his lap.

I dangle the pair from my finger and read the sentiment meant to warm my heart, but that instead chilled it.

"You killed a chicken because of a Christmas ornament?"

"Don't be silly." I snuggle into the crook of his neck, breathing him in as he strips the decoration from my fingers and takes my hand. "I didn't kill it; I just beat it into tender excellence."

Colin hums his agreement into the center of my palm, his lips lingering long enough for my breathing to spike. Placing my hand in the middle of his chest, he holds his firmly over mine and waits a few beats to speak. "There are so many things I want to say right now."

"But?"

"But I'm deciding which will make you feel better."

"Maybe I need everything?" The words get stuck on a lump in my throat I can't swallow away.

"Then let me start with the most basic and important to the foundation of our marriage." Tipping my chin, he pauses and then my eyes connect with his. "I love you."

"I love you, too."

"No." He shakes his head. "I love Charlie Carter. All of you, every complex and simple part that makes up the most wonderful woman who has agreed to be my wife. I wouldn't change one thing, baby. Not one curl in your hair or the curve of your hips, the sass that lives on the tip of your tongue or the brain that constantly questions the world. Not one thing." He maneuvers me so I straddle his thighs and then he cradles my face. "I know you're worried about our family, but I'm not."

"Colin . . ."

"Let me finish," he says, pressing a thumb against my mouth. "I'm not worried about where our family will come from. One way or another, we'll have children."

"But I can't . . ." I struggle for space, and he clamps down on my waist to hold me in place.

"In twenty-three days we'll be in the White House. Do you know what comes along with that?"

My sigh is loud and long because I don't want to play Twenty Questions.

"The best doctors in the world, Charlie, any or all of them. I can call in an army of experts to help us conceive. But I need you to know that it doesn't matter to me."

"That's not true."

His growl catches me off-guard, like a crack of thunder in the middle of the night. Wide-eyed, I stare as he catches me with his darkening gaze. "It is true. I have you and that's enough. Children, whether biological or adopted, are icing on my cake. All of my prayers have already been answered and then some. Tell me honestly, it's important for you to carry our child?"

He searches my face, and my breath stumbles into a cry. The dam holding my tears at bay since this morning finally loses its battle. Colin shakes his head, and I know he can't stand that they're falling.

I've held on to this burden, not knowing it was injuring me. It was just a fact of life. *Charlie can't have babies.* Years ago I was told scar tissue had built up and I had virtually no chance to conceive. My periods became so painful I was placed on a long-term birth control that held them at bay for months at a time, and when I did have one, it barely passed as a cycle. When we got engaged, I consulted a physician and stopped taking everything, only to be met with raging hormones and five days I wish away once a month. But I would endure symptoms a million times worse if only I could have one thing.

"I want your child growing inside me." The reality that I never will pushes the words out on a choking sob. "And I hate Shane-fucking-Roberts for taking that option away from me."

Wiping my cheeks with his thumb, Colin draws me close to kiss my eyes closed and murmur, "If a baby is what you want, you shall have one." He drags his lips to my ear. "I promise you."

FIVE

THE PROBLEM WITH MAKING babies is that we didn't try last night. I'm half-convinced I was kidnapped by aliens. Yes, that must be it. I was held hostage while a microchip was buried in my brain, and then forced to dictate some asinine rule about no sex before the wedding. *What was I thinking?* Apparently I wasn't. No sane woman marrying Colin McKenna chooses abstinence.

Ali thinks I'm crazy and this theory goes right along with her diagnosis—especially after last night. Lying in bed with a naked, two-hundred-and-ten pound, buffed-out god who can't keep his hands to himself has strapped me into a straitjacket. I wanted to give in. Oh, how I wanted to let those roaming fingers, and his mouth, dear lord his mouth, continue their exploration. My skin remembers them. Hours after the sun fought for purchase on the horizon, I can feel the path they followed up one side of my thigh and down the other.

Thank God Kyle and Fitz are in the front seat, focused on traffic, and not the flush crawling up my chest. Colin's leg pressed up against mine isn't helping matters. Laptop spread out on his thighs, cell held to his ear, he's giving the what-for to whoever's on the line. The President-elect is not a happy man, but that anger is not directed at me. His glance in my direction and gorgeous grin assures me of that.

After dropping Colin at his office, today's agenda includes a quick trip to the florist to ensure the centerpiece design is as planned. After that it's a rush around town for last-minute items for our short-lived honeymoon. Roughing it in Northern Virginia doesn't sound appealing, but being snowed in with Colin McKenna does. Oh, what his hands and mouth can do with more than seventy-two hours of wireless downtime. Speaking of which, the melodic tune of my phone reminds me we're not in the woods yet.

The number is unknown, but with the amount of wedding-related calls I get daily it's not unusual. My hello is drowned out by a grated, "You get two words. Yes, and no."

The hair at my nape doesn't like the sound of this and stands on end. That along with the tremor shaking my shoulders and I'm all ears. I glance at Colin, who remains embattled with diplomacy, and then out the window.

"Anything else and I will destroy the rest of your life before you've had a chance to live it."

Ella. There's no mistaking the venom in her voice. I've been snake-bit too many times to mistake the strike. "Yes?" I manage without faltering, yet I sink closer to the natural protection next to me.

"How much will you give me to resign?"

I freeze as anxiety pops out in a cold sweat on my brow. My voice, a Charlie Carter from a long ago conversation with John Montgomery, makes me sick to my stomach. Why would she have a recording of this? With my back now ramrod straight, I fight for distance and at the same time throw Colin a reassuring smile to alleviate the wrinkled brow my haste reaction caused.

"How much?"

"Name your price."

"No, you tell me what it's worth to you. And make it good, Montgomery, because you can't get rid of me that easy." No! No, that's not what I said. My gaze flies to Kyle. His head turns to watch the world pass by around us. Always watching. Always on the ready to enter into battle on my behalf. *"I didn't get involved this deep to walk away without my future taken care of."*

"A million dollars. It'll be in your bank account before closing time this afternoon."

My laugh is brittle and so disturbing I cringe away from it. *"Not enough."*

"Stupid girl. Colin doesn't deserve this. Two million. Submit your resignation letter now and it's done."

"Not enough." The anger in my voice is palpable, and I remember how it felt flowing through me at the time. I hated John for asking me to walk away, but that was nothing compared to the fit of rage boiling in my stomach now. *"Thank you, John. This conversation has helped me figure things out. More time is what I need and then maybe you'll see my value. I highly recommend that you come to the table before I get him to marry me, because when that happens, I will take Colin for everything he's worth. Dig deeper and don't call me again until you have the right number."*

Wait. What? I never said that!

My heart stops. Bumbling to a thudding beat, it starts again and I hiss, "What do you want?" I'm not a violent woman. Inner peace was important to find after conquering my past, but her newfound chuckle tests my limits.

"Meet me at the Lincoln Memorial at nine. Alone. If there is even a hint of your boy-toy or any other security, I will release this tape to the press."

I glance around. We don't exactly travel light anymore. Agents go where Colin does—lots of them, a car in front of us and one in back at all times.

"Your game is over, Carter. We'll talk about how you can walk away with a semblance of your dignity intact. These are my rules. If you break them, I will break you. Understand me?"

The past year flashes in front of my eyes. The University of Notre Dame and blueberry pancakes. Albany and the blizzard that followed. Blake's and Traverse City. The tornado that twisted my life into a violent path and Colin's steady resolve to see me through the turbulence. I find his eyes now—so full of love and trust. Looking into them, I see our future stretched into years of beauty, and the peaks and valleys that come along with every marriage. I will fight for him, just as he brought me to my rightful place by his side.

I'm going to have it out with the Montgomerys once and for all and be done with them. This is my life and no one is robbing me of it. No one.

I take Colin's hand in mine, and the strength from his grip reinforces my decision. "Yes. I'll be there."

WASHINGTON D.C. IS JAW-DROPPING. Steeped in history, secrets whisper from the walls of ancient porticos and monuments to the dead. The Lincoln Memorial is case in point, but today it's cold and alone. A lot like me. Grabbing my scarf tighter to my neck, I hold on to it and look around. The coldest winter in history has kept the memorial silent in the bright morning light. It's just the two of us.

Salt and ice burst beneath my feet with each step I take to reach her. The outline of Ella's petite frame is unmistakable. She stands square between two ginormous pillars that signify the joining of a union, when her mission is to break one apart. My pulse races—dangerous, just like this meeting.

"The location is a bit over the top," I say, looking up at the uncanny image of the sixteenth president immortalized in white marble. Foreboding, he sits in judgment of two women fighting for the same man. "We could have done just as well at the coffee house on Connecticut."

Her gaze cuts behind me and then to the left and right. "I'm glad to see you can follow simple directions. And this place . . ." she turns, heading inside and out of the wind, "is one where I can ensure what I have to say isn't heard by anyone but you."

"I think I heard enough over the phone."

She nods and glances over her shoulder, a malicious smile spreading as she dips into the darkness of shadow. "I was hoping to find a balance between dramatic effect and victory. It brought me great joy to play it for you."

I follow behind and mourn the loss of the sun when we're tucked in the corner of the vast room. "Is Daddy pacifying his little baby with bedtime stories again?"

Her laugh scares away the crows perched on the overhang. "My father has nothing to do with this."

Right. "Let's cut the crap. What is it you want?"

She circles. Her gaze travels up and down and over every inch of my body-hugging gray dress and the four-inch, pencil-thin heels that ground my leather boots. I shiver and this one is not caused by the weather. A smirk lifts the side of Ella's mouth and Cindy Lou Who just became Cruella Deville. Her black-and-white oversized tweed coat and beret lend to the guise. I clench my cell buried in the pocket of my jacket to text all Dalmatian owners to be on alert, but she interrupts before I can send a warning.

"What I want . . ." she says, stopping two feet away, "is for Abby to have visited her best friend that weekend ten years ago like she planned. They wouldn't have met; she couldn't have thrown herself at him like the tramp she was. With a little more time, I could have had him. I wish you were never invited to the press conference. Evan should have kept his opinions to himself. But I can't change the past; I can only manage the future. Tell me." Stepping closer, she searches my face until the scrutiny is uncomfortable. "Don't you find it strange that you look just like my sister?" Reaching out, she enfolds my escaped curl between two fingers and tilts her head. "So much like her," she murmurs, and what was a shiver turns to a tremor.

Stepping back a good foot, my hair slips from her grip and I shake away her creepy stare. "What I find weird is that you're punishing me because I do. Abby must have done a permanent number—"

"Don't apply psychology one-oh-one on me. She's dead and isn't standing in my way. But you are."

"Colin."

Her laugh is brittle. "Yes, you inane prat. Colin. It's always been him. God, I've done everything. Supported him from the moment we met. I even changed my major to political science to better support his career." Throwing her arms out, she screams to Lincoln, "I changed my life for him and he chose wrong!" Ripping off her beret, her hair falls to chin length, shorter than it was yesterday. "He always chooses wrong."

Talking to Ella is like being caught in a hurricane; sucking all the energy from those around her, she spins out of control. She paces back and forth in three-inch heels, arms flailing and temper rising.

"God, he's such a boy scout. But you!" She points in my face. "You are a lying cheat. I won't let you take him down the same road he's been before . . ."

I let her manic accusation sit in the silence surrounding us. Beating like a drum, it takes up time with my heart. Argument is a moot point. I'll never win with her, and I'm not inclined to try. This is more about preventing a rash decision, a choice that could induce a public outcry. Sitting in the White House may offer extensive benefits, but it also opens us to extreme criticism. Throughout Colin's time in public office we'll be held to the highest standards. I intend to live up to them. If doing so entails bringing down the house of Montgomery, then so be it.

"I think I've got it. You expect me to leave Colin, bow out of the wedding gracefully. Tell him I just can't go through with it for whatever idiotic reason I concoct. If I don't you'll release"—I wave my hand in a flurry of disgust—"the bogus tape to the public. Is that it?"

Cruella closes the distance, nodding. "You're not so stupid after all. But I have more. I have these."

Producing photos from the neckline of her coat, she hands them over. *Kyle*. We're on the street nose to nose, his eyes leveling me with warning to steer clear of Alex.

I can't hold down a bubble of laughter. It enrages her. A burning red haze flares up her neck. She tears the pictures from my fingers and then we both spin around at the aggressive tap of shoes on concrete.

"What are you doing here?" she asks, her eyes narrowing in on Joan and John Montgomery.

Tucked into a wool overcoat, John breaches our sanctuary. His wife is more hesitant, as if she'll burst into flame if she enters the temple. She chooses to hover on the outskirts, small standing next to a giant pillar.

"I asked them to come."

The commanding tone of Colin's voice washes through me like a raging river. A grin sprints across my face. Talk about dramatic. His timing could not have been more perfect.

I turn to find him. Colin in a suit is almost as sexy as him naked or shirtless and spread out on the couch, but the sexiest shit of all is the authority he exudes, cutting through the streaming sun with a powerful stride until he's swallowed by the shadows with the rest of us. His eyes are on mine, his mouth tilting in the smallest hint of a smile, and I know he's pleased with our plan, an idea we hatched within minutes of Ella's call.

Fitz and Kyle and a myriad of agents follow him, filing out of a door hidden in the corner to surround us.

What Ella thought was her smoking gun falls to the freezing concrete. Dead—just like her outrageous scheme. Proof of nothing more than a conversation between agent and ward. Friends.

"No," Ella sputters. "I . . . she—" Jerking her gaze from person to person, the storm brewing moments ago hits a frantic pace.

"I love when a plan comes together," I say, and bounce on my heels because this is getting fun. Leaning in, I whisper in her ear. "You've underestimated me."

Six

I'M TUCKED UNDER COLIN'S arm and looking up into the sun. His eyes shine down without doubt or mistrust; together, we've peeled away layers of insecurity and fear and we're strong. We can tackle any obstacle thrown in our path and destroy it. I squeeze in to his side; his heat and a hint of sandalwood warm the chill right out of me. But our reunion is short-lived.

"Can someone tell me what the hell this is about?" John says, narrowing in on Colin. "You pulled us away from a brunch with Senator Stanton and his wife to mediate a disagreement with Ella and *her*?"

He's refused to call me by my name since the phone call in question. I'd offer a guess he didn't expect me to hop on a plane and become engaged within twenty-four hours of his failed mission. He probably never suspected that I shared my recorded copy of the conversation with Colin months ago. Without a doubt he wouldn't believe I pleaded with Colin to remain neutral, to refrain from any action. Colin's standings had just gone on the upswing after the release of my personal address with Kathryn Hess. I had no desire for the public to perceive unrest within his ranks, and they would have if his top campaign advisor was terminated or suddenly stepped down.

After much debate, Colin had reluctantly agreed. He'd used John for the last leg of the campaign and into the general election. Very rarely was I within speaking distance of anyone in the Montgomery family. If I was on Colin's right side, they were in the back to the left. I never knew if Ella or John questioned the change in their standing. Until today, I'd enjoyed the complete separation.

"I . . ." Ella falters. "I have something you need to hear." A fraction of the confidence she held only a moment ago returns in her straightened shoulders as she holds out her phone, volume on high. All eyes are on her as it starts and my stomach rolls when my voice breaches the silence. It's horrible and even more nauseating to know this family would sink to an all-time low to drive Colin and me apart. But that's my innocence talking.

It's what Colin's told me all along. The underbelly of this city is cruel. Politics is a game of chess, except the precise rules are bent and broken prior to the end of the competition. The you-do-for-me-and-I'll-do-for-you backdoor promises made to propel forward misguided political maneuvers for personal gain, compromise the validity of the final act. What these heathens will never understand is that the queen always protects her king.

"Where did you get that?" John rushes forward, snatching the cell from Ella so quickly her arm remains hanging in the balance, fingers clenched around nothing.

John punches buttons, but my voice drones on as he tries to stop the recording.

"Sound familiar?" Colin asks, at the same time tucking me behind his shoulders. Kyle steps in and pushes me aside. Protected by both him and Fitz, I peek between them for a view of the festivities.

Joan's a statue. Lips pursed in red perfection, she watches in silent damnation. Her daughter's gone just as red in the face, a flush bursting through her pale cheeks. And John slips, literally and figuratively, stepping over himself to back up three feet. Shaking his head, he coughs out a lump in his throat and then says, "No. No, I've not heard that call before. Ella, how in the world did you come across something like this? I never . . . that conversation didn't take place."

"It was e-mailed to me." Her voice hesitates, just as she does when looking to the man she's loved for half of her life. "I got it yesterday from an unknown account. But it's real. It's real, Colin; you heard it. My father and Charlie—it's them. I know it is. She's using you!" Desperate, she throws herself at him and clings to his lapels. "Can't you see you're letting history rep—"

"Ella." She hangs on Colin's word, looking up with fading hope. "I may be a boy scout, but I'm not naïve to the ways of Washington and the people in it. I pride myself on steering this government in a direction that will see the United States prosper, not for the next eight years, but the next eighty." Colin tosses her hands away and backs out of reach. "To do this, I need a trustworthy team surrounding me."

"But you heard it . . ."

"What I saw is you bribing my fiancée."

Sweeping realization widens her eyes to the size of moons. She went too far, pushed too much. "To save you," she screams and stumbles forward. Colin is quick to sidestep her crumbling attempt at redemption. "I'd do anything, please. You know I would do whatever you need of me. I am your servant."

I almost feel sorry for her, but not really. This has been a long time coming. I should feel ashamed of the dizzying joy peeking out of my heart, but I can't find remorse anywhere. *Karma's a real bitch.*

Colin stares her down, distaste evident in the taut line of his mouth. "You're fired. We are no longer connected personally or professionally. Consider this a renege on your wedding invitation. And John?" He takes out a document from his breast pocket, even as Ella sinks to her knees. "I'll need you to review this and explain the content."

"Now?" he asks, sweat beading on his brow.

A stiff nod is all he gets, and then he shakes his head. "I don't know."

"Well then let me explain. This"—Colin snatches away the papers—"is a list of outgoing e-mails from an I.P. address of a laptop in your office. If you remember, the second computer you commissioned the campaign to purchase without my knowledge?" Colin goes on, even as John's continued denial hangs in the balance between them. "I assure you, the intel found by my firm has been vetted by our most esteemed colleagues at the Bureau. The same e-mail address forwarded a message to Ella Montgomery on Wednesday morning December twenty-eighth. The content of that recording we've all heard, so I won't bother you with the details." Flipping pages, he goes on to number two.

"Next is purchase confirmation of a cell phone in the name of Roy Smith. Know anything about that?" Colin dips down to capture John's lowered gaze. "Roy Smith," he repeats, and anger drives the two words into the ground. "I also have access to Roy's now defunct bank account, which sent sizable deposits to Shane Roberts. Fuck," he says, and grabs John's jacket, "I trusted you. We were family."

Colin closes his eyes for a second and then shoves John away. "Phil's good. Better than I gave him credit for, because he took speculation and drilled down to find proof that Roy Smith is John Montgomery. Created with a dead man's social security number, Roy was a perfect cover—except you used a computer that could be linked back to you with one random and buried invoice discovered in campaign logs."

"This is an absolute fabrication. I . . ." John stutters. "I haven't done any of this."

"Did you or did you not call Charlie last July and ask her to resign?"

Blank stare—for so long the crows come back to nest and hatch eggs. "I did, but that was . . ."

"I could go on. Once Phil found the computer, he cracked everything—a Facebook user account under the name of Sara Abbott, the release of Charlie's medical records to the press, the voice manipulation and additions to change your conversation with her." Colin drags his hand through his hair as if it can release the mounting tension. A dead calm falls over his features and radiates out to silence John's staccato breath.

Checkmate.

"As important as my political aspirations are, you found the one thing that will always take precedence. What you did to eliminate her from the equation and manipulate the trajectory of my life is inexcusable. So . . ." he straightens to full height and levels John with a stare that ages his old confidant by ten years in the span of a second, "we're done."

"You're making a mistake!"

Colin backs away from the man who in many aspects was a second father to him, and the waiting agents swarm in. John's fumbled pleas go unheard. They have him in handcuffs before Joan can swallow her pride and fight to drag Ella from her knees. Then, with head held high, she marches my way.

"Charlise," she says, but Kyle blocks her advance. I can't see his face, but if looks could kill Joan might be dead. Ella shrivels like the wicked witch on death's door and slinks behind mama bear.

"I can't figure out what game you're playing," Kyle spits out with acid on his tongue. "But let me be clear. It ends now."

My hand on Kyle's shoulder has him shift enough so I can watch the sharp rancor in Joan's eyes soften to the strangest hint of delight. Wind blasts through the opening of the memorial. The squall dislodges what appeared to be Joan's short bob into long, loose waves. My eyes dart between mother and daughter as my memory flashes to the coffee shop where Sawyer tucked Alex inside with a petite blonde. Not Ella but Joan. *He was with Joan.*

"Listen to what I have to say and know who I am," she says.

Kyle leans in and brings up an index finger to compliment his killer look. "I'm damn good at my job and that entails knowing exactly who you are. And I don't give a rat's ass what fancy family you were born in to. My kind of justice doesn't discriminate."

"Are you threatening me?"

"No, ma'am. I'm giving you the honest to God's truth. I don't believe for one minute your husband and spawn can be buried in shit up to their eyebrows and you're not tainted by the smell. Walk away and let this be the end."

One breath and two. On the third, Joan spins and drags Ella behind her as if she's a naughty two-year-old.

Bending, Kyle picks up the pictures of us, streaked with dirt from any number of shoes.

"Someone was watching." It's not just the steel glaze of his eyes that puncture my lungs, but the truth.

"Joan and Alex?"

His gaze snaps to mine. "The angle is wrong for someone at the coffee house to have gotten us at this perspective."

I sink into disbelief. "Then who?"

"Let me worry about this. Turn." He twirls his finger, and I shake my head.

"No, explain."

Smiling, he says, "Not my style. Leave it alone for now and let me work through it."

"Not my style." I cross my arms against my chest. "What's up with Joan? You've obviously already started to dig."

He throws his hands up in surrender. "Nothing. Absolutely nothing is wrong with her. She's squeaky clean, and that's what I don't like. Everyone has a past; I just can't figure out hers."

"Promise to tell me when you know?"

He tilts his head, and I can see the wheels churning into a decision. "All right, boss-lady."

"Okay," I say, as he slides his glasses back in place. "What will happen to Ella?" We both peer out of the enclosure to catch mother and daughter flying down the crosswalk, agents following behind.

"She'll remain free until we can connect her to Roy Smith and Shane Roberts. Right now, the only thing we have is the e-mail that was sent to her. It doesn't prove she participated in anything. Turn around."

I do and he peels me out of my jacket to strip the recording device he hid in the neckline. "You did real good," he says, draping the leather over my shoulders when he's done. "But you need to return to that seating chart. With the Montgomerys out, looks like you have an open table."

"Just remember this when it happens to you."

He grunts. "I can guarantee I won't have a power-hungry psychopath get arrested days before he's supposed to rain congratulations down upon my newly married self. Only you, my friend."

"What's life without a little action?" I shrug out my admittance that this is par for the Charlie Carter course.

"Have some compassion for the big guy. I think your attempt at espionage escalated his aging process. Go easy on him for a while, huh?"

"Right," I say, taking in the object of our conversation. He looks good to me—commanding, as he snaps off directions to Fitz.

He doesn't notice, but if he glances my way, he'll see a woman in love. Hands clasped in front of her stomach, legs crossed at the ankle and head tilted. Everything relaxes—my shoulders and heightened breath, my pulse and the nervous twitch in my left eye.

He took care of everything. The moment Ella hung up, I laid her plan at his feet, and then he flew into motion. Phil was closer to an answer than Colin had anticipated. Using Fitz and Kyle's connections at the Bureau, we were able to tie the faux identity to John and then the puzzle pieces fell into place. From there Kyle taped a microphone in my jacket and sent me in for my part—let Ella bury herself. Colin wasn't a fan of my face-to-face participation, but I wanted to end this as much as he did. With them hidden not twenty feet away, I was hard-pressed to envision failure.

It's over. A niggling apprehension sits in the bottom of my stomach. John will go to jail, there's no doubt. Ella doesn't have a chance to reengage in Colin's life, not after she went so far as to coerce me out of it. That's two out of three Montgomerys. What about Joan? Kyle's response to her scratches at the back of my brain. Could she have been so clearly separated from her husband and daughter's hatred of me?

The starburst glinting off of Colin's watch draws my attention back to him, and I tuck Joan away to think about on another day. I'm too far removed to hear what he says or see what he's pointing to, so I take advantage of my vantage point. When he slips his hand in his pants pocket it pulls the fabric taut against the firm globes that slide into powerful legs. Sexy in a suit is an understatement.

He must feel my eyes on him, because he turns, and heat fuels his stare—dark and dangerous in one instant and downright sinful in the next.

I swat a goodbye to Kyle's mumbled, "I'll get the car," and prepare myself for the new storm coming my way.

When it catches me, we're pressed hip to hip, and energy crackles around us. One touch and he owns me. The whisper of his fingers over my cheekbone has me panting and wanting. "Take me home," I murmur into his mouth as he brushes it against mine.

He laughs and nips my jawline on his way to my ear. "You have errands, as do I. I'll meet you there." He pulls away to check his watch. "At six."

My bottom lip pops out in a pout for the century, but it only broadens his grin. "Have I told you how proud I am of you? I'm in awe. Don't mistake me, I will never let you do it again, but I am damn pleased. Ella can't deny her intentions, and having the recorded proof will stop her from recanting the confession."

I wrap my arms around his waist and nestle in. "Now, we can get married and forget about them."

The hold he has on me is nothing short of fierce. With one hand braided through my hair and the other held firm against my lower back, he digs in, covering me in his presence. His heartbeat is strong beneath my cheek, but I know life can change in an instant. I've encountered the sudden impact more than most. I'm not sitting on the sidelines anymore waiting for the next curveball. There may be more Ellas or Johns or Shanes to cross my path, but I'm not afraid. I've fought my way into happiness too many times to get stuck in the potholes. I'll stand my ground and take what I want. And right now, that's Colin. I'm going to marry him and live the dream.

I lean back and tilt my head to give my own command. "Kiss."

The smile that peels across his face is priceless. It's sweet and disarming, the hidden side he saves for me. "Hm." He sinks into indecency, the line of his body molding closer to mine. "Careful, my love. We're doing so well to manage through your imposed boundaries. I would hate to breach them with only fifty-four hours . . ." he nips my bottom lip, "remaining through this sanction."

I laugh. "Counting down the hours?"

"The minutes, actually."

My eyes roll when his hands stray under my jacket, along my spine and to the sides of my breasts. Suddenly, they're aching and heavy, and my breath fractures when his mouth slides into place with a kiss so intense I can feel it in my chest. I'm ruined by the powerful thrust of his tongue and his complete abandon. And then he rips away.

"You," he pants into my cheek. "I'm terrified by how much I want you. More than that, how much I need you." He tightens his hold. "I'm obsessed with your laugh and with how you look at me, insatiable—exactly how I feel. I've never relied on anyone as I do you." I pry away only enough to see his eyes and the almost painful expression that cannot be smoothed away with my fingers. "So yes. I'm tracking the seconds until you're mine. And when you are, Charlie, when you belong to me, I will take you so hard time will cease to mean anything other than where my hands are and when they'll touch you again."

He kisses me deep, and with a longing that echoes his words. I hate that it has to last the entire day as we separate to tie up loose ends before we become affixed for good.

Each hour has my to-do list growing shorter and shorter. Last stop: honeymoon prep. Hours spent at Je T'aime, Washington's exclusive lingerie boutique, results in the perfect ensembles to drive Colin insane—in the best way.

Six turns to eight, and when reunited we have just enough time for leftovers with wine and a steaming shower. We fall into bed exhausted from the day, or maybe the year that has chased us right up to our I dos. I slip into sleep with my T-shirt tucked under my breasts so Colin's head can rest on my bare stomach. He loses his battle to stay awake while tracing words along my hipbone. *Forever is not enough.*

My whispered affection is lost in a dream that's over before I can remember it. Night passes to day. Vague impressions of love and loss weigh heavy on my heart as the subtle stroke of light brushes my lids from the outside in. The hint of sandalwood is replaced by something that doesn't belong under my sheets. I'm flat on my stomach, arms wrapped around my pillow with a chill covering my shoulders. Not once since sharing a bed have we been in one without touching.

Colin is gone, yet I am not alone.

SEVEN

ALI'S BLACK ORCHID PERFUME and giggle greet me when I stretch. She clutches a pillow, mimicking my pose.

"Morning, gorgeous."

"You're not who I was expecting," I say behind my hand to protect her from a yawn. "I wanted to wake up to Dark and Dangerous."

"Hm, he got called away earlier than expected, and I have the day off, so you're spending it with me." Instant disappointment crumbles my brow. Colin promised he was mine until the wedding but he's gone. "Oh, no you don't. Blink back those tears. I have something to make it all better."

I'm quick to rip open the handed over bi-folded page and devour Colin's artful script.

My dearest, Charlie:

I'm drowning in you, as much as one can sink into an abyss and forget everything but the object of his affection. Dawn turns to day and I can't bring two thoughts together unless you are a part of them. The driving force within my mind is to touch your ivory skin, let my fingers bare your flesh for my feasting eyes, and fill myself even further with you.

I knew no greater joy than when you agreed to be mine. Without doubt, our love is meant to be powerful and consuming and everlasting. There is more to us than this day or tomorrow—it is every moment of forever, and even that is not enough.

I promise for each minute we are apart, those that find us united will mean more than the ones before. Lay your head and rest with me. I'll bring you the peace you seek in your dreams, amidst your mind and heart, and when the sun gives you hope for a beautiful twilight.

Don't long for me, my sweet girl, as we shall be together soon, and then never be far apart.

Your devoted partner in life and love,
Colin

Hold back the tears—who is Ali kidding? After my second read-through, a river surges beyond the borders of my lids, soaking the pillow below.

"Damn, I knew he'd be too sweet. No crying; you'll puff yourself up like a blowfish." She turns, pulling a handful of tissues from the box on the nightstand to throw at me, and then I choke on a sob.

"We have so much to do . . ."

"Done, all of it." She waves a flourishing hand, as if magically making it all disappear.

I shake my head. "No, really. The guest baskets at the hotel."

"Done."

"I have to call the photographer, and D.J., the band leader, with playlists. Colin's tux; I forgot it in the rush yesterday. And—"

"All done."

"Everything?"

"Done."

"Colin?"

She smiles. "More like Betsy, his secretary extraordinaire. But did you think he would let you fend for yourself? Anyway, he took care of everything so you could spend the day with me. And we," she says, grabbing me into a chokehold hug that ends with me laughing and cushioned against her shoulder, "are spending the day at the spa.

Massages, mani and pedi, hair and makeup. Your man knows how to treat a girl right."

"I love him so much I'd like to tattoo the words on my heart," I whisper.

"I hope so, because you're about to say I do."

I grip her arm, holding onto my lifeline. "No, I mean, this sounds so crazy, but I can't imagine not being close to him. It would wreck me."

"Why would you think that's even a possibility? He loves you more than a human is capable of loving."

The whisper of my dream tickles my mind. In it, a gaping hole grew bigger until I couldn't see Colin on the other side of it. The memory suffocates the happiness out of my lungs.

Ali peels back far enough to search my face. "I know a lot of things, and one of them is Colin McKenna isn't going to let you slip away."

"You're right," I say. Forgetting the air of discontent, I breathe in her hair, sweet with a trace of coconut. "What about you and Evan?"

She barks out a laugh. "What about us? We're just, I don't know, friends?"

"Please, friends with benefits. The two of you are not fooling anyone. I see how he looks at you. It's all smoldering caveman—me want woman. Geez, I thought he was going to throw you over his shoulder on Christmas and unwrap you like his God-given present."

Tensing beside me, she grips my tee. "That man is a rolling contradiction. For most of his life, he's been an unrepentant man-whore, so it's hard to believe he wants anything other than a quick shake in the sheets. Don't get me wrong; I like him sweet, but I prefer him dirty. It's easier for me that way. No complications."

And there is the one crack in Ali's flawless veneer. Opening up to love is like an invitation for destruction. It had happened too many times with her birth mother coming and going until she made leaving permanent. Ali doesn't commit until it's a sure thing, and with Evan's track record, nothing is.

"You don't have to be alone. There's more to life than saving everyone else."

It's my turn to twist away, to see her eyes flash with an aching loneliness. "I'm a realist, Char. The chances I'll end up with a happily-ever-after are slim to none. I'm okay with that. Came to grips with it a long time ago."

"You're my best friend, Ali. And this last year, I gained another one. I'd never lie to you. Hell, I never dreamed of falling in love. But now that I have . . ." I grab her hand and hold it close to my heart. "Now that I have, I know the best part of a relationship is not the sex. Yes, it's mind-bendingly good. But waking up with him on a cold night is better. So is calling him at work just to hear him say my name, or holding his hand. Listening to him tell me about his day because he needs to share it with someone, and he wants that someone to be me, is better." I turn to face the fear mounting in her eyes. "Some people are worth taking a chance on. Evan is one of them."

"Maybe."

I shake my head. "Not maybe. He's a good man; I've been around for some of his stand-up moments. Think about it?"

She smirks. "When did you get so smart, Carter?"

"When I stopped letting the past interfere with my future."

She sighs, and tucks me under her chin. "I hate where we came from, but it's hard not to go down memory lane when you're getting married. Do you ever think about them? Your birth parents?"

I swallow down a sudden flash of regret: Georgette and Darryl Hilton. The year following the accident, I couldn't think of anything but them. I physically hurt from missing my life in Brighton and the two people who had loved me. When shock and pain wore off, I was stuck in anger, and I hated the memories. I hated them for leaving me in hell—a new day-to-day that was so far from the park across the street and the squeaking merry-go-round I would spin on for hours, or, Rusty, the stray dog who found his way into our backyard and my heart. If I closed my eyes, I could feel the nudge of his wet nose on my hand, and I hated it. I hated it because I was so sad.

They'd all been gone in an instant.

It took years to understand that my grief was overwhelming because the enormity of my love was just as great. But it was easier not to remember or feel or want, so I left thoughts of my childhood packed away in the box that followed me from home to home. And I never looked, because I knew it would hurt too much. Even now, it's sealed tight in the other room—shipped down with the few things I'll take with me into my future with Colin.

"Maybe I should," I whisper. "But I said my goodbyes a long time ago. Do you?"

"Hell no. That nut doesn't deserve my time." She shudders. "Fucking preadolescence. Why can't we burn those years from our memory?"

I shrug. "You're the mad genius. Figure it out, sister."

"It's at the top of my list, right under: *Get Charlie Married to Serious Hunky President.*"

"I love you."

"Ditto, but enough of this heavy shit—we've got a spa to get to."

My heart thunders into a gallop. "I'm getting married tomorrow."

"Yup. Let's get you relaxed and presentable so you're not a pufferfish when you walk down the aisle." She mimics one, eyes squinted shut, cheeks blown up, and I laugh. And then the doorbell interrupts our fun.

I bound down the steps to the door, where when opened I'm met by a blast of cold air and a huge paper bundle. A wide blue eye pops out from behind the bag stamped with *Flowers on Fourteenth.* Sawyer stands off to the side, sunglasses on, and I can just imagine what he put the poor guy through as he inspected the package.

"Morning, ma'am. Delivery for you."

Ali pops in to hand him a tip as I unload the burden from his arms. "Thanks," I say and head for the kitchen, smiling. They could be from just about anyone but my money is on Colin. My heart does a little trip, and my feet almost follow it as I stumble over to the island. Ali's right behind me, but she sits on a stool while I stand to tear open the bag.

"Oh."

I bet wrong.

A cold sweat breaks out on my brow.

BOOM! Freddie and a gun. *BOOM!* Colin collides with me and all I see is red. July comes back with a roar, and I shake my head to loosen it from my mind.

Red roses.

"I've got it," Ali says, scooping up the vase and heading to the sliding back door to heave it out in the snow.

I stay standing, watching, as paralyzed as I was that night, and she bends to pick up something from the ruined bouquet. Once inside, her cheeks are pink, eyes bright and checking me out on her way over. "You okay?"

"Yeah." I nod. "Roses get me every time. I hate them and their sickly smell."

"Here." She hands over a two-by-three card. "It's the only thing that made it out of the wreckage."

My attempt to smile feels more grimace than anything as I flip the envelope open and pull out a typed note:

Dear Charlise,

My heart is filled with so much regret I hope one day you'll hear directly from me. Until then, I wish you the happiness you deserve.

Sincerely,

Joan Montgomery.

I roll my eyes and toss the card down for Ali to read.

"The nerve of that woman," she says. "Come on, turn that frown upside-down. Get in the shower so we can go be happy and forget this crazy bitch." Ali rushes over to push me through the kitchen and living room and to the stairs. "Don't think about it," she whispers with a final love tap to get me going.

Don't think about it. That's easier said than done when the Montgomerys have a tendency to pop up everywhere I don't want them to be. Even when I think we're through with them.

WHISKED AWAY IN A limo, we sip on mimosas during the hour it takes to arrive at a lake house somewhere in Virginia, a place nosy reporters and curious well-wishers alike will never be able to find. As soon as we walk in the backdoor, staff rushes us upstairs and into a suite that rivals the poshest D.C. locale. Thoughts of the outside world cease to exist the moment we step over the threshold and we're treated to champagne and croissants. Sent into dressing rooms, we strip to our skivvies and then wrap up in satin robes.

Somewhere between the mud bath and the start of our massages, the white on white serenity is waylaid by the ultimate 80s. Ali's attempt to relive the rock-punk revival with air guitar and some Bad Religion has me rolling with laughter. She's good for my heart.

Spoiled is not the right word. Pampered and coddled come close, yet don't quite reach the extent to which we're babied and mollified. Colin wasn't playing. He went overboard, and I call around lunchtime to thank him. He's sweet, but distracted and eager to get off the phone. His text a half hour later is brief. *Everything is taken care of,* he says. *Don't worry, laugh and have fun.* I do all of the above. I'm buffed to a sheen, my nails are painted, and I'm prettier than I've ever been.

I've loved every minute of it. But a frisson of anxiety creeps in as the technician braids, twists and pins my hair into an elegant loose bun. That along with the makeup and I'm feeling every bit the bride, but I need this tomorrow, not today. "Not today," I remind Ali one more time and she waves, prompting me to enjoy.

"But the time," I say, pointing at the clock practically blaring we're going to be late for the rehearsal. "If we leave right now, we'll have seconds to spare." I half-smile at the stylist when she tries to hand me a mirror but dive out of my chair instead.

"Relax. I've got this covered. Have another drink." Ali tips hers up and grins. Of course she's drop-dead gorgeous after receiving the same attention I did. This reminds me to send her to the mortician tomorrow, even if I don't kill her tonight. *The maid of honor can't be prettier than the bride!*

Yanking on her hand, I manage to pull her up and spin on my heels for a look around the room. It's go time. From this moment on it'll be rush, rush, rush, and I don't relish the night ahead—separated by tradition.

"Alison Leigh Carter, I won't be late for my own wedding rehearsal. Focus up and find my dress!" I stomp my foot. I stomp it not once but twice when she doesn't move.

Holding up a hand, she says, "Easy, Sister. Don't get your feathers in a bunch. Or, your panties in a twist. Someone brought it up. Look by the window."

Oh, thank God. I sigh under my breath, reassured by the garment bag hanging there. I'm on it in a second, yanking the zipper down to get the show on the road. We're on the verge of twilight, the suite bathed in the late afternoon sun. It streams through the open plantation shutters, playing tricks on my sight as I peel back the bag. I swing around to find Ali, stunned by the turn of events. This can't be right.

"What has he done?" I ask, breathless, because my heart is racing a mile a minute. "This is not mine. My dinner dress is emerald green—to match my eyes. Colin loves that color. This isn't . . . it's not . . ." I bat away tears, and it's like looking in the mirror as my sister does the same. "What has he done, Ali?"

There's nowhere for my hands—not my hair, not my cheeks, because they're all done up. Twisting them in a knot in front of my stomach is the best I can do, and then she grips my shoulders.

"What's happening?" I whisper.

"He's giving you what you've wanted, but never thought to ask for." I shake my head, speechless as my brain gets stuck on the graceful gown waiting in the wings. "A wedding filled with family and good friends, not the public and their spectacular ideas."

"Oh, God." *Colin.* He'd do anything for me. Rip the sun from the sky if I needed him too. I'm overwhelmed, weakened in the knees by his generosity. "We're getting married today?"

Ali's chin trembles, and she rapid-fire blinks to save her mascara. "You got it. You're minutes away from being a Mrs."

"He's here?"

She nods.

"Right now, he's here? And Mom and Dad and Ian and Sammy and . . ."

At this pace she may need a neck brace.

The enormity of what he's done sits on my chest as the day clicks into place. He didn't get called away anywhere but to plan a second wedding that will happen before the first. *I love the shit out of that damn man.*

"Let's get you ready; we've only got minutes to spare," Ali says, squeezing my shoulders. "I can't believe you had that last drink."

I laugh as the stylist sweeps in to place a flower in my hair. Guiding me into a room, she hangs my surprise gown from a hook and hands over the scantiest lingerie. *Colin did take care of everything.* When she steps out, locking me in privacy, I enjoy the soft slide of lace and then draping silk. As I turn and take in the curve of my hip and the plunge that leaves my back bare for Colin's greedy hands, I get lost in perfection. Smooth lines cling to my thighs only to fall into a pool of white at my feet. The front dips to show a hint of cleavage and barely whispers against my stomach. It's glamorous and exactly how I pictured myself walking to meet him.

This dress is more than my style. It's a statement. He's stripped us bare and removed the pretense. We can do this, and we can do it our way. I don't doubt each detail will be flawless. This is what Colin McKenna does.

Ali peeks in. I smile, and she steps in to look over my shoulder. She's statuesque in the barest hint of blush pink, covered with black lace. From shoulders to wrist and down to her knees, she's demure, everything except for the daring drop in the back that's reflected in the mirror on the far wall. Her hair is swept to the side, curling into a waterfall over her shoulder.

"Something blue from Colin," she says, while guiding a delicate platinum necklace in place. Settled between my collarbones is a blue, cushion-cut diamond surrounded by twisting rows of brilliant white stones. It matches the earrings he gave me for Christmas. "Something old." Holding my hand, her fingers brush over my engagement ring. Colin's grandmother wore it every day for fifty years, and I couldn't be prouder to wear it for the next. "Something borrowed, from Gram," she whispers, holding out a fine handkerchief embroidered with clovers.

Running my hand over the swell of my hip, I turn and say, "Something new."

Tearing up while giving me the onceover, her "no crying" warning is muffled by my hug. A sister is a precious commodity that I'll never take for granted. "Thank you for always being exactly what I need."

She nods and squeezes harder. "We'll always have each other, Char, husbands or not." Peeling away, our eyes lock for a sweet second. "Come on, let's get Dad."

A knock sounds, and he surprises us by tipping his head into the suite. "My girls." We rush into his open arms and after a moment, Ali slips away. I'm left with the first man to bring stability into my life. I lie my cheek on his chest and pick at his tie.

“Thank you.” I catch the sob just before it chokes out of me. Gram’s hanky comes in handy and I dab at my eyes. *Lord, if I’m a mess now, give me five minutes and I’ll be unrecognizable.*

“Charlie-girl.” His voice is soft, just like the fingers rubbing my arm. “I wasn’t there on the day you were born, but I know you were beautiful. The moment you stepped into my world, you brought me great joy. I’ve watched your struggles turn into determination to find your way. You welcomed us into your life as a family; we’ve supported and celebrated and treasured every moment since you gifted us your heart. Your contagious laugh makes my smile linger after hearing it.” I nod in time to his steady heartbeat. “I love being your father. And I could only give you away to a man who will care for you as I do.”

Pressing a kiss into my forehead, he says, “Now is that time.”

Eight

Every day within the last year narrows down to this moment. I blink into reality as Dad murmurs reassurances that he won't let me tumble down the steps. With each one, I take in the ceremony site. Pine sprigs tied to the railing bring the outside in. White orchids and the barest pink peonies sit in delicate array on every open surface and are bound into the bouquet I clutch in front of my stomach. Daylight comes to a close with a bright burst through the wall of peaked windows, blurring the rows of chairs and the guests in them. Candles of varying size flicker on either side of our projected path.

As we hit the landing, my lids fall closed on a breath, and the music changes to Pachelbel's Canon in D. With the first strum of the chords, I hear the rush of bodies stand and an almost simultaneous inhale from around the room.

A sudden peace settles within me, taking away the tears I've held in since this wedding was revealed. There is nothing but a satisfied happiness as I open my eyes to find my beloved.

My Colin.

It all comes into focus and he's there, at the front—hallowed by dusk. For so long I ran away from truly feeling. Now I find myself eager to get to the man who makes me feel more than I ever thought possible.

"Ready?" Dad whispers.

"There is no other way for me but into his arms," I murmur, and make the first move into my future.

Everything around and within me falls silent. I'm struck by how handsome he is, clean-shaven and with his hair pushed back into waves, a lone piece curling on his forehead. I've seen him in a tux plenty of times, but never at the end of an aisle waiting for me with tears in his eyes. Blinking them back, he takes a step forward, as if he's anxious to have me by his side. I smile when his jaw clenches along with his hand into a fist next to his thigh. The whole time he devours me with his eyes. *I wanted Dark and Dangerous and apparently I'm about to marry him.*

"Not fast enough," he says, and my grin grows. His brow crumbles for an instant before recovering with a joy reminiscent of my own.

"Come and get me," I dare through a whisper and then giggle when the man who exerts control over all things loses it, lunging to meet me when I'm just halfway down the aisle. Dad chuckles and murmurs "smart man" as Colin comes to a stop inches away.

"May I?" he asks, without moving his gaze from mine.

Taking my bouquet in hand, Dad says with a quiver, "Love her every day."

Colin cradles my face, his thumb skimming over my bottom lip. He looks anything but gentle.

"Every minute," he says, and then he kisses me.

The world stops spinning. It is only us, clutched together before we say I do. My hands grasp his lapels, at first to draw him flush against me, and then one snakes its way to his nape to keep him in place.

I relish his sigh and the touch of his tongue, the firm grip he has on my lower back, and when his groan vibrates into me. In minutes, this man, the perfect man for me, will be mine to have and to hold from this day forward. *Mine*. If possession is nine-tenths of the law then we're already committed, but I'd like to hear the words and have his signed consent just the same. My breath takes up time with my accelerated pulse, and reason checks in as thoughts of stripping him of his tie flitter through my mind.

On the verge of panting, we lean our foreheads together and smile. My heart bursts at his whispered "I love you," and it's only then that I become aware of our audience. Evan's laugh and Ali's hoot that I'm sure comes along with a fist pump. Gram's *Hank Carter, you pay attention to all this romance,* and Aiden's *now that's how yeh get married, lassie*. The chorus of awe pushes me into motion.

"Couldn't wait another night?" I kiss him again, murmuring against his lips.

"I would marry you every day if I could."

My heart falls into my stomach. It's a miracle I don't fall from a romantic swoon as Colin starts us toward the setting sun. Wrapping my hand through his extended elbow, he holds onto it, and I keep my eyes glued to his until we're next to the officiant.

"Today we promise ourselves in front of the law and tomorrow before God and the entire world," he says, nodding that we're ready to begin.

I'm sure I look crazed when my gaze swings back and forth from Colin to Ross Gallagher, who's in attendance to tie our knot. The Chief Justice of the United States Supreme Court tilts his chin to stare over the rim of his tiny readers. "He has always gone after exactly what he wants. I can see that hasn't changed."

"No, sir." I look into Colin's storm clouds raging next to me. "And sometimes I help him get carried away."

"A good match then." Opening his book, it all unfolds as if we've practiced it a million times. Turning toward Colin, I slip my hands into his strong and sure ones, his strength flowing into me as it so often does. I stand taller and straighten my shoulders. The words have been repeated by the ages, yet they remain sacred and somehow special as they bind us together.

"I promise to love and comfort you, honor and keep you, for better or worse, for richer or poorer, for as long as we both shall live."

My "I do" trills into the hushed silence only to be broken by my mom's sniffle.

Colin grins and then pledges the ultimate commitment. Straying at the end, he closes his eyes and swallows. Seconds pass and his hold deepens, as if he's trying to pull me into his thoughts with fingers twisted through mine. When his lids blink open, the blue I seem to live in shines. "I've waited for this feeling, this fullness, this relief that I could give wholly of myself without regret or question. The minute I saw you, I knew you were different, and I was petrified I would fail, that I wouldn't be enough. I'm not afraid anymore. I promise each day I'll love you more than the last. I will care for you and pick you up when you stumble." Nearing combustible levels, he leans in and I believe every word. "Never doubt me; I will be true to you, Charlie. You have my heart and it belongs to you for all of time. In this life and into the next, I am yours."

I try; I really, really do, but tears race to my eyes, big dollops that can't be batted away. *He belongs to me*. Ali peeks over my shoulder with Gram's hankie and Colin takes it, tilting my head back so my vision is filled with only him. The gentleness missing when he first saw me at the end of the aisle is with him now. Drowning in his own emotion, he wipes mine away.

"Don't cry, my love. We have no end; this is only the first moment of a lifetime more, and I will cherish every one. Come on the journey with me."

I may be his shelter from depravity, but he became my wings. I soar now into an unbelievable reality. I scan his face, each angle and plane that I've studied many times before. I'm struck by his eyes, glowing as if the sun can shine at midnight. He soothes me in a way that I'm only beginning to understand. What was a relationship begun in a rush of heated longing evolved into the steady beating of a strong heart. We're made to stand the test of time.

No matter how crazy it may seem, Colin loves Charlie.

"You're beautiful." Desperate to rush on, I wait for a beat, taking my time to get it right, just right, since he's done everything to make me perfect. "You know my soul better than I do because it's like yours. We are the same; that's why we fit. Where you end, I begin." Placing my hand to his cheek, a shiver burns down my spine as he nuzzles into it. "Thank you for believing in me and pulling out all of my best parts. But most of all, thank you for being beautiful and amazing and mine."

Leaning in, his lips hover a whisper away and he breathes in not once, but twice before murmuring *forever yours* and then stepping back to put decency between us.

Just as twilight draws to a close, Colin slips a band on my left ring finger. Lifting it to his mouth, he seals his promise with a kiss. Using as much confidence as he exudes, I declare my fidelity and glide his in place. My stomach somersaults as his thumb caresses the white-gold and his gaze rakes over me. It's just a look, yet at the same time so much more. As if he was missing that piece and now he's complete. And he is.

The unadorned ring is a perfect fit, but it's what is on the inside that mirrors our love. Something he said to me when we first met, something that lives between us will lie against his skin for all of time.

"*I breathe you.*"

I say it now, knowing what he meant that first time, what he felt but couldn't understand. What it means to find the one person who fills all of the gaps and makes you whole.

Colin's nostrils flare. In a fractured heartbeat, his hands weave in my hair and his mouth is on mine, hot and heavy, as Justice Gallagher declares, "I now pronounce you husband and wife."

Holy cow—husband!

Any idea I had of a sweet kiss is out the door, smashed by his urgency and the first sweep of his tongue. At the second more daring foray into my mouth, I groan and my fingers lace around his neck. The weeks of forced chastity come to an end a day early and by the hand he moves to my hip, I'd say he'd like to consummate our union right now. When he draws me closer, I know I'm right as the burgeoning length of his erection digs into my stomach.

I let him devour me because it's our truth. This is how it should be. Intense and hungry, we play. Charming and chaste are for tomorrow. Tonight I can be his in our own way—cheered on by those closest to us.

My smile interrupts his growl. As do my hands, when they slink against his chest to press for a hint of distance, forcing his lips to slow and slip to my cheek where he lights kisses up to my ear. "I need you. Alone." He swallows his desperation and I laugh. Underneath his tux, his heart pounds as he drags in air.

"Only a few more hours, and I'm all yours."

The smile that lights his face is breathtaking. Forehead to forehead, he says, "For all of time."

Turning with ridiculous grins, we face an explosion of cheer at the declaration, "Ladies and gentleman, it is my pleasure to introduce Mr. and Mrs. Colin and Charlie Carter McKenna."

Charlie Carter *McKenna*. I gape at Colin. I told him one night, as we lay outside looking at the stars, about becoming a Carter. How my hand still remembers the first curve when I signed the adoption papers. It's a day I'll never forget, nor will I forget the enormous relief it brought along with it. In one instant, I went from not belonging anywhere to having a home filled with laughter and love. *They were mine*. Taking their name was an important part of my recovery. I feared losing it when I married Colin, losing a little part of myself that came after so much sacrifice.

Now I don't have to.

My grin returns and I beam at him and then Dad and Mom, who no longer try to hold in their tears. Gram, more beautiful than ever in her purple party dress, blows me a kiss. Gramps waves and elbows Ian, who does the same to Sammy. My family: now extended to include Colleen and Michael, Ryanne and Brett and Uncle Niall, with his brilliant smile. Behind them, clapping and letting loose a piercing whistle, is Aiden, Blake and Carla cringing next to him. To the right are Fitz and his wife, then Kyle. Changed into a tux, he's off the clock. But it's the wide-eyed brunette squeezed into his side that makes him look so good.

“Ready?” Colin asks while snaking an arm around my waist, his gaze as hot as the hand resting on the swell of my hip.

“I was born to be yours, Mr. President. So, yes.” I snuggle in and take advantage of his backside with a quick pat. “I’m ready for the first step into the rest of our life, husband.”

“Then by all means, wife, let’s begin our journey.”

The smack to my ass propels me forward and into a full-out laugh.

Our wedding is perfect. Always touching, never an arm’s length apart, we’re hugged and kissed by all. Set to the side on a grand piano is our wedding certificate that I’m first to sign. Colin may have blessed hyphenation but I discard my given middle name and replace it with Carter. I want him to know I’ve entered our union fully aware I’ll always belong to him. My husband nibbles my neck as McKenna flows with ease, becoming my name too. He steps forward and I hand him the pen. Only after he adds his signature with a flourish does he pause and sigh.

Wait staff rush forward with champagne. Colin tucks me into his side with one hand, using the other to grab a flute, first for me and then another for himself.

“To us, my love.” The gentle clink of his glass to mine rings true.

I nod. “To us.”

It’s crisp and zips to my stomach with the same restlessness I feel. I want to jump and shout, throw my head back to scream my joy about this night and the man wrapped around me. Instead I ask, “How did you do this?”

I look around in wonder as the ceremony chairs are whisked away and replaced by tall cocktail tables. Someone’s home, an enormous log cabin with a family room open two stories high, was transformed into a chapel and now a reception. One wall is lit by string after string of white lights; on the opposite, rocks climb to the ceiling and logs wait to be lit in the hearth. Flowing along with drinks are an array of appetizers, and everyone eases into a good time.

Colin scans the room, and then leans in for another kiss. "How isn't important," he murmurs against my mouth. "I wanted this for us. Intimate, so I can have my hands on you every second. If you haven't noticed, I'm greedy where you're concerned. I hated to think of sharing you with four hundred people and television cameras on our wedding day."

"Thank you. I love it," I say, draping an arm around his waist to mold myself into the line of his body. "Almost as much as I love you."

His gaze lands on mine, and we share a moment. A thrilling, stomach-churning, heart-pounding, my-life-will-never-be-the-same moment. The silence may as well be a novel. Chapter after chapter play out in the clench and release of his jaw, the subtle sway of his eyes as he searches my face, the parting of his lips, and the swift inhale that I feel along every nerve-ending. When he stares at my mouth, it speaks volumes: Kiss me soft and hard, short and long, dirty and sweet, tease me, but more than anything—do it forever.

"That." I pull him down by the neck. "That right there felt like your teeth sinking into my shoulder."

Broad and looming, he pulls up to full height so he can lean over and tilt my head back. "Like that, do you?"

"Yes," I breathe out in a rush.

"Good, because I've got plans for you," he murmurs into me. "And they start on your knees . . ."

Oh, God.

Colin chuckles. "He can't save you tonight, bunny. I'm hungry. But before I sink my teeth in you, I want your mouth on me." Light as a feather, he drags a finger from my temple to the object of his current affection. "I want that sweet-as-sin mouth to take me to the back of your throat."

I lick my lips and remember the clean, musky maleness. "It's been too long."

"Then let me remind you."

“Here?” I look around and catch the occasional smirk, our family humoring us with a minute alone.

“Now.”

Pressing his cheek to mine, he whispers. Explicit details, placement of my hands—tongue and lips, too. I’m coiled tight. It’s a long chapter with a very happy ending. By the last page, I’m breathing heavy with my fingers clutched in his hair. The champagne is long forgotten and barely hanging on in the limp hand at my side.

“Not fair,” I moan into his neck, living and dying in the hint of his cologne and the sweet nectar of him.

A rumble rolls in his chest. “Neither were the last ten days.”

“Payback?” I ask.

“Payback.”

The word flickers a flame along my skin just as the fireplace sparks to life, and the string quartet tucked into the corner warms the atmosphere even further. Mission accomplished. I burn for him. In my angelic white dress, I want the devil to take me, and he knows it.

Our celebration goes on and I melt into the blissful torture.

NINE

LAUGHTER DISSOLVES INTO MUSIC. Stories are passed around. And over the next couple of hours we mingle, nibble on the food and each other. I can't stop smiling. A photographer I hadn't noticed earlier hovers outside of conversations, clicking the night into memories. Every time Colin dips down to brush his mouth on mine, or I stand on tiptoes to taste his jaw, she captures it on film.

At some point, conversation stops as we dance, or more like sway, to a rendition of our song. I sing to him as I often do when we're alone, sometimes while playing the guitar and others just like this. I stare into his eyes or at his lips as he licks them. The words of the song tremble when his strong fingers tease my bared skin and then dig into my backside, too low to be proper. Then again, we've forsaken etiquette. When his breath fans my ear, I lose myself in his whisper: *"So damn exquisite. I can't wait to see your face in our children."*

I trust that he will. Squeezing my eyes shut, I bury my head in his neck and hum. And breathe. And let it sink in that we are a family now. Tonight we started something more significant than his work or my past. Our beginning starts right now, and we can shape the rest of it with decisions made together.

As the final notes of "At Last" vibrate, the not-so-subtle strike against crystal prompts us to part enough for our lips to meet. At first it's a soft brush, and at the next pass the pressure is firm until I open to allow him in. We're tangled in more ways than one. If I say *I love you* again it won't be enough. It's not merely a statement, or a feeling—it's simply more.

Dad steps in. His eyes meet Colin's, and a silent message passes between them. Colin nods and presses his mouth to my temple, lingering long enough for me to hold his cheek and inhale his scent. Then he's gone, leaving me to slip into the safety of my father's arms while Colin swoops in to dance with his mother.

"You're glowing."

I try to straighten a grin away. It doesn't work. "I feel alive."

"You've earned this happiness, Charlie. There is no need to stop your smiles or hide your feelings."

Dad's right. And I won't. I won't shelve my emotions. Loving Colin isn't only easy for me, but for my parents, too. Their affection was cemented when he took every step necessary to ensure my well-being last July. Later, Colin asked their forgiveness for proposing without prior approval. He didn't have to beg. Not because he'd be hard to say no too, which he is, but because his actions speak for him.

On a campaign run through Michigan after our engagement, we stopped for a quick visit. They saw his love in simple gestures—the brush of his thumb against my lip, or kissing my palm and then pressing it against his chest. And even more so because he slowed down so I could show off my ring to my family. So I could have a normal moment and look at bridal magazines with Gram and Mom.

Dad told me his respect for Colin grew that day, and I catch him now, chuckling at my husband's lost look as Colleen transitions into Michael's arms.

He glances my way and gets serious. "Your mother and I trust Colin to take care of you and I trust you to know when to come home. Life experiences set the differences within us all. It's okay to take a step back every once in a while to find your feet again."

"I love you," I say into his neck, squeezing a breath out of him. This is the happiest day of my life, but tears keep clogging my throat. "I won't be gone too long; we'll be up for a visit soon."

"I miss you already, Charlie-girl. Before you make your old man cry, go." He waves me on. "Put your husband out of his misery."

Colin is midway to my side when Ryanne overtakes him, and Aiden slips into my open arms for a dance just as Dad vacates them.

My greeting is muffled into his shoulder as he draws me in. He smells clean with a hint of campfire, as if he's never far away from the forest any lumberjack would die for. With his burnt umber hair slicked behind his ears, and matching beard trimmed, he cleaned up into a presentable gentleman. Well, almost—everything except for the fingers strumming along my spine.

"You're antagonizing him," I admonish with a smile.

"Aye, lassie." Aiden barks out a laugh. "It's easy to do where you're concerned."

Colin's snarl reaches us as he and Ryanne sweep by, too close to be anything but a threat. Dragging his gaze to his friend, Colin mouths *I'm watching you* and then spins his sister into an elegant twirl.

"There was a time when he wasn't so serious," Aiden says, watching Colin watch him.

"In college?"

"Yeah. He and Evan were hell on wheels back then. All above board, don't get me wrong. But they came up with some shit." Aiden shrugs, his cheeks burning red. "I damn near pissed myself when they duct-taped me and Alex together after passing out."

"Alex?" I ask, snapping to attention.

"Yeah, we were easy freshman prey back then. Damn, it set Alex off." Aiden shakes his head and looks into the flicking flames warming the room.

"What did he do?"

"Not much he could do. Colin may have been easier back then, but he owned that campus. Everything he touched was golden; he was head of the class. Alex couldn't take him on the debate team or the rugby field, and Colin got his girl."

"What?"

Aiden's blush reheats. "Ah, Charlie. I'm sorry. I shouldn't be talking about this on yer weddin' day."

"No," I say, with more force than a hammer to nail. "I don't mind. Go on."

Feeling the pressure of my stare, he stammers out, "St . . . Steffie Ross. Alex wanted her since summer orientation. They went out for a few weeks before Colin showed an interest. As soon as that happened, she didn't know who Alex Miller was."

"Did Colin know they were dating?"

"I don't think he cared to. He wasn't close with Alex, so if Steffie didn't tell him, then he wasn't asking."

"Why didn't you?" I ask, sharp enough to match my sudden nerves. "Tell him, I mean."

He winces. "Honestly, I didn't think it was a big deal. Steffie made her rounds, if you catch my drift, but Alex, he fell hard."

That's why he hated Colin. *And it's why he went after Abby.* The puzzle piece drops into place. *An eye for an eye*. I shudder against the thought.

Aiden takes up nonsensical chatter, and I sink into my own thoughts. But it's more like a black hole of knowledge. There's something I'm missing—a break in the connect-the-dots preventing the whole picture from coming into focus.

So many moving parts: Shane, Alex, Ella, and John. I had thought of the latter as the lead. Yet, maybe I'm wrong. We're embroiled in a game of chess and if Alex and Ella are pawns, then one has been knocked out of play, what does that leave on the opponent's field and who is the mastermind? Alex—but could he design the enormous stage? John—the king. He was sacrificed, leaving the queen as the most powerful piece. *The queen*?

Joan.

My eyes snap to Kyle, dancing and laughing with his girl until she turns green and rushes off the floor. It might be funny, Kyle left standing with his arms caressing the air, but the wreckage she left behind is too pathetic to enjoy. In the worst rendition of The Robot known to man, he tries to recover his cool and slide away with little fanfare.

"Thanks for the dance, Aiden." I kiss his cheek and follow Kyle out of the room and down a long hall.

I find him, head bent, fingers on the handle to the bathroom. "I'm coming in, angel," he says, only to be met by a groan from the other side.

"Probably not a good idea." I pat his shoulder as consolation.

He bangs his head once and then looks up. "I could hold her hair or something."

"You're smarter than that, cowboy." I choose the nickname Faith used earlier, and it drives his eyes to slits. "No woman wants her man watching a pukefest. It's very unattractive."

When his shoulders fall in a slump, I pat them and then nudge him out of the way. "Faith?" I call, opening the door just wide enough to slide in. She's hunched over on the floor, a pooling heap of red dress stark against the cream marble. Easing down next to her, I relieve the hand holding her curls back. We sit in silence, as her breath and heaving chest calm, until she turns, cheek resting on her stretched arm. Even lying against a toilet, I can see why Kyle fell so hard.

Her shining eyes offer hints of spun gold woven through their brown depths. Chocolate velvet frames smooth, sun-kissed skin. "I'm sorry," she says, in a raw whisper.

"No worries." I reach over to flush and then stand, dragging her with me. It takes a minute, but after rinsing her mouth and washing up she looks more human than Martian. I hop up to sit on the counter, handing her a brush from the goodie basket next to me.

"This isn't exactly how I envisioned meeting you," she says, her gaze flicking away from mine. "Vomiting at the President and First Lady's wedding, wow. Let me die now and crawl in the casket."

"Well, lucky you. Because I'm just Charlie, so there's no need to kick the bucket."

My heart catches when the beginning of a smile crumbles and tears well, ready to fall. "I don't have the flu, and I didn't have anything to drink."

I'm a quick study, and connect her health and sobriety to a double line on a pee stick. I nod and rub her arm, because what do I say? I'm not sure she's ready for congratulations and *it's going to be okay* is a meaningless platitude.

"Cat's out of the bag, I guess." Faith straightens her shoulders and tosses her hair back. Wiping along her lower lashes, she says, "It was the first time we, uh, you know . . . had sex. I thought he was just a hook-up, but as it turns out, he wanted more. Even before"—she motions above her stomach—"even before knowing this."

I pry the brush away and take her hand. "This is so cliché, yet I've found it to be the truth. Everything happens for a reason. You may not be able to understand it right this second, but down the road you'll look back to this moment and the light bulb will go off. Doesn't matter why, what does is that you are."

"Yeah, I am," she says. "Life's messy that way."

"It doesn't have to be a bad thing."

"But how can it be good? I've known him all of a minute. Which I get, and hindsight is a bitch, because I can see I shouldn't have wanted to sleep with him within the first hour we met, but I did." Squeezing my fingers in a death grip, she says, "I wanted it and then I wanted him. I still do—more now than ever."

"Then there you go. You're just going about things in a slightly unconventional timeline."

"Slightly?"

"Everyone can make their own right way."

She smiles. "I like you."

Sliding off the counter, I say, "Good, because I've already decided we're friends, and it would be awkward if you didn't."

"Thanks, Charlis . . ."

"Charlie. Always Charlie, or I'm kidnapping this killer dress in six months. Ransom will be weekly babysitting duty with little Jessie James. Prepare yourself; he might come out with guns blazing."

Her eyes go wide, and then the sun shines through in a smile so big it burns a dimple in her cheek. “Jessie James Sommerton. That’s kind of a horrible name.”

“Yet so right at the same time.”

We giggle and try to squish through the door side by side. As soon as he sees us, Kyle busts out of a lean against the wall to take back ownership. I can read a *thank you* in the clear waterfall that is his eyes as he buries Faith in a hug. *You’re welcome,* I mouth and turn back to the party, only to be stopped by a hulking groom at the end of the hall.

“That’s one fine-looking husband, if I do say so myself.” And I do, taking him in from head to toe. He lost his jacket and rolled his sleeves to elbow-length, collar open with his loosened bow-tie hanging on either side. Looking at perfection never gets old.

He scoffs and reaches for my hips. “You’re coming with me.”

“We still have to cut the cake.” I laugh as he gets hands-on, backing us into a shadowed den to lean his ass on a desk. Spreading his legs, he nestles me between them and finds my breasts at eye level.

“The only way I’m eating cake is if the frosting is dripping from your body.”

I sigh and wrap an arm around Colin’s shoulders, drawing him even closer, so close his breath goads my nipples into tight buds. His hand sweeps up and down my back. More potent than the wine or fire, heat flares in my belly, and I shudder when he teases the line of my G-string.

I’m seconds away from an indecent make-out session that would cause even Gram to blush, and desperate for a distraction. The chess game I thought of earlier is pressing for further discussion in my mind. I want to learn more about one particular player. “Tell me about Joan Montgomery.”

He grunts, glancing up and out of my cleavage. By the looks of it he’s none too pleased with the request. “Why the hell would we discuss her on any night, let alone this one?”

“I have a feeling . . .”

“Then let me give you another.”

Leaning in, he sucks on the swell of my breast. My gasp is sharp, but not as shrill as Ali’s whisper-scream, “Not here!”

The distraction I asked for breezes into the den like a storm. Colin and I lock eyes and smile. Entertainment comes in all forms and tonight, it’s Evan and Ali. One of them is bound to get swept away by their sparking tension.

“Why not?” Lit in the doorway by the licking fireplace flames, Evan shrugs into nonchalance, and it sends my sister into a narrow-eyed hellion.

“Because . . .” She hisses and steps forward to grab his lapel. “I’m not interested.”

“That’s a lie.” He digs his fingers into her hip, dragging her forward.

Pushing away, she says, “Give me time to finish.”

“Oh, sweet Ali. I’ll always make sure you finish first.”

Mouth falling open, she takes a second to fume and in another she gives in. She slams him against the wall and they clash into a kiss.

It’s not my giggle that gives us away in the corner of the room, or Colin’s groan as I turn and shimmy my backside into his already tented trousers. It’s Kyle when he flicks on the light, Faith tucked in behind him.

I giggle at his *oh shit* expression that eases into one of goodwill. “Meeting of the minds?” he asks us with a raised brow. At the same time the blonde beauties come up for air, dazed but not surprised by their audience.

“The smartest ones,” Colin murmurs, running a finger along the curve of my arm. Ignoring my shiver, he does it again. My retaliation is swift and close to his groin, and then I relax into his grunted chuckle.

“I’m so sorry. We didn’t realize . . .” Faith says, staring wide eyed at Colin.

“No need to be, honey.” Ali tugs her dress in place. “You can’t help you were dragged into a room full of blue balls. Well, all of them except for your guy. He looks pretty healthy.”

Evan throws out a point, covering Kyle’s *bet your ass I am.* “Hey. Don’t bring the color of my nuts into this. It’s not them; it’s that you’re fucking sexy—all the time, Al.” I’ve never heard him whine and it’s fabulous. “Fuck.” Running his hands down and then back up his face, he grabs at his hair.

“I know.” She pats his chest, but looks at Faith. “Since Evan is speechless, ask him.” Ali nods to Colin and Faith’s eyes pop with the shake of her head. “Go ahead; ask him about Charlie’s pre-wedding preparation and how he’s managed.”

“Jesus, woman.” Evan groans.

“I . . .” Faith shakes her head. “I can’t ask the President about blue balls.”

I laugh into my hand and then bend over; it grows until I cry. The best tears of all. This night is a dream come true, far away from the pressure to perform in a big white dress in front of hundreds of people I barely know.

Colin folds me in his arms and I look around. Evan hauls Ali against his chest. He whispers something in her ear that pulls out the brightest smile I’ve seen from her all day. Faith’s man holds her as if she’s every baked good in the U.S. and Canada combined. My love, with his chin resting on my shoulder, is pressed so tight to me I can feel the buttons lining his shirt branding me as his. Our fingers tangle together to rest on his thigh, his thumb circling my engagement and wedding rings. For once I’m not nervous about tomorrow or moving into the White House. I know with certainty that whatever comes next in this wonderful and crazy life, we’ll hit it head on, together.

TEN

Charlie – April

PRESERVE, PROTECT AND DEFEND. With those words, my life changed irrevocably. I held the bible, the weight of Colin's hand pressed to it as his voice vibrated with certainty. He is President of the United States and we live in the White House. Months after he carried me over the threshold, these facts still sit just left of surreal.

Even as I bound down the steps and into the foyer to greet a touring group of students, I find the collective gasp strange. I'm Charlie with a dash of princess, because I live in a castle with the prince. Our home is starched in tradition and the amount of history that lies in each inch is breathtaking. Lit by large chandeliers, the checkered marble tile, red carpet, and impressive pillars are formidable. The memories of powerful men who once lived here, who now line the walls in portraits, are daunting.

But it's hard to ignore the truth when living with the constant flash of cameras and the reporters who follow my agenda. *My agenda.* I have responsibilities outside of being the president's wife. Scrutiny and judgment, power and influence—they're part of the package and I have taken advantage of it all. I've found my passion, and it's not only Colin. I have four years to impart my message, to leave a Charlie Carter McKenna legacy to shape the futures of women that share my past, and soldiers who need more than they have now.

Finding my voice is electrifying. Helping others find theirs is humbling.

Three months of volunteer work at Washington's newest military rehabilitation center, a heavy dose of reality and working with recovering veterans, brought me to this moment. One I'm not sure my husband will appreciate. A camera flash sparks and so do my nerves. It's time for my appointment with the President.

Life in the district is fast. One minute I'm posing for pictures and whispering in the ear of a wide-eyed twelve-year-old boy "Look in the corner of the Red Room and you might see President Lincoln." In the next, I race away. It's a long, but easy transition from home to hub: the West Wing. I weave between suits and ties. Many faces are familiar campaign staffers who accepted regular positions on Colin's team; others are press or visitors lost in the maze of offices.

My husband broke tradition by reallocating space for me on the first floor, in a corner opposite to him. The previously designated suite for the first lady on the east campus felt like the other side of the Earth from where we are now. If he'd had his way, I'd be tucked next door with easy access to his personal suite, yet I predicted he'd get little work done with less than ten feet separating us. A last-minute reluctant agreement landed me here.

Bigger than I deserve, the white walls and built-in bookshelves are a subtle backdrop for the traditional yet modern beige wood desk that sits center-stage. A crystal chandelier and light blue accents, including two chairs sitting opposite of mine, clearly define it as feminine and entirely different than the deep umber markings of my male predecessor. Colin wanted me comfortable, at work and in our personal residence. A makeover of both locations was his way to ensure I was.

Molly sits at the small conference table by the window, riffling through the pages of a bound brief, and highlighting key points of my presentation. After the inauguration, I was pushed to select my own staff. A long line of positions missed their meaning, so I decided I needed just one. And the one became my friend.

"Just in time, Mrs. First Lady." She glances up and whistles.

I turn to show her the dark lines on my stockings that travel well past the hem of my skin-tight pencil skirt. "I'm not trying to distract him, but a little persuasion of the Charlie Carter variety can't hurt either," I say over my shoulder. "He couldn't possibly say no to this, could he?"

"It's called coercion. And yes, I can confirm the President will have a problem with you rolling around on a mat with that." She points to a picture of a buffed out Navy Seal who's been teaching me self-defense.

"He's harmless." I wave away her lifted eyebrow as if she's questioning my sanity.

"Uh-huh, tell that to the eighty-seventh infantry he singlehandedly rescued in Iraq. Did you know he already has a medal of honor and it appears he may get another? The list goes on. To top it off, he's a feast for the eyes. If I wasn't already taken I would lap the frosting off of him and call him cupcake."

I giggle. "It's true. Women everywhere will thank me for this, and Caden Lawless may just receive a few marriage proposals in the process."

"Try selling it just like that to your husband and you're sure to get house arrest."

"Oh, right." I remove my forgotten accessory from my clutch and slide them on. "That's what these are for." The Nurse Carter glasses come in handy a second time. I let them slip down my nose as I look at her over the rim.

She coughs out a laugh. "Are you trying to disable the man? He won't be able to walk to his one o'clock."

"My goal exactly. I've been missing him the last few days so I'm taking advantage of every minute I have." A lump sticks in my throat. It's not the 55,000 square feet of White House space that's wedged distance between us, but the constant moving pieces of his position. He's needed here, asked to be there, consulting with them and meeting with everyone except me. But I'll see him tonight; it's fine.

Molly taps her highlighter on the table to bring me back to the now and not last night when Colin's meeting bled past dinnertime.

"It's Wednesday; everyone in the White House knows the evening belongs to you. What are you planning for date night?"

"I've got a new risotto recipe and a side of lace I'm going to try on for size."

"Perfect." She squares the edges of three binders with her robin egg blue painted nails. "Okay then, here are three copies of the final proposal. If you need the presentation, which I'm predicting is a no, it's on here." She hands over the files and a flash drive. "Oh, one last thing—here's the info on Aubrey Tayler, the war widow you've agreed to meet with on Friday."

"Thanks." I tuck the stack, added file and all, in the crook of my elbow, like a school girl walking to class. "Wish me luck."

"Goodbye, hot stuff," she calls after me as I head down the hall.

I flatten a smile when Communications Director Eric Brady does a double-take. His loyalty to the President has stopped him from looking me in the eye, let alone taking a sideways glance. Causing his jaw to drop is a feat unto itself, and he's not the only one. I tried extra hard to look stunning today and apparently it worked, but the nerves hit regardless of my swagger. This is important, and I need Colin's blessing to move forward with Katherine Hess.

Aligning forces with her was not on my radar until my eyes were opened to a community most people don't think or talk about. They needed a voice and I happened to have one on a very large, national scale. We're prepared to produce a documentary capturing the struggles of recovering war veterans as told through their hard work and raw honesty. In the end, it will bring two close-to-my-heart topics together: self-defense and physical rehabilitation, starring yours truly.

Coming up on the Oval Office, I knock on Betsy's open door. She knows everything about D.C. and the people in it, first and foremost—the President. If I want my husband, she can find him.

Head down, phone to ear, she looks up with a finger in the air. A white 70s shag and a glare make her as formidable as the man she protects, but in the moment recognition takes she warms into a smile.

Ending her call as quick as I popped in, she says, "Mrs. McKenna, so nice of you to stop by. Are you here for the President?"

"I am. He squeezed me in between his appointments."

Before she can reply, the door to the Oval Office swings open and Kyle stomps out in a haze of agitation. There's nothing easygoing about his drawn lips and scowl. The red hue fueling his combustion drains from his face when he spots me, and he stops in his tracks.

"Easy, killer." I step forward and peek around his shoulder. "Everything okay in there?" Colin has minutes of wiggle room in his calendar, and I don't want to miss what little time he set aside for me.

"Boss-lady, what are you doing around these parts? The motorcade will pick you up at the front."

"Don't deflect. Did you piss him off?"

He looks to the floor and then behind him, sheepish. "Me? Nah, it was just some intel that came in. Come on, I'll walk with you."

Sidestepping his outstretched hand, I say, "Thanks, but Colin is expecting me. I'll be out in a few."

"Charlie . . ."

But it's too late. It's too late for my heart not to be broken because the office is empty. The looming carved Resolute Desk is cleared of any work. Two couches mirror each other, the presidential seal bold and in full color on the rug beneath them—very patriotic, even more regal, and extra vibrant with no one in the room.

Oh. Okay. I turn to find Kyle and Betsy standing and staring through a moment so awkward it hurts my chest. It's hard to ignore the blush burning up my cheeks, I'm sure more noticeable for the light pink sweater that's now cinched too tight and fueling my fire.

"He left through the back," Kyle mumbles.

I nod, hugging the binders close as if they were a shield, a protection against the hurt that has crept in more than once during the last few months. "For something more important than me."

"DO YOU REALLY NEED to clear out the restaurant?"

Kyle levels a stare my way. "For the record, it's only one of three rooms and yes, we do—every time. That along with security inside, on the perimeter outside, and having everyone in the place vetted against a list of terrorists and White House fanatics. So stop asking and get to eating."

He points to the only guest allowed to remain in the back of Tao. This place is Ali incarnate—modern and smart, cream walls and leather furniture that match the pale tone of her hair. Red accents, the same as her lips, line the walls. She's done up today in a black pencil skirt and a skin-tight sleeveless turtleneck. With her hair tucked up and under to mimic a short bob, she channels Marilyn Monroe, and I'd like to know why. Lunch with me doesn't warrant lipstick.

"I don't know how you talked me in to this," I say as I approach, and then give her a quick hug. "I hate sushi."

"But Evan loves it." Her grin is so broad it must knock out the waiter as he slams down water glasses.

"Ah." My heart sinks, even when I know hers must be racing. "And he's joining us?"

She nods as we sit. "I haven't seen him in a week, and today is my only day off. He's got a few hours while Colin is at some meeting. Just enough time to eat and have my dessert, too. Oh," she says. "Oh, honey. I'm sorry. Is this bad? Should I call and cancel? I didn't think you'd mind. But you do. Yes, of course you do. We hardly see each other alone with these boys around all the time. I'll call him."

"Ali." I sigh, as she pulls out her phone.

"No." She bats away my attempt to grab her cell. "I totally get it."

"Stop." Success comes in a swift snatch. Her eyes narrow as they did in high school during baseball season. Behind the plate, I could hold my own with quick hands and a good arm that rivaled her hand–eye coordination at short-stop. "I'm happy Evan's joining us for lunch and I'm sorry for this." I set her phone aside and wave around my face. "Blame hormones or Colin. One or both are responsible."

"You're missing him."

I hate when tears blur Ali into a toddler's first attempt at finger painting. "Yup." Swallowing my feelings is easier said than done and I have to use the menu to fan my eyes. "Call me silly. I see him almost every day, but stringing minutes together here and there isn't making for quality time." *It's okay*, I say to myself in a chant. *I'll see him tonight.*

She tugs the menu from my grip, setting it aside, and then my hand is in hers. "We knew it would be tough."

I nod and bite my lip to hold in a full-out cry. "I know." My voice wavers. "It's just a bit more difficult than I thought. It's fine though; we're fine." The water comes in handy as I drink it down and wash away too much emotion. "Enough of this Debbie-downer business. Things are good with Evan?"

It takes her a minute of review, weighing my change of direction against her further questions. "Really good. Better than I thought possible."

I squeeze her fingers and release from her grip. "Is this when I should say I told you so, or do I save that for my speech at your wedding?"

"Hush your mouth, Sister," she says, and then breaks out into a blush to rival her lipstick. Ali blushing? Dear sweet Jesus, mark the moment in the bible. The last time this happened she was stuck in the confessional for so long, Father Thomas had to ask for a respite before he could continue.

"Damn."

"I know, right? I don't fall in love, Charlie. This is crazy."

"Enjoy it, Al; it's the best rollercoaster you'll ever ride."

"Speaking of riding. . ." She beams over my shoulder, and I roll my eyes. Evan leans in to kiss my cheek and then slides in next to Ali, his arm rounding the back of her shoulders as he does. As always, he's dashing in a black suit and tie.

"How's my girl?"

"I'm fine, thanks for asking," I say.

He grins, but can't stop staring at Marilyn.

"Yeah, so I'm going to pee while you two finish having sex with your eyes. If the waiter comes, order me a burger, because raw fish isn't my thing, okay? Okay, great. I'll see myself out." I laugh and grab my clutch.

It's an easy path to the ladies' room when no one else is around. The hustle of late-lunch traffic picks up when I pass through the main dining area. Tao is a horseshoe, with the kitchen in the center. Even though I teased Ali, I like it for the backroom they save for business meetings. It's easier for security to empty a small space than desecrate lunch service just to feed the First Lady.

In the restroom mirror, I check my eyes to ensure my feelings aren't running down my face. I miss Colin. Today's failed connection is at the bottom of a growing list. Last week he was stuck in the situation room as he and his team worked on negotiations with a volatile Middle Eastern country. He'd missed my apple pie that night and the indoor picnic I'd planned. Before that it was a long line of senior leaders who had needed to speak with him, so I'd attended the ballet by myself. *It's always something.*

Kyle calls my name through the door. With one last glance at my eyes, I slide my clutch off the counter and with it, someone's leftover newspaper I hadn't seen falls to the floor. The headline lands face up: *Unrest in Europe. Terrorist Threats Rise*. A quick scan of the article outlines unsuccessful attempts with more suspected attacks over the coming weeks. U.S. citizens are warned to cancel travel plans. I grab the paper and walk back in a daze. *Europe in four weeks.* It's a tick burrowing in the back of my mind, and it bothers me as I sit and sip my water. Evan and Ali are too engrossed in each other to notice my distraction. The waiter comes for our order and with a small carafe of Sake, but I stare unseeing out the window.

"What's up, Sister?" Ali snaps her fingers in front of my eyes.

Storm clouds brew, rumbling into a dark gray and my stomach churns with them. "Europe in four weeks." I pull the paper from my lap and push it across the table. Evan's brow tightens down as he scans it over. “Why is Colin going overseas when the region is so unstable?”

He tilts his head, as if I’ve had too much wine. “That trip’s been planned for months, Charlie. As a new president he needs to establish ties with Munduozzi, Aguillard, and Cameroon. They’ll discuss many things, including terrorism.”

“And this is the trip he asked me not to go on.”

“He’d prefer you didn’t. Relations are strained right now with some countries. From Colin’s perspective, the farther away you are the better protected you’ll be from becoming a target.”

“A target?”

He nods. “It’s complicated. The President’s trying to keep you safe.”

“From what?”

He stops, piercing me with a serious stare. I’m not backing down, and level him with one of my own.

“What am I missing?” Ali asks, hesitant as she flicks her gaze between us.

“Kilpatrick,” Evan says with little inflection.

Damn, my heart. It rolls around like a WWE wrestler as my pulse picks up. “He’s worried.”

“Everyone is. But add the President’s overprotectiveness of his wife and we’ve reached nuclear threat levels.”

“Okay, okay.” Ali holds out her hands. “Who is this guy and why is Colin threatening war over him?”

Looking around, Evan only continues when he’s sure the room is clear but for Kyle and Sawyer flanking the walls. “Kilpatrick is former U.S. military special ops. Five years ago he turned sides and is now the leader of the most aggressive terrorist cell we’ve seen since Bin Laden. I’ll spare you details of tactics he’s used to persuade the opposition to do his bidding. It’s not pleasant, and neither are his latest threats.” Slamming back a shot of Sake, he looks at the empty cup as if disappointed it wasn’t a stiff 100 proof whiskey. “His specialty is infiltrating sects. What appears to be a friend is very much a foe, and you won't have a clue until it's too late."

I push away my glass, too nauseous to drink. "How does he do it? Get the people to follow him?"

"Everyone has a motivation. He finds it and plays it up. If it's greed, he'll pass along more money than it's possible to spend. Revenge? You get the idea."

"And Kilpatrick has threatened Charlie?" Ali grabs Evan's sleeve, her knuckles turning white through the force of her grip.

"I never said that."

"But it's been implied." Her eyes flare, incredulous.

"If there was a direct threat, the First Lady would not be having lunch at Tao. She'd be in a safe house with the militia surrounding it, a thousand-deep on each side." He looks at me and then Ali. "It's no surprise the President and his family are targets; they always are. The quickest path to break a man is through the one he loves."

"You're right." I swallow my fear and look at Kyle. I trust him with my life every day. He'd die for me, but I pray it never comes to that. He has too much to live for, and he's leaving tomorrow to go get her.

"Colin is in a tight corner, Charlie. Balancing your well-being and the future of every person in this country is a lot of pressure."

"And what about him? Why is no one stopping the President from overseas travel?" Panic tightens every muscle in my body and I stay tense with unease.

"It's day to day, but as of now the intelligence is clear. His trip is a go."

It doesn't sit well. None of it does. I want to hide away in the tunnels below the White House with machine guns strapped to our backs. I'm not one for guns, but self-preservation seems appropriate in this scenario. Colin is not the only one worried, but this is our life for the near future. Fear of living it isn't the answer; following the rules is. "We have the best intelligence in the world. I trust it to keep us safe; if not, I'll end up medicated and rocking in the corner."

Evan smirks. "He'd make a deal with the devil if it meant keeping you safe. I'm praying he won't need to make that call."

"I'm sure he won't." But a trickle of anxiety remains through lunch and our goodbyes. It follows me into the limo, and while I learn to put power behind my punch at the rehab center. I expel my angst in each jab at a newfound friend who I see more than my husband.

Exhaustion doesn't free me from apprehension, even as I return to the residence and sink into a hot bath. I force myself into happy thoughts with candles flickering on every surface. Maroon 5 and a little "Sugar" drown out the buzz of evening White House deals and the last group of tourists. I sink into thoughts of Colin and take my time remembering his hands and his mouth and his body. He sticks with me while I slide into black lace. I feel him wrapped around me in the kitchen with each soft stir of the risotto, and as I sneak a glass of wine before he arrives. His breath is a whisper on my neck as I set our places in the dining room and dim the lights.

At seven I'm done and sit in front of the fire to wait for him. Pulling a pillow and throw from the chair, I lie down and relax, watching the flames flicker and remembering when we would dance in Georgetown. To whatever was playing, it didn't matter. As long as he held me and we moved together.

Missing those days, I find comfort in our space. It reminds me of him because I borrowed his townhouse style for the renovation. The colors and mimicked furniture brought a little bit of home into the second floor. The tall walls of the long and narrow great room are the same gray, punctuated by stark-white crown molding and built-in bookshelves. They're lined with pictures of our weddings and family and other mementoes we've collected along the way. At eight I get my phone and send him a text.

I love you, Colin McKenna.

Resting my head on the feather-down pillow, I think of him and startle awake thirty minutes later when his *And I you, my love. Be home late* buzzes through.

But it's date night.

My lip crumbles in time to the thunder outside, and I let the tears come. They wash the disappointment away only to get stuck in a lump of sadness in my throat. I storm into the kitchen and heave the risotto, pan and all, into the trash with a rush of anger. Standing in front of the sink, arms straight to hold me up, I mourn the night and the man I want so bad my heart aches.

Looking out the window and into the sky ripped in two by lightning, I wrestle with missing him and hating his job. Yet I know of its importance and how hard he fought to get to this moment. Begrudging him that will only see us grow apart, and I'm not willing to go there. Ever.

Dragging my sorry ass to bed, I'm stopped by the flurry of feet on steps. "Mrs. McKenna?" A slight southern drawl announces it's Johnson about to break through my door.

Shit. I look down at my breasts spilling out of the barely-there bra. Racing to our room, I grab Colin's work shirt that's waiting for the cleaners. I roll my eyes as I sink into his musk. Sanity saves me from smothering myself in all things McKenna, as does my name when it's called again.

"Here." Running into the living room I salute Johnson and his partner for the night. Richards, I think is his name. They have the decency to turn away after their gazes meet my legs, and I twist the cotton closer to my neck.

"Ah, ma'am. Please stay put; we're on lockdown."

My chest tightens every time. It's been happening more and more often. There's no privacy during these stints as the Service investigates a threat to the White House or someone in it.

"What's going on?" I ask. Sitting on the couch, I cover my bare skin with the blanket I pulled out earlier. Kyle would tell me, but he's off, and I don't know these men well enough for them to relay White House secrets.

"Please, ma'am. Continue with whatever you were doing."

Tears coat my eyes and I look away. "Nothing. I was doing absolutely nothing." With strangers staring at my back, I take my

Kindle from the side table and hope to get lost in someone else's dream come true.

ELEVEN

IT'S POSSIBLE TO MISS someone you see every day. Colin's position changed our lives in many ways. One of which is time. There's not enough of it. Up at the crack of dawn yesterday, he didn't fall into bed until I had long fallen asleep. This is where I find forgiveness of his oversight. Running the country is more important than dinner.

But *I miss him*.

I find myself awake, just to stare. Watch as his features lie peaceful, his lips full instead of pulled in a tight line. Brow and jaw relaxed into the sweet man that hides behind the powerful president.

Our personal suite is huge, as is the four-poster bed, and he seems a mile away as the sun breaks from the horizon. Lord, he's a sight in the morning, lying on his stomach with his arms pushed under his pillow. The rigid muscles of his back are barely relaxed and the round swell of his ass is visible above the sheet I pull down inch by loving inch. I remember the feel of my feet wrapped around him. His skin as my nails dig in, the sweat that coats it as he moves within me.

Oh, my. I fan myself, smiling. And I do the only thing a wife can do when she wants to be close to her husband—I act as his alarm clock and slide on top of him. Aligning my curves with his hard plains, I press my nose between his shoulder blades, right below his nape. His fists loosen to accommodate my fingers as they wind through his.

"What are you doing, love?" His voice is sexy as sin as he unravels from sleep.

"Touching you everywhere." I kiss and then taste him with the tip of my tongue—male, musky, and mine.

We let time pass, Charlie loving Colin in the simplest way: with him perfect and hot underneath me. Reality settles in with a ray of light breaching through the curtains to streak across us—a reminder that the Earth continues to revolve whether we want to join it or not. I prefer not.

"Hm," he murmurs and rolls to bring us chest to chest. I bite at his chin, reveling in the rough brush of his whiskers. "You're my favorite wake-up call."

He's tired. Red rims and the barest hint of shadow confirm it as his eyes find mine. Hidden inside the clear blue sky, with a slice of amber in the left, is a gentle longing mixed with need. Tucking a fallen curl behind my ear, he watches as his finger feathers over my lobe, following my cheekbone to my mouth. When he runs it along my lower lip, I open and take him in, sucking hard enough to power his heart into a hammering beat beneath me.

I stop and let him go when his face falls into an aching pain, recovering quickly with his expressionless expression. Kissing his cheek, I pop up to straddle his waist. "Tell me."

"I want more time with you."

Oh, Colin. I place my fingers over his mouth to hold the statement close. Our love is a living, breathing thing, and it needs to be fed and nurtured for continued growth. He knows this as much as I do, and he's stressed by the need to feed our gluttonous desire. I smile and bend to kiss him again, this time on the lips, first the top and then the bottom and then our tongues slide together, playful, only to run on repeat until I can't breathe and it's my heart threatening to explode.

"That can be arranged," I murmur into him. "I'll talk to Betsy and get on your schedule."

He laughs, but it's hollow. "I don't want you worked into my day; you're more than an appointment, baby." In a second, he sits up, taking me with him. With his hands buried in my hair, he tips my head back. "I need to figure this out."

"Don't worry about me; I'm doing fine."

"But I'm not."

"Colin?"

He shakes his head, closing his eyes at the same time as our foreheads touch. "I just need more than five minutes to love you. Sunday, it's yours."

"The whole day?"

"Every second." And we both know that even as he says it, it's a lie. We don't own our time anymore. It belongs to the world and whatever urgent issue needs his attention.

"Then I will hold my calendar, Mr. President. For you and only you."

My thanks comes in a kiss. He's thorough. Deep and hungry one minute, light and loving in the next. When his true alarm wails on the side table, he remains glued to me while swatting it off. He walks us into the master bath with my legs wrapped around his waist and my fingers running through the silk strands of his hair.

The mundane becomes intimate. Our eyes lock as we brush our teeth. Shaving his face becomes a joint affair. Propped on the granite counter, I layer on the foam and then study his steady hand as his razor scrapes him smooth. In the shower we stretch the minutes, touching, washing, and teasing smiles into memories that will see us through to the night.

I yelp and leap ahead as he smacks my ass post towel-dry and then turn on him. And, oh shit, he's cute, and chiseled, and tall, so tall I look up into his growing smirk—wicked man. I move slowly, he moves slowly, and we round in a circle, the hunter stalking his prey. Except this time, I strike first. He dodges my quick hand, laughing. It takes three tries and a loop around our room before I wrestle the cotton from his hips and use it to mark victory on the back of his thigh.

"You'll pay for that." He stalks forward.

"I'm counting on it." I sidestep his advance and let my hips exaggerate their sway while moving into the huge walk-in closet. His mumbled dissention is music to my ears while I watch him dress. He does the same until the tension suffocates me.

"What are you doing today?" we ask at the same time, and finally break into grins. "You first," he says, nostrils flaring when I slide lace panties in place. My breasts are next, and he misses a button as my bra covers them.

"Molly and I are putting the finishing touches on the Easter Egg Roll, and then I'm headed to the rehab hospital for Defense Against the Dark Arts training. By the way, did you know gouging out eyeballs is the best way to escape from an attacker?"

Colin grunts and fumbles with his knot. "You're spending a lot of time with him."

"It's for a good cause. And that reminds me, I need to speak with you about the documentary," I say, stepping forward to save him from a clothing disaster. "I like this tie." Heat burns into my cheeks as I remember the magenta silk around his wrists.

"Someone made it my favorite," he murmurs, chin up and eyes on mine. I ignore my racing pulse and finish, tugging his collar down to complete perfection.

"You're very handsome, Mr. President. It's a wonder I let you out of the house without my supervision."

"Come with me," he breathes, his nails sinking into the soft flesh above my ass.

"Back to bed? I think I can squeeze you in my schedule."

"Chicago."

The air evacuates my lungs in a rush. "That's today?" A new reality weighs heavy on my mind and heart. He's leaving.

Tipping my chin as it sinks farther to my chest, he says, "Come. Cancel your plans and be with me."

"I can't." I shake my head with growing disappointment, and turn to the long line of outfits hanging on the wall. "I've agreed to speak at the Smithsonian on your behalf tonight."

If not for Molly and her boyfriend, Brendan "Hollywood" Carlyle, gaining an invite, the festivities would be dry with upper-crust society. But Hollywood's considering a career change. More so, now that Molly's accepted a position in D.C. with me. Colin had offered to introduce her boyfriend to Jonah Stratton, the man who knows everyone who is anyone in Washington, before being called away to Chicago. Now I'll do it for him.

I bend to slip into slacks and my ass runs into Colin's groin. He grunts and his hands clamp down on my waist to manage my wiggle. As I right myself, he takes over work on the clasp and then pulls me in flush against his rock hard body. "I'll get someone else to do it," he murmurs against my ear. "Evan—he owes me a favor; if not him, then Parker's wife. Let's get out of this city and breathe."

I weave my fingers through his and turn my nose into the crook of his neck to breathe him in. "You and I both know it's not that easy. They've advertised my attendance. If I show up somewhere else, the press will go crazy speculating why I bailed on the fine arts. I'll be fine. Besides, Molly has an uncanny ability to find fifty-year-old scotch that makes every dinner party a good one."

"I don't know why I let you hire her."

"Yes, you do," I say, rounding on him with my mouth a whisper away from his.

"I do?"

I nod. "Because it was my decision, and I didn't ask for your permission."

He laughs. "True."

"*And* she's exceptional; you want the best for me."

"Always." His lips linger and he breathes out *always* once more before sitting on the lounger to buff out the scuffs from his shoes. I slip into a camisole and then pick up his jacket from yesterday, checking it for anything that shouldn't go to the cleaners. In the breast pocket I find a *while you were out* reminder note and my stomach falls to the floor. Joan Montgomery: Wednesday, lunch at Patrick's Steakhouse in the private dining room.

Frozen and clutching a ridiculous message that should mean nothing, I stare at Colin. Focused on his task, damp hair falling to his smooth forehead, he carries on as if he hasn't a care in the world. Yet, that's not the case at all. The Montgomerys will never go away. And

I'll forever remain in the dark as to why they're like a bad case of fleas that can't be eradicated. It's a bitter pill to swallow, and by my tone I make sure he knows I don't like the taste.

"So, Joan Montgomery gets lunch and I have borrowed time in the morning?"

I fear for his neck; it snaps up far too quick not to dislodge vertebrae. What was smooth is now creased with three lines as his gaze narrows in on the pink slip. Closing his eyes on a sigh, he takes too long to formulate a response.

"Don't feed me a line of bullshit, Colin. In fact, don't say anything."

Frustration bubbles up in the form of a sprint out the door with no place to go. A better option would be to stay and talk it through like an adult, but I'm mad. If I'm honest with myself, I'm jealous of the family that continues to take up precious seconds of his life when he can barely spare me a minute. He catches me by the arm just as I step through the archway to the living room.

"Stop for once and listen. I don't have time to hash this out . . ."

I stare at his fingers and their steadfast grip. I love this man, more than the stars that saw me through my nightmares when I was a child, but I hate taking second place to anything but his job.

"Of course you don't."

"What does that mean?"

Jerking away, I find myself across the room, the battle line drawn by the velvet couch. "I waited for hours and as it turned out, I tried my new mushroom risotto recipe by myself. If you care to know, the California Riesling was a perfect match." I choke down tears as last night catches up with me. He stares with a blank look and wrinkled brow, confused. "You don't even remember," I whisper. "Date night."

"Charlie." Regret lies heavy in my name, yet I drop my eyes. I can't look at him for fear my wall will come tumbling down.

"I know you're sorry, and under normal circumstances this wouldn't happen. But I have a hard time understanding how that woman made the schedule and I didn't. You may not want me to be an appointment, but it seems that's the only way I'll be more than passing time."

"For Christ's sake, it was goddamn lunch."

"Why was it with her?" I scream. "What could she possibly have to say to warrant an hour of the President's day?"

"Not now, Charlie. Not yet," he says, and the words stab into my heart.

"Well, at least I know where I stand." *Payback*, I think as he flinches, and then I hate myself. I hate where we are, but I can't stop feeling betrayed.

"I am sorry I missed your risotto." He steps forward, tentative, swallowing his apprehension. "I'm damn sorry I missed the lace that went along with it. Excuses are futile, so I won't placate you with one now. Baby, your best interest is always at the top of my mind. I'm asking you to trust it still is and in time, I'll share the conversation I had with Joan."

"Mr. President?" Fitz calls from the hall, knocking at the same time.

I stare at Colin's tie as he comes closer and stops within touching distance. When he tips my chin back, I squeeze my eyes closed, a coward to his honesty. He strangles out my sob as he growls "look at me," and I fist his shirt to hang on when I do.

"I'm asking for your trust."

All the time in the world seems to pass by in the moment he waits for my nod. He searches and beats it into reality by sheer will and the desperate clench of his jaw. There's really no question. My belief in Colin lies deeper than the Titanic ruins on the ocean floor. Lunch with a sworn enemy and missing dinner are bundled up into a giant ball of hurt that has yet to unravel. But it will. It will and then I won't have this desperate urge to tie him to the bed and punish him for forgetting me. Or maybe I should, and it would make us both feel better. The thought of spanking his ass brings about a grin he accepts as forgiveness and I'm crushed against him—washed in sandalwood and comfort and left with no answers.

With his fingers digging into my hair, he growls his apology. "Every day begins and ends with you, Charlie. It's by sheer determination I produce any form of coherent thought when we're apart. In seconds, my mind strays to your mouth and what you'll whisper in my ear when I come home. And home is wherever you are, nothing more." He pulls away to meet my eyes. "I'm sorry."

"I know." I stretch to kiss his cheek. "I believe in you. I also believe Joan is a manipulative bitch, so when I find out you had lunch with her it's a hot poker to my stomach. I'll let you share whatever is happening on your timeline, but it doesn't mean I like it. And it doesn't get you out of trouble for hiding it in the first place. If Joan calls again, tell Betsy to transfer her my way. I've got a lot on my mind, and I'd like to give her a piece of it."

I study his expression, trying to figure out the pain rumbling behind his storm clouds. More gray than blue today: different. The last few months of working non-stop are catching up with him. "We'll talk tomorrow night. I'll tell you everything when I have more time." He glances at the door. "I have to go."

The brush of his lips against mine does little to lift my melancholy. Nor does the minute he's away to grab today's suit coat or when he returns for my hand and we walk to the door. My funk grows with each step and thoughts of the hours we'll spend apart. *I'm fine.* It's a new mantra that doesn't stop my heart from bleeding out sorrow.

Goodbyes are never easy. Today the separation feels downright wrong, and I have to nudge him past the threshold so I don't break down and beg him to stay. *Talk to me*, I'd say. *No secrets, remember? I want some of your time, please*. But the answer would be *not today.*

Not today.

"Be safe, husband," I call, with a stupid wave that falls to my side. He turns, jaw rigid and eyes burning. One of these days, his smoldering look might make my heart stop. Until then I'll take a mental snapshot and hold it in my pocket for the minute I need him.

Losing Colin is an instantaneous pang in my chest. At the same time, my stomach flutters as I walk in the kitchen and stop at the quartz island we've used for more than food preparation too many times to count.

Memories like that make me want to chase him onto the helipad, even though the thunder of the blades announces his departure in Marine One. It happens that fast. The President doesn't wait in lines at an airport; it comes to him in the backyard.

The annoying squawk of an alarm reminds me it's time to check on Dr. Beckman's fertility plan. I head into our room, stopping next to the bed to turn it off on the side table, and then pick up Sara's picture. I placed her there when we moved in so Colin wouldn't feel as if he had to forget his first family because he started a second with me. At three months old, she was beautiful with a glowing smile and red curls. A mirror of Abby's features, and with a twist of fate, mine as well.

I shake off a wicked sense of déjà vu and pop into the bath to pee on a stick. In the time it takes to clean up our morning antics, I have my answer. Two lines equal two days. Forty-eight hours for fun and maybe our own baby. Colin's schedule is an instant obstacle, but it doesn't take a rocket-scientist to solve this problem. My plan is hatched with a smile and a call to Betsy. Waiting until tomorrow to play it out brings back the doldrums, so I head into the kitchen to focus on omelet preparation.

Eggs and cheese are nothing compared to thoughts of Colin eating with Joan. *Why?* It's a simple question I can't answer and it drives me crazy. I need something more distracting, so I fire up Kyle on the phone.

"You're kidding me. I reminded you ten times I'm off the rest of the week."

"I love you too." I tuck the phone between ear and shoulder and carry breakfast to the table. "And no, I didn't lose my mind between yesterday and today. I'm just checking on your progress. Forgive me if I find this an exciting time. By the way, stop bouncing your leg, you'll throw the jet into a tailspin."

He laughs. "I'll land in about an hour. You may want to call Faith to work her through a panic attack that should hit . . ." he pauses and I'm sure he's looking at his watch, "right about now."

"Hey, I get it. Moving is huge. So is change, and she's had a lot to take in these last few months, starting with your super sperm. Cut her some slack."

"Consider it done. Thank the big guy for me; flying in the McKenna private jet makes the whole trip a lot easier."

"He was happy to lend it out. Captain Green isn't getting much fly-time these days. When will you be home? I'll stop by with Gram's chocolate cake and a gallon of milk. The three of us can get punch-drunk on sugar."

"Saturday, and she'd like that."

"It's a date. Before I let you go, can I pick your brain?"

"That depends; what are you drilling for?"

"Your research on D.C. family history and our favorite people to hate." I have time to eat in the length of his pause, yet I shove my plate away.

"Boss-lady, do me a favor and let this one go, okay?"

"Why?" I spring off the chair to pace. Why is that always the answer when I ask?

"There's nothing there. I've looked and Joan's clean."

"Then why hasn't John gone to trial for conspiracy, or whatever the hell he's charged with, for working with Shane Roberts? We're missing something, Kyle."

"He's in jail; there's not a chance in hell he'll get out. Justice takes time in this country; you know that." Kyle sighs. "And on another note, you don't need to look for missing pieces. Your husband would dive off the deep end into an empty pool if he knew you were intent on digging this hole. Let it go and let me tell you if there's anything you need to know."

"I don't like being kept in the dark."

He lets out an exasperated sigh. "The dark? You're bathing in goddamn florescence."

"Alright, okay. Here's me letting it go." I fake releasing a helium balloon in the air. "Anyway, I'll call Faith later and work her off the ledge you're sure to put her on."

"Charlie?" he asks, and I can just see him pulling his hair. "Let it go."

"Done. Safe travels my friend." At that I end the call so he can't try to talk me out of . . . what? What exactly is he trying to talk me out of? The gray rug beneath my feet begs for a reprieve, and it comes from a knock at the door.

I'm there in seconds, pulling Molly in by the hand with a rushed, "Hi."

"Good morning to you, too. I've never seen you so anxious to finalize a ball toss."

My mood is not lending to fun and games. "Did you bring your laptop?"

"Sure, I always . . ."

"No, not that one," I say, pointing as she pulls it from her bag. "The government tracks every word you type."

"And they'll care about balls why?"

"Our research is more historical today, and I need to do it on something that can't be traced back to me."

Sinking down on the couch, she scrutinizes my statement through razor-sharp eyes and the fresh-cut straight line of her bangs. "What are you doing, Charlie?"

I cross my arms and look down, taking my stand. For months I've let other priorities plan out my agenda. In January, it was the inauguration and our move. February was full of learning the way through our new life and fertility tests. Colin kept his word and found the best doctor. March brought with it a laparoscopy and stent to clear the way for babies. Before pregnancy happens, I need to make my play and figure out why Joan keeps popping to the surface. I'm not going out on a limb here. All of my escapades will be done in cyberspace, not at high noon with the press following.

"Colin once told me that history predicts the future. If that's the case, it houses all the answers I need to put the past where it belongs once and for all. I intend to find answers to my questions and I need to know if you're with me?"

Twelve

"I WANTED TO CYBERSTALK Joan Montgomery, not have cocktails with her," I mumble into my drink. Sparkling cider is a far cry from the bitter burn I long to warm my stomach. It's also tabloid fodder. If the media gets wind of this, I'll be front-page news with a bun-in-the-oven.

Molly laughs as I glare at my glass and envy hers with a not-so-subtle lick of my lips. "Why are you torturing yourself?"

"Because Dr. I Will Get You Pregnant Within The Year If You Follow All Of My Rules told me one glass of wine per outing, and I downed that an hour ago—my remedy for pre-speech nerves."

"You sure it wasn't because of her?" Hiding behind five hundred guests at the Donald W. Reynolds Center for American Art, Molly points to the matriarch of my nightmares.

"Quite possibly. I'd rather speak naked in front of Jame Gumb than be alone in a room with that woman."

"Who's Jame Gumb?"

"Buffalo Bill? '*It rubs the lotion on the skin or it gets the hose again*'? Gah!" I wave her arched brow movie ignorance away. "You're missing my point."

"The point where speaking naked in front of some random dude is more appealing than coming face to face with Colin's former mother-in-law?"

I tip my drink to her. "That's the one."

"Okay, you need something stronger than cider to help you make sense of Joan Montgomery."

"I would agree, however, motherhood calls. And listen, I've worked it out in my head because I can't think of anything else."

"That might pose a problem."

"Why?"

Rolling her eyes, Molly points to Hollywood as he stalks our way. Dark and dangerous in his own right, he parts the crowd as if it's the Red Sea and he's bringing forth followers to salvation. His dimpled chin and all-American good looks has women drooling and staring at his ass in a tux. "Because if you're thinking about Joan, you are not thinking about the sexy times with the President that will bring about all those babies."

"Point taken, but listen . . ."

"To what?" Hollywood leans in to brush a kiss on Molly's cheek and up to her ear. Whatever he whispers heats her into a deep crimson, the color of the night and one meant to pay homage to women in the arts. When the carpet was rolled out, it brought foreign dignitaries, A-list celebrities, and just about anyone in D.C. with half an ounce of influence. The sad part is Jonah may have more to do with it than Georgia O'Keefe or Suki Sherman, who's in attendance.

Colin has known Jonah since he took a seat in the senate, and Hollywood met him tonight to shoot the shit and get a feel for politics. At forty, Jonah is a finance and media wizard with the power to shape the perception of anyone in this town—good or bad. Most events like this see intelligent people turn into preening peacocks vying for attention.

It's worse than the zoo, and I can feel the eyes of every animal on me. My floor-length ruby gown may as well be non-existent without Colin. I'm exposed. The peacocks are more like vultures and they swarm, waiting for the perfect moment to dive and tackle their prey. Ramsey Nichols is one of them. He makes a habit of attending any event where he can finagle his way into the pockets of Washington's elite. Raquel is replaced by her polar opposite—a blonde pixie young enough to be his granddaughter. As usual, having a companion doesn't stop his eyes from devouring my chest.

"Charlise." He takes my hand. Instead of brushing his mouth against it, he hovers, eyes popping up to mine as he presses down. Dinner crawls up my esophagus as his tongue flicks my skin, and I rip my fingers away from his grip.

"Mr. Nichols, I had no idea you were keen on the arts. I had you pegged for film." *The kind without scripts.*

He chuckles. "I find pleasure in many things."

"I'm sure you do. Oh, but that reminds me, where's Raquel? I assumed she'd be the star of your show."

Pixie preens as if she's won a prize, but Ramsey's eyes narrow. "I thought you'd heard." I shift away at his snarl. "She returned to an ex. When the most powerful man in the world calls—his whore answers."

What? Colin? Indignation burns into my cheeks like a swift fire. I shake my head to deny Ramsey's stupid comeback, but a high-pitched whimper releases instead. In Kyle's absence, Agent Johnson steps in, and Ramsey blinks back in surprise. Hollywood saves me from trying for another fumbling retort. Placing my arm through one elbow, Molly's in the other, he weaves us through the throng. We're held up ten feet later when I'm forced into an excited hello with Missy, a Delta Burke wannabe I met last year. The current contestant for my new best-friend-forever kisses my cheek. "Do stop by later, Charlise, I've got to get you over for lunch." A half-hearted smile is my only promise. Peacock for sure.

When we're tucked into a more private space, I mumble "thanks" and sink further into a day-long depression. Tomorrow is a million miles away, and I want my husband. Stepping away from Molly and Hollywood, I turn for a bit of privacy and what I hope will be to hear his voice. I pull my phone from my clutch and press one on speed dial. My mood tanks even further when it goes to voicemail, but I'm quick to send a text: *Dear CM, Wish you were here. What are you doing that's better than me*? I add a winking emoticon and hit send. No immediate response, and my heart cracks like the goddamn Liberty Bell.

I miss him.

Burrowed next to a huge Ficus tree growing indoors, two out of three agents who escorted me here protect our circle. Sawyer's missing. Dragging my gaze away from the perimeter, Hollywood says, "Forget Ramsey; he's an asshole, Charlie. Now, what were you ladies carrying on about before I so rudely interrupted?"

There go Molly's cheeks, miming the color of the tinted light shooting up to the ceiling five stories high. Bathed in red, the steel and glass ceiling branches out into a spider's web pattern and I shudder. For the first time in months, Fourth of July in Texas rattles my thoughts. The punctuated flair of long-ago fireworks reminds me I haven't spoken to Sylvia in weeks, and it might be a good idea to find time.

"Charlie and I were dedicated to research today."

He's a smart man. Scanning first Molly's face and then mine, he waits for one of us to break our silence. The hum of muted conversation takes up space before he tips his head in apparent frustration.

"If you won't share, I'm sure the President will be more than forthright with the records of your search—when I tell him that you two are up to something."

Molly shakes her head. "That might be hard to do."

He looks at her through sharp slits. "Explain."

"Because we used your laptop." She tries on her slyest smile.

Hollywood curses under his breath. "Then I suggest you spill it or I'll work the evidence out of you."

I roll my eyes when she purrs and melts into his side. "If you two start talking about spankings, I'm leaving."

He laughs. "Alright, go on."

"Think of it as game-day preparation. I need to know my adversary's past moves to know the one she'll take next."

"Stop with the riddles and lay it out straight. Who and why?" He points, with his scotch in hand. "And get into details so I follow your logic."

Irritation with Colin's former mother-in-law wells up into verbal vomit. "Joan Montgomery. Because she's everywhere I wish she wasn't. Tonight for instance, she wasn't on the guest list that I was aware of, yet there she is." I point to the far side of the room. "Kyle, who's a motor-mouth, is tight-lipped about her and Colin." Rage simmers under my skin as I sputter my indignation. "They fine dined together at Patrick's while I worried about his safety. It's like Joan's hovering in some goddamn omnipresent capacity, directing the lives of everyone around me. Why, you ask? That's what I'm trying to figure out, and other than Molly, no one seems to take me seriously when I ask the same question. So I'm finding out for myself."

"And what did you discover?"

I shrug. "Nothing screaming *I'm a monster*. An only child, she was sent away to Foxcroft Boarding School, and when she graduated she went Ivy League for college. First Yale and then she transferred to Notre Dame, where she met John. Her family has more money than the Queen of England, which I found interesting. I had just assumed John was rolling in the dough, but as it turns out, he prefers to roll around in the sheets."

Molly looks like she swallowed an oyster and gags. "Gross."

"I agree, but it appears he had a long line of female admirers."

"And how did you come by this knowledge?" Hollywood asks, and then downs the last swallow of his drink.

"Easy—Wikipedia. An affair was reported twice; at the tail end of his first run it was suspected and his numbers plummeted because of the rumors. The second go round for a senate seat, a campaign staffer came forward, and he lost his place on the ticket when his affair was broadcast nationally. But all of this brings us back to John so I didn't dwell on him long."

"Not necessarily," Hollywood says, looking around before closing our circle. "What would you do if Colin cheated?"

The hair at my nape prickles as pain and rage rumble into volcanic spray and shoot out of my eyes.

“Whoa,” Hollywood laughs, holding up his hands as my laser beams try to sear him in two. “I’m not comparing you to her, and no way would Colin touch another woman. My point is your reaction. Everyone has one. The question to answer is what Joan’s was.”

“I don’t know.”

“Might be a good place to start, but also think about your husband’s reaction when he finds out you’re poking the bear.”

“I’ll tell him tomorrow when he gets home. I’m not trying to hide . . .”

“Come on. That’s so far from the truth you’re on a deserted island with no hope for rescue.”

“Fine,” I seethe, reaching my boiling point. “I used a different laptop because everything I do is monitored, and I didn’t need Kyle knocking on the presidential suite asking questions. Besides, I’ve already picked his brain and it’s locked up tight.”

Exasperation is apparent in the subtle shake of Hollywood’s head. “Be smart about this, Charlie. That could still happen. It’s not a long stretch to get to you through me. If you’re looking at things someone doesn’t want you to, you’re not exactly in stealth mode.”

I sigh. Ditching my cider when a waiter passes by, I glance at Joan. Petite, she stands proud with a starched air of Washington aristocracy. It’s not in my nature to hate. It takes time and too much space in my brain. Not the Kerrs, who turned their head and feigned ignorance, or Shane Roberts, or the drunk driver who killed my biological parents. If I spent my days plotting revenge I’d have remained a victim, and I wanted desperately to survive. I hated what they did, but I forced myself to forget and move on.

What if Joan didn’t? Is it possible she’s wallowed in John’s infidelity all of these years? Waiting to exact a plot that would see him in jail for the hurt he caused? She’s not exactly shattered by his absence—with Champagne in one hand, a man closer to my age than hers is hanging onto the other. They’re laughing, and she glows, whether it’s from her sparkling gown or losing the baggage she’s carried around for almost forty years is anyone’s best guess. Gazing with wide eyes, she flirts with her boy-toy and holds up an empty glass. She watches as he runs to do her bidding. Seconds later, she steps back and then nods to the shadowed entrance of a hallway. Goosebumps pop on my arms as she slides into the dimmed light.

A gut reaction has me moving in the same direction, and I don't stop when Molly calls after me.

"Charlie?"

"Girls' room, I'll be right back," I say, picking up my skirt to lengthen my stride. The entrance is clear on the other side of an area nearing the size of a football field and I'm at the fifty-yard line. To avoid as many people as possible, I stick to the outer perimeter, throwing smiles when I catch someone's eye but not slowing down. I have no intention of chatting with anyone, including Joan, but I want to know who's talking to her. After John's arrest and the scandal that followed, no one came near her. Divorce papers and publicly denouncing his actions placed her back in favor that's more Mellow Yellow than the popularity of Mountain Dew. Nearing the door, I stop so quick Johnson's open suit coat feathers across my bare shoulder.

"My apologies, Mrs. McKenna," he mumbles.

Tossing my hair, I turn and cock my head. What I hope is a brilliant grin nearly crumbles as his baby face falls, mouth parting, and I fear it may be more Cheshire cat creepy. I point to the label for women only. "Could I have a few minutes to freshen up? I won't be too long."

He glances at the sign and nods. "Certainly, ma'am."

Pushing the door open, I feign entry but dash down a few yards on tiptoes when he turns his back. The slice of angst I should feel at ditching him evaporates. *Ma'am*. Could there be a more awful word in the English language? Anywhere past twenty-nine and you're labeled for life. Law enforcement should place the word next to bullying in Webster's dictionary and arrest all partakers for verbal abuse.

Veering to a branch on the right, I slow down. The hall opens into pocket galleries with portraits hanging along each wall. Working on my gut feeling, I keep going until the sounds of the celebration become a low hum, and the steady stream of the air conditioner is my only company.

My gut reaction must be indigestion. There's no one here but Mrs. Copley—a stunning early nineteenth-century portrait of a wealthy Rhode Island woman, brought to life by the dim lights glowing from the ceiling overhead and denoted as such by the plaque next to the painting. Her dress is as red as mine, but I'm not cinched nearly as tight as her corset.

And then I am. It's as if the strings are pulled and I can't breathe when Joan's whisper grows louder. *Oh, shit.* I slide into a small alcove and close my eyes to the many Mona Lisa-like smiles. *Leave the detective work to Nancy Drew,* my heart screams as it jumps into discomfort.

"We're covered. In no way can I be tied to him, and you'll have left the country by the time the picture comes together," she whispers. "I see no reason not to move forward as planned. In situations where the pieces are moving fast, action is called for."

A garbled male response, "Su . . . mission . . ." is broken up by the soft vibration of my cell. *Colin.*

Clutched in my hand since I sent the text, I bumble to turn my phone off and slip farther in the corner. An instant adrenaline rush spikes and I can't hear above the pulse pounding in my ears. I sink into the wall and pray it's possible to be mistaken for a portrait because there's no hiding here. Seconds pass. The shuffle of feet and clipped heels work in the opposite direction.

Curiosity killed the cat, and if it doesn't, then Colin will. Scratch that—he'll tan my hide and like it. I roll my eyes, but remain paralyzed, chin to chest, listening to the welcome sound of silence. Edging out of my hiding spot, I look both ways down the larger gallery. Alone but for the many painted eyes following my escape, I pick up the pace and race toward the exit. *Too close*. Spying on Joan isn't a crime, but maybe her mission is.

What the hell, Charlie? Let it go. I should. I know, and I will. I'll tell Colin everything tomorrow and wash my hands clean. Done.

I believe it too, even more when a shadow jumps into mine from the adjacent hallway and my scream echoes off the walls.

Sawyer. Thank God.

"Foxtail is secure," he pipes into his sleeve and levels me with a Kyle-like glare. I can't read his expression; his eyes are dark and even more so as they fall into slits. "Mrs. McKenna, if you wish to take a tour I would be happy to escort you."

"Done," I say in a panted whisper, hand over my thundering heart. "I've seen enough, and I would really like to go home now."

Waving me forward, he follows and I try to settle the uneasy vibration keeping my nerves on high alert. A welcome distraction buzzes in my hand, and I read Colin's message. *Dear CCM, I'm meeting with an old friend for dinner when I'd rather have you. Think of me, my love, and I'll be with you in your dreams.*

Oh, God. Tomorrow cannot come soon enough.

Thirteen

Nothing but silence rouses me from a dream, yet conscious thought ticks into place, first with the subtle hint of sandalwood under my nose. And then it's my heartbeat. It picks up time when I sense him, when I feel the weight of his stare. I can't help but smile and it gives me away from slumber to giddy girl, excited by the surprise of her first love's kiss.

"Welcome home, Mr. President," I whisper, and open my eyes to all that's good in my world.

He's here, sitting in a chair pulled up next to the bed, legs crossed, forefinger and thumb tugging on his lower lip while he watches me. I'm not immune to his broad shoulders covered in a cable-knit sweater, or his eyes raking over my prone figure, the details of which are hidden by a sheet. One side of his face is thrown into sharp relief by the hall light I leave on when he's not home. He's split down the middle, light and dark, good and evil, as if the devil is whispering half-truths in one ear and he's falling victim to temptation.

"You're an angel when asleep," he whispers.

"And what about when I'm not sweet as a dream?"

Teasing doesn't bring about the smile I hoped for. It tugs down his brow. "Everything—you're my morning and the sun on a cloudless day, twilight and the stars that follow. Nothing could be more than you, Charlie."

I would tear up even if I hadn't been missing him like a moonless sky. This man has my heart. He owns it, owns every piece of me. Yet the look on his face belies any comfort taken from our wedding vows and the intense possession he's found in them for the last four months. He's nervous.

"It's a good thing you feel that way, because I'm not going anywhere. Till death do us part, and all that jazz." I smile, rolling up on my elbow to get a better look at him. "Marrying me twice makes it quite permanent."

His lip twitches. "That thought may have crossed my mind."

"I'm sure it did."

He looks to the side table and the picture of Sara, staring so long the seconds become a minute. "I couldn't stop thinking about you and the way I left. It didn't sit well so I came home to talk with you."

"Are you sure it didn't have anything to do with my disappearance into fine art?"

Finally, a smile, but it's short-lived and ruthful. "Maybe you own a quarter of my decision to change my plans. Why the sudden interest in early-American modernism?"

I shrug into my chin, and the collar of his shirt-turned-nightgown brushes against my cheek. "It was very educational, but I was more interested in Joan Montgomery."

His jaw works back and forth, as if tasting the flavor of my comment. The curl to his upper lip would indicate it wasn't very appetizing. It may be the time to lay our bets on the table, but I was hoping to get him inside me before we played the odds. I've missed him, and talking about the wicked witch isn't a soothing bedtime story. I don't want to do this when my pulse is racing hot. Not when he's a foot away with hours before sunrise stretching in front of us. Not within the forty-eight-hour this-is-the-best-time-to-make-beautiful-babies window. But as my mouth opens to tell him so, he beats me to the ground rules.

"I've walked this line before—my career on one side and my family on the other." His brow crumbles as he moves forward. With his elbows on his knees, he takes the hand resting on my hip to weave our fingers together. "I'm sorry. I never meant to hurt you or make you feel as if you are not the most absolute important person in my life," he says, his chest heaving on a breath. "Everything I do is for your protection and happiness—everything, Charlie. Don't ever forget that your well-being is paramount. I don't want to hurt you."

My Colin—he carries the weight of the world and the burden of Abby's past selfishness. Her response to his career involved the ultimate deceit. But we're blazing a new trail, balancing the personal and professional, and finding a way to make it work for us.

"I've known you for sixteen months. To most people that's the blink of an eye, but that's when I started living, really noticing details. I *know* you. I've spent almost every waking minute studying you, and not for my own fan-girl moments, even though you are dreamy."

"Dreamy?" he asks, his brow arching as he does.

I smile. "Mm, so much better than blueberry pancakes, but I digress. It was my job to market McKenna to millions of people while I worked on the campaign. It wasn't a hard sell because I know your lip pull means I'm-worried-about-Charlie, and I'm on to your feel-the-most-show-the-least superpower. You're the real thing, Colin McKenna, and I'm proud to be your wife. I tucked trust in an envelope called my heart and gave it to you a long time ago. So we can fight, and feelings might get hurt, but I will always be yours and I will always come back to you. Even if my mind is a million miles away, my love will be right here." I pull free from his increasing grip and press my hand against the center of his chest, basking in the steady thrum underneath my palm. "I know you worry about me more than you should."

He shakes his head, falling into raw emotion. "I only want to help you live a life full of love and protect you from regret."

"And so you have. I never tried to find the extraordinary—quite the opposite, in fact. I wanted to blend into mediocre, but since meeting you, magical things keep happening."

I'm greedy for one more miracle. Fertility plan or not, there is no guarantee of success. But I want him. I want him open and raw, sharing his love and every frustration in a primal drive to mate and make a family. I want him to take it out on me in the thrust of his hips, and to feel it with his nails digging into every part of my flesh.

"Come to bed." I slide my fingers down the marbled texture of fine wool, not thick enough to hide the muscles trembling under my touch, to rest on the hot and pressing outline of his erection. It's been too long.

He sucks in a breath, pinning me with his eyes. "This." His hand is on mine, curling my fingers around him. "You, having your mouth on me, sinking into you and losing myself—I've thought about it all day. Reality is so much better."

"Colin . . ." I sigh and he stands. Our fingers slip free from connection. Nothing is better than Colin loving me. And he does so well, with the weight of his stare as he takes the back of his sweater and pulls it off in one tug, tossing it to the floor. Exposed are the rippled planes of his abdomen and the chiseled indent tapering into his waist. I'm quick to strip, the sheet, his shirt, leaving me naked and stretched out under his hot appraisal. I arch from the mattress, rubbing my thighs together as his belt whispers through the loops.

"Trust me," he says, holding the leather out for me to see. But it's more than trust and a not-so-subtle request to tie me up, rather an appeal for me to yield in all things, submit and know that he will take me to the end with care and at his pace. Not mine, because sometimes I sprint and the course is marked for a marathon.

I offer my hands.

He appears dazed by my concession. His lips part to speak, but he pauses to look at mine instead. Then he's quick to take advantage. Worn from constant wear, the strap slips around my wrists, twisting once and then twice, and with his gentle jerk my hands are above my head and knotted to the headboard. I'm pulled taut, but even with the tight hold digging into my skin, it doesn't hurt. It fuels my need, and the slippery wetness slips down the crease of my backside. *Oh, my.*

"I'm going to remind you how good it is to be mine, my sweet, Charlie," he says, tracing a finger along the curve of my elbow and down, down to curl around my nipple. I swallow a cry when he flicks the stiff point, and I lift into his touch. "But first," he whispers, lying his forehead on mine, "I want you to ruin me."

Just as his breath warms my lips he's gone, ripped away as he does the same to his pants and boxer briefs. He's so hard everywhere, muscles tensed and glowing in the faint light behind him. My pulse skyrockets when he straddles my waist. With his cock in hand, he strokes up and down and inches his way to kneel near my face. There's a struggle in his eyes, the need to use me and love me at the same time.

I grant permission with the tip of my tongue and the light flick that caresses his swollen crown. He moans. Gripping my hair with one hand, he feeds me with the other in a slow drive forward. Cautious, he pushes in and out in short strokes, yet with every thrust, his control slips and so does he—to the back of my throat. Far enough to take his pleasure and spur on my own.

The desperate hunger lying dormant all week unleashes as I lick and suck, urging him deeper with the curve of my tongue, breathing in his clean musk.

I love it; I love him and watching him lose his mind in the tight clench of his jaw and his finger running along my straining lips as he says, "Perfect." In the flex of his hips and the muscles coiling beneath when he jerks faster and faster still. His eyes glass over. And even though I want him inside me, I want to taste the life that lives within him, so I hum, murmuring my approval for him to come.

Falling forward, his hand braces against the wall, and he punishes my mouth for goading him on. I'm so full and yet empty at the same time. Each thrust, every swivel is a direct line to the throbbing beat taunting my clitoris. I want him to touch me, rub out my need until I scream around his. As if on cue, he swells into a tight vibration and I swallow, begging for more, arching from the bed to take him there.

His lips part on a gasp, and he jerks free.

"Fuck."

The word is as hot as his stare.

Up and down, his chest rises and falls as he catches his breath, all the while holding his pulsing erection at the base. Circling his fingers around it, he holds back his release and checks on mine. "You want me to come in your mouth," he pants, reaching behind to slide his fingers into my slickness. A guttural groan rumbles from his chest, and he murmurs *so wet* as he dips into my opening. I can't look away from the reverential awe in his gaze, as if he's surprised my desire is as urgent as his. But his admiration is short-lived. His lids sink into a look that's anything but gentle, and he slaps my clitoris. "Answer me."

Oh, God. I'm going to come. "Yes," I cry and tug my arms.

He smiles. Dark—dangerous—and so thoroughly mine, I buck my hips and beg. "Please."

The smirk never leaves as he stretches, rolling down so we're pressed together, my legs spread wide to cradle him and welcome his hard length next to my wet heat.

"I know what you need because I know everything about you." He licks my lips, and then sucks on them until I writhe, lit up like a livewire. "Everything, Charlie, and I could not want you more. My wife, my love, take all that I am."

He watches me fall into a silent groan when his hips rise, dragging his tip through my swollen flesh to press against my entrance and spread me apart, so slow, pushing in and giving me a fullness I've only ever known with Colin. Oh, for the love of all that's holy. I can't look away from this gift, my husband, and his eyes storming into decadent darkness. I breathe through the pleasure with his mouth over mine, not yet a kiss.

Dipping down, he nips at my jaw and neck, latching onto my pulse to suck a cry from my lungs. "I'm not going to be gentle tonight," he says, his breath feathering over my ear. "I want you to feel me tomorrow. Remember where I was and what will be coming to life inside of you."

I moan and tug my arms; I want my hands in his hair and all over him. Without the distraction, I zero in on his hips held tight to mine and the urgency simmering under my skin for friction. "Please." I grab his ear between my teeth. "Let me touch you."

He draws up to his knees. Empty. Cold air smacks my skin in his absence and I'm twisted on my stomach just as quick. With one hand on my neck, his other holds his erection as he taps it against the crease of my ass. Once, twice and then he leans in, pressing into the one place he's never gone before. I exhale a rough breath, wondering if I'll finally have a first time with Colin.

"One day soon, love," he says, slipping lower and sinking into my tight channel. I curse the bed as the tip of his thumb pushes past the ring of muscle into my backside and I know now what it means to be full. I'm stretched thin, almost at my breaking point, and he's only just begun to move. Slow at first, a steady tempo to ratchet up my need.

In.

Out.

Fast, faster—demanding.

Every thrust is deeper than the last until the flush of awareness centers on the slick friction and the impending explosion he promises with each lunge forward. But it's not enough, and I find myself mindlessly begging for *more* and *harder*, both of them—thumb, cock, please, *please*.

He laughs. Bending over, he licks across my shoulders and never misses a beat. I'm lost in sensation. Held tight by the strap and his hand, I need to move, find his rhythm, so I grind into the best sheets money can buy, and they burn like burlap on my overheated skin.

"That's it, get there." Colin grunts with each stroke, pressing me farther into the mattress, and with every pass my clitoris is set on fire. "Oh, fuck yes."

There is nowhere to go. Pulling taut on the leather, I tuck my forehead in and ride it out. Tense, lost to the sounds of his breath punched from his lungs, the slick sounds of my body taking him in and my cries, my pleas—it's too much. I try to tell him, my mouth open, my heart racing, but I can't speak. I can only feel—*too much.* His fingers dig into my hip and I'm done, pushed past the brink so fast, so hard, I scream, pulling against the strap with my head thrown back as he rides me into raw feeling.

"Oh, Charlie, you're coming, yes baby."

When he rips his thumb from my ass, I explode, and he falls on top of me. Taking my breast in hand, he wrenches the aching peak, and I arch from the bed and into a pleasure so blinding I fade to black.

Muscles twitch with aftershocks as Colin's cock slips free, leaving me empty while he remains hard and unsatisfied. But my mind drifts, floating in la-la-land despite the work he does above my head. When the world rights itself and I can center my thoughts, the sheets are to my back and his chest is against mine, but more than that my hands are free to roam. And they do, up and down his arms, his taut muscles strained as he strokes into me again, long, deep, this time chasing his own pleasure as he gives me so much more.

"So good," he whispers against my cheek. "So sweet. Come for me again."

"I can't," I cry and wrap myself around his sweat-drenched body, loving his heat and his hold. But when he moves, really moves, punching his hips harder, faster, demanding I give in, I do. I do and I will; I surrender to his need to own every part of me in a slow, rolling pulse that runs through me and around him.

"Oh, thank Christ," he says, suspended for a second. Then he loses himself in the brutal pace of his hips. With his head falling into my neck, he presses a groan there and shudders out his release one hard thrust at a time until he's spent.

A minute passes, my body ticking in time to the seconds, and finally he drags his mouth along my collarbone and neck and up to kiss me. Hard and insistent, he takes me in a desperate drag of tongue and teeth. He pulls out, only to immediately fill me with his fingers, three of them, pressing so deep he keeps all of his come inside. Reaching up and in, he finds my spot, swollen from the constant drive of his cock moments before. I gasp when he rubs it over and over, and my hips willingly match his tempo.

"Oh, Charlie," he says, rubbing his rough cheek against my lips before finding my eyes. "Are you sore? Am I too much?"

I watch him, the intensity in his stare, the hard clench of his jaw as his fingers work me over, and it doesn't matter. Nothing matters but this, Colin lost in me, possessed by me, and there is no way I'll give up this bit of control. It's how I'll always know he's mine.

"Never."

A strangled moan tears from his throat as he moves faster, plunging and circling. Ripping away, he rears back to his knees and onto his stomach. Wrapping his free arm under and around my waist, he pulls me forward into place, the perfect place for him to kiss and lick and suck my clit until I'm mindless and begging.

"Colin," I whimper and watch his eyes. He holds my gaze as he worships me, sweet and dirty at the same time. I arch into the mattress and moan as his tongue flicks and then I'm wrapped around him when he latches onto my inflamed bundle of nerves. There's nothing to do but clutch his hair and grind into his face, loving how he loves me with his wicked fucking mouth.

"Oh, God," I cry and thank him for soundproofed walls at the same time. "Right there, don't stop. I'm so . . . so . . . *yes* . . ."

I forget to breathe when he uses his teeth and stars light my way to the other side as I come and come all over his hand. We're both panting and white-knuckled—his grip into my inner thigh so hard I *will* feel him tomorrow. *Mission accomplished.* But he's slow to bring me down, taking his time to massage me into tremor after tremor. Each one pulls his seed deeper inside and closer to making the baby I so desperately want to bare.

"Good God," I whisper, and he groans, as if it's hell to move away. "Colin." I tug this time and he releases my clit to kiss his way up my stomach, and then each breast, and finally my mouth. I find myself on his tongue and drown in the sweet musk of us for what feels like hours.

Time has a way of interrupting perfection.

As I pull away, he rests his lips on my forehead as our breath slows. *Wow, holy wow*. His chest vibrates into a chuckle and he rolls off me, arms splayed above his head in his own surrender.

"Yeah."

I giggle and tuck my boneless self into my favorite place with a huge grin pressed to his skin. The man with endless energy and who knows exactly what to say and when to say it, is speechless—ruined by his wife.

Fourteen

Friday

Charlie – 0900

I'm not sure who destroyed who. Last night ended in the early morning hours, limbs entwined, hearts pounding, breath panting, and sheets pulled free from the corners. For the first time in weeks, we slept through dawn and into day. Colin finally rolled out of bed to shower and dress, leaving me with thirty minutes to relax and grin my ridiculous satisfaction to the ceiling. I can't help myself. It grows with my eyes closed as I stretch into a delicious ache.

Once before, Colin fell into this kind of visceral need, after a difficult decision stripped his control because there was no good choice and he had to pick the better of only terrible options. A man died that night. He took me then, letting his vulnerability slip between us in a primal sensuality that stripped us bare—and brought us closer together.

"You're making me wish I could call in sick," he whispers in the smooth caramel tone that starts a pulse at the apex of my thighs.

The mattress dips and then his lips press against mine. I sigh, opening for the tip of his tongue to play a game of cat and mouse. Minty fresh and devilish at the same time, he taunts me—I go after him. In a heartbeat I'm lost in fresh scent, sandalwood and sex. The sweet rhythm is forsaken for dark lust, my hands in his hair, fingers raking down his neck and rounding to his tie to hold him in place. We're crushed together, licking, biting in a rush of renewed desire.

He grabs my breast, palming and then pulling, gripping until I'm hot beneath him.

Then he stops. As quick as we began, we're over, and my body screams for him to get me off one more time, insatiable. On a groan, he tears his mouth from mine and leans his forehead against my lips. I feel the weight of his stare on my chest and stomach and then below as I kick free of the cover to get closer to him. I spread my legs wide, knowing he won't be able to help himself.

He groans and then he's there, caressing my branded inner thighs—marked by McKenna as his fingers and teeth scored my flesh all night long. The brush of his finger over the tip of my clit has me cry out, one hand buried in his nape, the other gripping the sheet next to my hip. I lift into him as he dips in to gather and spread my heat up and around. Then game on. Mouth open, my hallowed cries barely escape before I'm breathless and creaming over the edge as his quick fingers get me there in record time.

"Holy," I say, panting. He cups me while I pulse and come down, watching as I wet my lips.

It's as if my release cools him off as well. His eyes are bright, teasing in the morning sun streaking through the window. "Do you think that will last until tonight or should I stop by around lunchtime?"

"That depends," I say, straightening his knotted tie as he moves to hold himself above me, his hands pressed to the bed on either side of my shoulders. My gaze drags along the corded muscles of his neck—shaved smooth—settling on his lips, swollen and red from my kisses, "on when tonight begins."

I don't want the haze of sadness I felt last week to overcome the perfected bliss I found in the early morning hours, yet I need to know if I should prepare for a lonely weekend.

"Sooner than you think."

Confusion settles in my brow, but he just smiles, smacks a kiss on my lips and walks away, leaving me naked and spread out to shiver through the chill in the air while his sexy ass steps into the bathroom. I groan when I get up, and then smile. Every muscle in my body aches, especially my thighs and what sits in between them, but it's the kind of ache that will have a silly grin spike on my face every time I move. The rush of water fills the silence as I slip his discarded shirt around my shoulders. But then he's at the threshold, watching. His wrist is up, fingers working to clip in a cuff link, and I want nothing more than to strip him, to peel back his sleeve to see the rippling veins of his forearm pulsing against his strength. Then I'll move on to his chest. Damn, my ovaries are taking notes and then they're jumping, begging for attention as confidence becomes a sexy-as-sin smirk.

"What's going on, Mr. President?"

He walks forward, placing his hands on my waist to bring us hip to hip—*such a nice place to be*. "I've rescheduled my appointments after three. We'll be in the air heading toward Camp David by four." His breath sweeps across my cheek and over to my ear. "I'll have you back in bed by six."

I swallow. Hope is a dangerous emotion. "You can do that? Just leave?"

"For you, yes. I'd build the damn lodge myself if it meant I'd get you alone."

What can I do but wrap my arms around his head and bury myself in the crook of his neck? Being draped around Colin like this reminds me of the campaign trail, when we spent every minute together. I hadn't thought I'd miss that time so painstakingly it's a pinch to my heart. Since the inauguration, we're ships passing in the night. I hate it so much, I want to build a goddamn foundation and nail him to it. But this, this offer to leave Washington and give me his time, it's more than everything.

"I love you."

"Ah, baby." Raking his fingers along my back and into my loose hair, he presses his lips against my temple. "It's not possible for me to love you more."

That pinch, the one in my heart—it's a vice grip, as are my arms in one last squeeze. I pull away, running my hands over his chest to smooth out his shirt and vest and straighten his tie. Anything to feel him under me for even seconds more.

He stops my ministrations by tipping my chin. "We have a lot to talk about. I'll tell you everything, answer any questions you have. Can you wait until tonight?"

I nod, reaching up on my toes to kiss him. "I will. I'll wait for you."

"Good. Now tell me your plans. Where are you off to?"

I have to think. After last night, my schedule seems a million miles away. "Oh, I'm meeting with a war widow—which reminds me, I need to talk with you about the television documentary. It's good . . . really good." I've lost the salesmanship I practiced a hundred times. I blame him for blowing my mind, and the look he levels at me—all smoldering mogul and trouble waiting to happen. I have to force my gaze from his mouth and the full lips practically begging for my kiss. *Damn this man.*

"If it's important to you, then it's important to us."

My eyes narrow, suspicious. Maybe I need to sex him up every night. "It is?"

He laughs. "Yes. I read the proposal you left on the table. I agree it's an excellent concept." His brow pinches down. "So who is with you today?"

"Sawyer and Johnson, along with a legion of men."

"You know it's necessary . . ."

"Yes, because you're worried."

"And not just because I'm worried. Terrorism is boiling up in our backyard . . ."

"I'll be fine."

"I won't apologize if it's overwhelming. Kilpatrick's threatening retaliation for an attack led by our Army two months ago. We took out two of his training camps and captured his second-in-command, by my order. His response is an attack at LaGuardia.

Fucking American soil—it's a miracle we intercepted the intelligence at the last minute. A goddamn bomb, Charlie. He's not stopping and he's getting closer . . ."

"I'll be home in less than two hours."

"It's one thing if he comes after me, and there's a possibility he will, but you? God, if he comes after you I will lose the ability to walk the line of this office and preserve the oath . . ."

"Colin."

He breathes out a sigh. "Just do everything Sawyer says."

I nod. "Everything."

His kiss is more than a goodbye; it's a reminder to heed his warning and a promise of what's to come. After devastating tongue action and then a brush of his lips against my cheek, he's gone. I mourn his absence for a second and then get lost in the fantasy of another night like the last one. I may not be able to walk straight, but I might get that baby after all. Unless . . . I peer down at my stomach and pull apart the cotton to stare at the flat surface.

"Anyone in there?" I giggle at the silent response, but wrap my arms around myself and smile all the way to the shower, through my blow-dry, and as I slip into an emerald shirt-dress. The military collar is apropos for my lunch date, the neckline not too low and the hem not too high.

I head over to the side table for my phone. Slipping it into my pocket, I find myself staring into Sara's eyes. Our life is crazy busy, as if the fast-forward button is on auto-select, and the days fly by. But Colin and I are strong, ready to find time for a family. Our path is different than the chaos surrounding Sara's paternity and Abby's infidelity. I'll make sure it stays that way. I've no desire to resemble her any more than I already do.

More than I already do. A pang pinches my heart. For the first time in forever I want to revisit my childhood, delve into a history lesson and the parents that brought me into this world. I've not far to go. Down the hall, the spare bedroom remains untouched from the family living here prior to us, so I'm engulfed by blue walls and boxes. It's no secret I would be fired if ever hired by a moving company. Labels are not my thing, so it's not until the fifth one that I find what I'm looking for.

Emotion curls into a ball in my throat when I pry the lid open to find my past. A long-ago buried childhood bundled up in one twelve-by-twenty package. I let a gasp go as Teddy peeks out in joy. The bear I took everywhere looks upon me with a smile I haven't seen since I was eight. I bury my nose in his worn neck, hoping to smell the spaghetti my mother made on Tuesday nights. Disappointment that I don't is short-lived when I pull out a jewelry box, and a tarnished gold locket hidden inside.

The pictures are faded but detailed enough for a rush of fresh tears. My dad's blonde mop-top and the flash recollection of Mom saving money by cutting his hair at home. His jaw is set, rigid, lips drawn tight. For just a minute I sink into history and try to remember his laugh; nothing comes but a revolving door. He would leave in the morning for work and return late from a hard day, spending most nights in the garage rebuilding an old car.

And then my heart stumbles on a pretty brunette with eyes similar to mine. Mom's hair is full, with the wavy curls I tame every day.

I don't dwell, falling to my knees and diving into the mounds of pictures filling most of the box. Some are sweet and bring forward a smile or a sob that blurs years into yesterday. Christmas morning by the tree, missing front teeth, birthdays with candles brightening a homemade cake, our dog Rusty snuggled next to me in bed. So much to take in, yet I do, with trembling hands and an open mind.

The last treasure lining the bottom is an old photo album. Brittle, the bright purple paisley cover peels away at the corners. My eyes narrow at the first page and a cold sweat breaks out on my brow. I look closer at the rallies reminiscent of those I just lived through. Red, white and blue bleached into pastels. Signs strung across stages, people vying for a handshake, and a common candidate front and center in all of them.

“No,” I cry, flying through the pages with a pulse thrashing to a scary beat. “God no.” *Please, please*, I whisper in desperate denial at what stares back at me. My mother, my beautiful brunette mother, Georgette Hilton, snuggled into an embrace with a Senate candidate.

Held tight and beaming by a young, confident red-headed John Montgomery.

Colin – 1030

THE TIMING OF MY good mood could not be worse, as evidenced by a report not five minutes old citing the movement of three radicals hiding out in rural Pennsylvania. They’re missing, yet I can’t stamp down my damn grin. *Charlie*. I pinch my lips closed and force my focus on the document at hand.

“When did we lose sight of them?” I ask National Security Advisor Stacey Price, but glance at Evan sitting next to me. He’s no better off. Blue circles rim his eyes, as if he hasn’t slept in a week. I’m betting he hasn’t, if his Carter is anything like mine.

“Oh-nine hundred hours, sir.”

I nod, throwing down the useless facts. “And how in the hell, after months of surveillance, did they disappear out of thin air?”

Voices explode around the table. The situation room breeds stiff responses and the requisite to be heard; everyone has an opinion. Standing at the head, I watch reports surface on monitors beyond the rectangular table filled by people charged with keeping the country safe.

“Enough.” My tone brings on silence. “What’s the chatter?”

“Heightened concern for brush fires in Santa Monica.”

Shit. Also known as an exchange between terror camps, and my pulse lurches. I narrow in on General Hill. “I need to know if this is in any way related to Kilpatrick.”

“We’re looking, sir.”

"Look harder. What's the recommendation?"

"Increase the national security level, force con Alpha."

"Done." I point around the table. "I want airports on alert. You have one hour before we're back in this room. If I don't have specifics we're moving to Bravo, and we'll need to communicate the added security. I'm erring on the side of caution unless you tell me otherwise. One hour," I repeat and slide out the door, Evan on my tail.

Something is happening.

The bristling awareness at my nape confirms it. "How hard is it to keep an eye on fanatics in the Cumberland Valley?" I ask, bounding up the steps to the Oval Office.

He huffs. "Our satellite bombed out. In the thirty minutes it was down they could have gone anywhere."

"Have Brady work up a formal communication and let Carla know she may need to pool the press in an hour to give it. If we go to Bravo the world needs to know."

"Mr. President," he says, and I'm not surprised by the formality. It's crucial in the West Wing so boundaries are clear and personal lines don't bleed into business. "Given this change, is traveling to Camp David the best idea?"

Bypassing staff and their greetings as we make our way down the hall, I nod, salute when needed, and rub the tightness out of my chest. "It may not be, but I've got to find time for Charlie." It's not just her disappointment that worries me. We need to talk.

"I'll make it happen."

Betsy is the last person between me and the door. "Hold my calls," I say, and push through to a job that became comfortable faster than I thought possible.

It's happening now.

The thought crushes my conscience as I glance toward the flag behind my desk and then out the windows on each side of it. A cloud rolls in front of the sun, dipping the room into darkness.

Charlie.

One second.

Whoosh.

Whap.

A bullet cracks the glass.

My heart lurches.

Another round snaps and splinters the bulletproof glass in a pristine burst—two holes.

My breath is knocked from my lungs.

I'm laid flat as Evan tackles me to the ground.

Fitz barges in the room, phone in hand.

"Code black," he screams. "Repeat, we are on full lockdown. Shots fired. Crash the gates!"

Agents rush in, guns drawn. Military guards barricade the back door I used an hour ago. In a dizzying rush, adrenaline hums and I push to my feet, throwing Evan off and storming past the arms reaching to herd me out the door. I pant and fist Fitz's lapel at the same time fear expels from my stomach.

"Find my wife—now!"

Fifteen

Charlie - 1030

I'm quite certain my world is about to implode. A timer was set thirty years ago and the alarm has sounded. It still rings in my ears, drowning out the constant rumble of tires over concrete. Leaving the White House far behind didn't bring clarity; it left the Virginia countryside in a rushing blur through the motorcade windows.

I don't know what to think about Georgette and John, so I try not to. *One thing at a time*, my motto modified to get me through the interview with Aubrey Tayler. After that, Colin will help me reason through the mystery surrounding my life. He's my buoy, but the water is so rough I'm lost amongst the swells. I'm alone, fighting the nerves clawing my skin to escape in the opposite direction.

The first heaving cry comes out of nowhere and catches me off-guard while it rolls up my spine. As does the sudden jerk to the left; my shoulder stings from the crack into the door. It happens again and this time it's my temple connecting to the glass with enough force that I fade in and out of a dark cloud. Starbursts blotch my vision when I open my eyes, and we fishtail to a stop. Raised voices, Johnson and then Sawyer's, are muffled by the dark window separating the front from back.

Pop, pop, and silence.

My heart races.

I'm dazed; my head pounds.

Black on black bleeds together in a haze of interior leather and carpet, but I've enough sense to reach for my phone. My pulse sprints into each second as I fumble for it in my pocket. Just when the cool cover is in my hand, light rips into the shadows and I'm blinded for the second before Sawyer fills the space.

Large and looming, he bends down, glasses covering his eyes. "Mrs. McKenna, change of plans. Come with me."

What? No. I stare at his grip on my arm because it's wrong. The sinking pads of his fingers shouldn't hurt. *Everything Sawyer says*—my promise roars into reality.

He tugs. I press one—Colin. My hand is pulled away when he hauls me from the car. I stumble, looking over my shoulder for Johnson and the other agents that should be swarming us. I'm alone. Nothing but a dark sedan and budding trees line the deserted highway.

"What's going on?"

"The White House is under attack; we've been routed to an untagged car. Get in," he says, opening the back door of the new vehicle. A strange driver sits behind the wheel.

He's lying. I swallow my fear. "Where is the President?"

"Get in the car."

"Where is he?" I demand.

The sun beams past the glint of his glasses and his eyes are called to attention, dark and full of deceit. In a split-second decision, I bolt in the opposite direction, hoping to buy time and figure out where we are.

Sawyer laughs. I surge forward.

And then I scream. The sharp burn steals my breath as he grabs my hair, wrenching my back to his chest. I'm pinned by his arm.

"I knew you would make this fun," he seethes in my ear. "But now is not the time for games."

I'm stunned by his brutal hold and the amount of animosity in his tone. "Why are you doing this? My husband will find me and he'll kill you," I cry.

He twists his fist until my eyes water. "Someone has to atone for his sins." Step by step, he drags me to my fate. Even digging in my heels isn't slowing him down. "Killing you is a shame, really." He chuckles, a low rumble I feel as he presses closer. His mouth rests by my ear. "All those fertility appointments we take you to, fuck, you're a bitch in heat. Maybe we can both dip into that sweet cunt before I put you down."

Oh, God. I scream and he pulls to bare my neck. The pinch is followed by freedom. The world slows down and instead of running, I mumble. A litany of words tumbles from my mouth even as my lips become heavy and my lids do the same. I tip my head to the sun. It's stunning in the clear sky, so bright the overflowing rays reach into the deepening blue at the outer ridge of my vision: *my Colin.*

Sawyer growls out a roar and pats me down. My phone—gone—crushed under his foot.

Darkness descends. My legs crumble underneath me, pitching the world upside-down, and in my heart I fear I'll never see my love again.

Colin—1130

SHE'S GONE. THE THOUGHT cripples my brain even when I should be absorbed by incoming intelligence. But it all means nothing. The shots fired at the White House were a decoy—of that we agree. The target was my wife. Bile rises, burning my esophagus with the truth.

Charlie has been taken.

I don't need CIA narratives to confirm it. The aching emptiness in my heart did that when the first bullet hit the window. Tentacles of fear strangle the life out of me one breath at a time. I have never known its full strength before now. Every memory has become a blurred slide clicking into place, the vibrancy bled dry in comparison to the bright terror of this moment. She's gone. Not since Sara's death have I felt this helpless, paralyzed by my failure to protect her.

A nuclear bomb could fall on the emergency operations center and I would survive, whole and ready to lead. Sequestered with my staff and those key to ensuring the well-being of the country, everyone is safe except for the most important person of all.

"Mr. President?"

Evan. I've been expecting him. Protocol dictates the Chief of Staff will share news of events that could shatter the commander in chief. I swallow because his crumbled brow and hallow eyes say it all. "Is she alive at least?"

He nods. "We believe so."

Relief and desperation pitch my pulse into an unnatural pattern. "Who?"

"We don't know that yet." He holds a hand to my shoulder to keep me in place. "We're on scene where the motorcade was taken. The first and third cars were seized, two agents wounded, the other two missing. Mrs. McKenna's car was found five miles farther down route-sixty. Johnson is dead."

"Christ."

"Every agency is working on finding her. By your order, a net was cast: roadblocks set up and all transportation suspended from the district and neighboring Virginia counties. They're not going anywhere."

"That leaves a lot of ground to cover, houses to search. Get Carla ready. I want the kidnapping broadcast on every goddamn station every second until she's found."

"No."

I straighten my shoulders and singe him with my stare.

"Don't let this out. Not yet. We all believe it's Kilpatrick. He wants you to fall in front of the people, become vulnerable to the world. You need to remain strong, the voice of reason in a time of uncertainty. If word gets out that your wife is missing and you play into his demands, any number of threats will come in. Every family member in this administration will become a prime target, and you'll chase your tail the entire term. No one can know."

"I have to call her parents and Ali."

His nostrils flare. “No one. We can’t know how they’ll react to the news or explain a rush of family to the White House, not when we’ve closed the district. Right now, we’re working under the guise of an imminent terrorist attack and we’ve asked people to stay home. Do not share this until we know what we’re dealing with.”

“Fuck.” I hang my head, running a hand along the migraine forming beneath it.

“Listen.” Evan’s eyes hold a fraction of the fear I feel behind my own. “We will find her. When we do you can release the truth, but now is not the time.”

“I want the Carters under surveillance; my family, too.”

“Consider it done.” He turns his head by a fraction and nods to Fitz who steps from the room. When he connects with my gaze again, he crouches and lowers his voice. “There’s more. Evidence is pointing to an inside job, the missing agents and Sawyer. Mrs. McKenna called you when it was happening, and the recording confirms it.”

“What?” I scream, and pat my damn pockets for my phone like a simpleton. Evan hands over a device, headphones attached.

“Not here. Step into the den,” he says, motioning toward the door.

In seconds, I’m in an underground version of the Oval Office. Sinking onto the sofa with buds in my ear, I know why he insisted on privacy.

Fucking Sawyer. I will kill him with my bare hands. I close my eyes at the sound of her voice and cringe time and time again. Balling a fist for my mouth, I hold in a groan. ‘*Maybe we can both dip into that sweet cunt before I put you down.*’

And then it’s my Charlie. Slurring words I know she wanted me to hear. I choke on them and listen on repeat.

My nights were so dark until you lit them up, the brightest star in the sky. I’ll look for you and find my way home.

The fear is back. Terror surfaces in my ragged pulse because I’m afraid no matter how hard she tries or how many agencies or squads are out there looking, she will not come back to me. Something is happening so out of my control, and I'm helpless to stop it.

"Sir?" Evan steps in only to blur by emotion I can't blink away. "We have something you need to see."

I'm up and at the door in a second. I push him out of the way and my breath catches in my throat as Charlie is shown on ten different screens in the situation room. With the lights down, it plays like a horror movie, but this is my life. Ten of the sharpest minds in the country watch my beloved wife lit by a spotlight, suspended amongst the pitch-black. Her head hangs. Cable ties bind her ankles to a chair and her wrists together on her lap. She's surrounded by a halo of her red hair, yet it's not enough to conceal her torn dress and how it falls from her shoulder.

Sawyer steps in, fisting her curls to rip her chin up. I rush forward, as if I can save her. But I can't; I'm fucking held hostage by the same government I lead. A cry burst from her trembling lips, shredding the final string holding my nerves in check.

"Say it," Sawyer growls. "Or I will cut you and he'll watch you bleed."

I love you, she mouths directly to the camera and then her eyes empty as if the lights are turned off. My Charlie hides in her mind. "My name is Charlise Carter McKenna," she says with no inflection. "I'm being held by Logan Kilpatrick and his army. Mr. President, you have twenty-four hours to release Kingston Quade. If he is not given in trade for me by tomorrow at ten-thirty, my life will be taken in lieu of his."

The screen goes blank, and I welcome the rage. It fuels my mind and a plan for retribution. This is not a normal quid-pro-quo. A happy homecoming is not stacked in the deck, whether I produce Quade or not—of that I'm sure. The United States of America does not negotiate with terrorists, but by the grace of God and with swift action they'll know not to fuck with my family ever again. I will destroy Logan Kilpatrick, and anyone else that has laid a hand on my wife.

I will find her. They will die.

Every eye in the room is on me, waiting. I find Stacey Price. "You have five minutes to get me whomever you've tapped to profile Kilpatrick. I want him in this office, along with phone records and all the intel available on Sawyer."

"Sir, the FBI—"

I cut her off with my finger pointing first to her and then all of them, one at a time. "I don't give a fuck who's working on this; I will be involved. Get me everything you have or consider yourself relieved of duty. Evan." Anger settles into a plan and I need one person to help me put it together—the one person who studied Charlie and the people around her. "Get me Sommerton. He has some explaining to do."

Sixteen

Charlie—2030

Time is a strange foe when it has an expiration date. Left alone to suffocate in the dark, minutes could be racing away or remain suspended in slow motion. I've nothing to do but count my breaths to hold the silence at bay, and whittle against the tie around my wrists.

I hurt, my head more than anything, and when I lose track of numbers, I think I may slip out of consciousness. The rigid line of my spine aches, held tight against an unforgiving chair, but hope remains. Colin always saves me. It is in that thought I find peace and know this is not my last day.

That doesn't defeat the terror tapping on my psyche. As much as I long for the next minute with the hope that it will bring freedom, I fear that it will not. So I sink into the faraway place and the protective bubble where I don't contemplate the past or what tomorrow may bring. It's just me and my numbers until the black steals my mind once more.

Little has been said since Sawyer stormed out, leaving me to a deafening silence. I strain for the slightest noise, but let my other senses take over when there's nothing to hear. The air is heated, the stale flow confirming it when it stutters through the register with a whir—an old house, or maybe an unused one. Smooth plastic digs into the meaty pads above my thumbs and rounds my wrists, zip-ties there and on my ankles.

A faint squeak sounds off in the distance of the house, so subtle I ignore it the first time, but it comes again and again, forming a pattern I can't ignore.

My pulse sprints. Fear bristles under my skin and there's nothing I can do to stop it.

Someone is coming.

The floorboards sink in a desperate moan just outside the door. My breath hangs suspended, waiting for the handle to twist and the hinges to grate. It happens so fast it's a quick squeak, and I shy away from the dim glow when it stings my eyes.

The click of a tongue and an admonishing hum I've heard before. "Charlise, dear girl, I'm so sorry the accommodations are appalling."

My gaze snaps in the direction of the familiar tone.

Joan.

Even blinded by the sudden light shining from the ceiling, I know it's her. "What . . . how?" I blink her smile into focus, cruel and snarling at the sides.

"Surprise," she singsongs with such glee my stomach turns. She's dressed in black as if she's attending a funeral, and I think she may be planning to. *Mine*.

"But why?" I ask, dumbfounded by the amount of hatred needed to go to this extreme.

Joan tilts her head and stares. Her gaze softens for a second as it moves over my hair and face, but when she catches my eyes hers narrow.

"Your naivety was charming at first; now it's simply annoying." She crosses the room to fix her hair in the mirror suspended above a table, and the nature of my prison becomes clear. A masculine Victorian sitting room, as stated by the curved lines of gold-rimmed furniture and navy wallpaper. In its prime it must have been expensive, but now the corners peel. It's as big as my condo was. On my left, double doors open to a cavernous bedroom. It's cloaked in shadows, but from what I can see it has the same antiquated feel.

She looks around. "I always hated it here.

The Abbott mansion. I swallow as a puzzle piece falls into place. "Was this yours?"

"Of course not, darling. I didn't belong here. Nothing was ever mine. Not a room or the family that occupied the space. They made that very clear. No," she says, taking a step forward to run her manicured nail along my cheek. "I found my future with someone else, and I was happy until that slut did, too."

I gasp on the other side of her backhand, rotating my jaw to massage the sting away. *Oh, crap that hurt.* But I've no time for aches and pains. She's crazy. The need to keep her talking pushes me into questions.

"What does that have to do with me?"

Joan stares, a solemn contemplation with pursed lips and steely eyes. After a moment she shrugs. "You would like to know before you die, Charlise? You want answers to the questions plaguing your life?"

My heart lurches, but I force out a "yes".

She shakes her head and crosses her arms to peer down her nose at me. "For a long time I couldn't decide if I hated you or if I wanted you to be mine. Take you away from her as punishment. An easy lie could have had you birthed from a relative or his sister. After all, you and Abby could almost pass for twins; no one would have to know the truth of your maternity. Everything was on the side of Montgomery, except for your eyes. I couldn't look at you and not think of her. So I decided to track you—wait for the perfect moment to conquer the beast who played me for a fool." Joan's cackle is back. I shy away from it, as I do the dots that are now connected. *I don't want to know.* Closing my eyes doesn't help. The picture forms, and I whimper against the truth.

"I wanted Georgette to suffer," she hisses. "But then I learned John was. He actually loved that bitch." She paces back and forth in a whirlwind of energy, the rhythm upsetting my stomach.

"Years passed. I celebrated your mother's death with a party. A grand one in a celebration of life where I made John give a speech. It was lovely, but he cried. Charlise, he cried—in front of me he mourned his mistress. The only man I ever loved was never mine; his heart belonged to a Michigan whore. So I waited for the right time to break him. Then Colin desecrated my family—my Abby and Sara dead because of his indiscretions."

"That's not true! It was Abby and Alex."

Her hand makes contact with my other cheek leaving a searing burn in its wake. "Shut up! You know nothing, stupid, stupid girl. It was so easy to manipulate all of you. In the race of their life, I threw you in the path. Who do you think turned Evan on to your articles?"

I flinch against her clap.

"Yes! I sent them to him with your little bitty picture attached and I knew he wouldn't be able to resist showing Colin. He'd always wanted another chance with Abby and so you were typecast for my retribution. One plan and I could take them both down—John to jail with overwhelming evidence of his guilt to kill his bastard child and Colin, broken by the death of his newly beloved." Her brow crumbles and she shakes her head, crazy. "Your boy Shane was an added benefit, but I didn't anticipate Colin jumping in the line of fire. No, that made the game more difficult. Once you were surrounded by federal agents, I had to broaden the field."

Who? Who could she employ that has the scope to pull off a coup this size? Coax loyal men from their sworn duty to the country as well as the President. Breach government guards to help Joan Montgomery get to me. My shoulders slump as another piece falls into place.

"Kilpatrick."

She winks. "Yes. He gets his guy back, and my dreams finally come true. I've been called many things—resourceful is one of them. With a little digging I found Sawyer. Your husband's bad decision destroyed his family when his brother was killed months ago. Easy as pie to persuade him with money and retribution—an eye for an eye, it works every time. And look where we are now." She twirls. "Thirty years later, I've made the final play."

She's sick, and my stomach churns with it. "You think you're the chess master."

"Not chess, Charlise. This is not so complicated; it's dominoes, dear. And the last one is about to fall." Back to the table, she picks up a small knife.

Gulping down my racing pulse, I hold her with my stare as she comes closer.

"It's not me you need to fear." She clips my bindings, first my chest and then my ankles, but she leaves my wrists bound. I track her as she stands and turns toward the door. From buoyant to morose in a second, her head falls forward as one palm lies flat on the panel, the other covers the knob.

"You think Colin is your salvation. I know you do, because I thought I'd found mine, too. Think again. No one is ever who they appear to be. Not even you." She turns, ice blue irises twinkling like the chandelier overhead. "There is one man who knows my grief—felt it on the same level. I had to give him a gift. He's been the only one who understands my pain, the loss too great to overcome. It's been years, but he's still so in love with Abby."

Her face blurs as my head swims. I struggle to keep the darkness at bay and watch as she opens the door. "Goodbye, Charlise."

Relief rushes through my veins as she closes me in alone. I don't care about what she's talking about; I need time to think and breathe and form a plan. Colin. Oh, God, I wish he could hear me. I pat my pockets as I've done a hundred times. No cell. Sawyer smashed it. I look to the side table and the ancient circular dial sitting there. It's a crap shoot, one that results in stars lighting my way and no tone. I lean against the table to catch my breath and form a plan. *Joan's knife*. I drag my eyes to the door, and that's when I see him stepping out from his hiding place in the bedroom.

Alex.

Run!

Lunging forward, I swing the door open wide with my tied hands; it takes a second to get to a full sprint. But everything slows me down. The unknown corridor, my heels, and the panic barreling up my spine and into my mind—*not fast enough, not fast enough.*

He's coming.

His roar meets me at a turn and I slip to my knees, scramble to find my footing and pick up the pace. Go, *go faster.* I scream and fly down the hall. I pump my legs until my chest burns and so does the air when it scrapes down my throat. The staircase, oh God, it's three feet away. I grab the rail and use it to propel myself down, slipping for two, gaining footing for four, and then tumbling in a tight ball of agony. My head counts each step as it thumps and thumps. I jam to a stop at the bottom.

A slow fog mutes my thoughts. I was running, but now I'm not. Each breath is sharp, stabbing a pain in my ribs on the way out.

"There you are, precious." I squeal when he grabs my hair and yanks me to my knees. "No running from daddy," he says, peeling my head back until I see his eyes. The honey brown is a sweet rancor. I gag and he pulls harder.

"Oh, Abby, how I've missed our games." He clicks his tongue and then says, "But we have all night."

I scramble to get my feet beneath me, but fail and whimper over every step as he drags me back to the room. The burn, my head, my hair—he's scalping me. "Please." I'll beg. I'll do anything—*don't do this*. "Please," I say again.

We're at the top, the hall much longer as the floorboards grate against my hip. The rug slows him down. He tugs harder and my sight fades.

The blue room. Weathered scraps of paper peel from the wall. Awareness overwhelms me. I'm on my back, arms above my head and legs spread wide, knees bent and hanging from the bed. Alex fumbles with his belt between my thighs.

"No!" I scream.

Fueled by a surge of adrenaline, I pull back and kick him in the crotch as hard as I can.

Clutched over, he howls, "You bitch!"

I do it with both feet this time to his hunkered shoulders. *Not again, never again.* I say it over and over as I fight for my sanity. I slide down, and my legs crumple beneath me. No, no, *no*. "Get out, Charlie go." I say it as I crawl and I scream it when he's got my hair again. He yanks me up and throws me back in place. I'm breathless, with a black blur hanging around the edge of my sight.

His hand rounds my throat.

I match his steely stare. "You'll have to kill me."

"Don't fucking push me, Abby."

Enough. I struggle from his grip but it's too tight. "I am not Abby, you goddamn nut case! I'm Charlie Carter McKenna and I love Colin. I love Colin McKenna," I say it to him and in reassurance for me. "I will always belong to him. I will always belong to Colin McKenna."

And as Alex Miller looms over me, growling, a hand under my dress to rip my panties away, the other squeezing the life from me one second at a time—I slip into a peaceful darkness with Colin on my tongue.

SEVENTEEN

Saturday

Kyle—0100

FIVE MINUTES.

Anger keeps me centered. Misguided as it may be, I curse Charlie. Because if I do, she's still alive, a tangible target. At the end of this mission, I'll place blame where it belongs. Then I'll tell her how ridiculous it was for her to miss baking my cake and welcoming Faith to the neighborhood. "Selfish, boss-lady," I whisper to the tree, as if she'll answer. She'd have some sarcastic retort that I wish I could think of myself, but I can't because no one is quite like her.

Night goggles are a pain in my ass. That's what I'll tell her, first thing. Everything is green, and I hate that color. I stop and cue the team behind me with the quick flip of my wrist held high. Closing my eyes, I listen to the rustle of brush and the new growth of leaves whispering in the breeze. There it is again—*snap, crackle, pop*—and I got your ass at sixty-degrees north. I like guns, and I level one at the target and fire. It's that fast, and I feel nothing when he falls but the added weight of a number in the good guy column.

Four minutes.

"Almost there, boss-lady, and you better be ready to go. Get your shoes on." I keep up the commentary, much to the dismay of Seal Team Six. They only agreed on the tag-along because the President forced their commander's hand. But let's face it. I'm not new to this rodeo, and I was damn good at special ops until a sniper took me out of commission years ago. And that was just a fluke. If I'd been at the top of my game and not nursing the flu, he never would have gotten me. At least I like to think so.

The woods surrounding Abbot Farm is an armory full of men to protect Kilpatrick's treasure. A sure bet. Capture the President's wife and you can demand anything. In this case, it was Kilpatrick's right hand man, but I'd wager it was more about bragging rights. With success, he could drill fear into every politician in the world. But he chose wrong. He got involved with the wrong woman, and in minutes his head will explode. I'd like to be there to watch it happen.

At the exact same moment, agents will apprehend Joan Montgomery at her home. Bitch is probably knocked out with Ambien and sleeping on silk sheets. I'd bet Kilpatrick never thought we'd connect him with her and if we did, tie her to the mansion that's been empty for nearing forty years. But I've studied her, up one side and down the other. When I got the call, I knew she was part of the madness and exactly where they were holding Charlie. We just needed time to get the satellite pinned on the address, the teams coordinated and the plan fine-tuned.

The fun part is the clearing, an open playing field where they can see us if they're looking. Surveillance showed two guys on the roof, but if played to plan, the sharpshooters will take them down now. Two soft thuds later and we're on track.

Three minutes.

It's a clear shot to the side of the house. I've got my mind set on Sawyer. The low-life, traitorous bastard, is mine and I want him to look me in the eye and see the flash recognition when I save the world his bit of oxygen.

Seconds later we're in the side door and split off into our assigned pods. The voice in my ear simplifies my path and announces the enemies as they come in to play: one more down on my right without a sound.

Two minutes.

Up the butler's stairs to the second-floor landing and there is Sawyer, kicked back in a recliner watching late-night television. That anger I mentioned earlier, it's no longer misplaced but zeroed in on fuck-face, and I tell him so. "Say goodnight, sweetheart."

I've no time to enjoy his reaction. I end him just as screams pierce the silence. I lunge forward, counting doors. In my ear, confirmation comes—the house is clean except for whoever is with Charlie.

One minute.

One man remains.

And I'm going to kill him dead.

This place is a museum, down one hall and left on another. She's in the second room on the right and the floorboards announce my arrival, as does the ancient knob screeching on the turn.

"I'm in," I say, gun drawn as I scan the room. And then I shake my head in disbelief. "You beat me to it, boss-lady."

Charlie—0100

A WOMAN CAN ONLY take so much before she has to take control. Hallucinations have come and gone; now I'm just plain tired. I want Colin and fresh sheets. Clean clothes would be nice, too—something to protect me from the chill and Alex.

I've given up on rescue as time slips away. It's dark, so I rely on the house to tell me when he's coming. And he has, over and over again. The first time he stood by the bed, watching. The power of his stare was heavy on my exposed stomach and thighs. The dress I'd donned a lifetime ago was torn clear to the waste, leaving the sheer details of my lace bra as the only cover for my chest. His breath pushed out in uneven bursts, but he didn't touch me.

In the next visit he came closer. The air swirled around my feet and he dug his fingers into my inner thighs, spreading me open. I ached, not from his touch but from Colin and our night together. I thought of him then, as if it could buffer me from Alex as he mumbled *broken* and *fix me*—everything else was too random to understand. Gagging almost gave me away when the slapping sound of his hand told me he masturbated. I prepared myself to feel his come spurt on my naked flesh, but instead he got angry and his speech more chaotic. His outraged pitch rose with his furious pace. It took everything within me to feign sleep or death, repose from kidnapping. *It's exhausting.* And then he screamed and left me alone with the chill in the room.

The third time he proved more daring and prepared for an attack. One hand held a knife to my wrist, slicing through my binding, and then he spread me open, an arm on either side. The other traveled up my leg and onto the curve of my waist, the pad of flesh saved for my husband. He tugged at my ring finger, trying to pull my wedding band off. I wanted to kill him then. Rage hummed beneath my skin like a sick song, thrashing and driving to a wild beat. "I can't look at you," he sputtered. "I can't," he said and began to cry, the sick, wet tears of the unstable.

He disappeared.

I plotted.

This time the door swings open but the bright burst behind my lids doesn't come—the lights stay off. When the floorboards announce his entry and the air swirls, I wait and wait for his hand to climb higher and for the knife to glint on the soft skin of my navel. For the first time since I was taken, I forget Colin and focus on my training. On Alex with his face hovering over my stomach and the revolting heat of his breath, on lying still and hoping my racing heart doesn't give me away. I concentrate on striking with the strength of a mother saving her child from the hands of death.

I'm fast, too fast for him to respond. My thumb scrapes his nose and then gouges his eye—not bad for a blind try. I revel in his scream and grab my salvation that he's dropped to the mattress beside my hip. Palm to hilt, blade up, I swing madly and fight to drive it through muscle, past bone and into his organs. Once, twice, until he's limp and whimpers as he falls to the floor.

I scramble to the far edge of the bed and test my feet, cool on the naked wood. Breathing heavy, I close my eyes and listen, listen to the house and for what comes next. Alex crawls to the corner, a distant moan telling me when he makes it there. Panic simmers in my stomach when the floorboards groan, the knob turns and the door opens.

On instinct from day after day of training, I raise a fist to my nose, the knife held lower in my other hand, and adjust my stance into my defensive pose. I'll save myself or die trying. I won't let Joan or Kilpatrick or Sawyer cheat me out of my life, not without a fight.

Breathe, Charlie.

"You beat me to it, boss-lady."

I can't move. I just stare at the dark and give God my worries, because I can only feel the numb joy of being found.

Charlie—0105

"SUSPECT DOWN. ALL CLEAR."

"You're late," I whisper and shiver alongside Kyle's chuckle.

His words spark a flurry of action. The lights pop on. My fist falls and I close my eyes against the invasion. More feet, more bodies fly in the room and I stay still, locked in place, listening as they make quick work of securing Alex.

"Think you could drop the knife for me, Charlie?"

Knife? I dip my head and look, blinking against the reality that I may have killed a man. The blade drips blood as do my fingers, with spray cast up my arm. The weapon is heavy, an anchor taking me under as I feel every bruise, every word, every hand gripping my hair, every minute within the last day. *Everything hurts.* I let go of the knife and follow it down, my knees giving up just as I do.

Kyle catches me before I hit the cold wood. My head to his heart, legs scooped up, he cradles me and mumbles over and over *you're okay*, as if repeating it will make it so. We're on the move, voices all around, a blanket laid over my shoulders and a medic taking my wrist for a pulse. She follows beside us asking questions I can't answer—too dazed to speak. Kyle never stops. I know the sound of the stairs; I lived them with my body one at a time. He crosses the foyer and exits into a wash of fresh air that stings my cheeks and speaks the language of freedom.

I'm fine until I hear him. But at the first rumble and then the tortured groan, tears race to my eyes faster than Kyle's feet move to transition me into his arms. *Colin.* His touch is feather-light, yet fierce at the same time. I can't look, so I bury myself in my favorite place and cling to him, hands in his hair, lips to his thundering pulse. I sink in as close as humanly possible, knowing, feeling the thick blackness reach for me once again.

"Don't let go."

"Never," he says, his mouth pressed to my ear. "I'm here; I will always be here, my love."

I slip away, comforted by his truth.

FROM NIGHT TO DAY, lights rouse me to the point of understanding that people exist outside of my head. As do the sirens that send it pounding like a woofer. I want the knife back when some lunatic pulls my lids open and shines a torch in my eyes. When I raise my left arm to knock it away, the best I can do is tug and squirm; the right side is just as secure. I whimper.

"Hush."

Colin. He soothes me with a kiss to my forehead and whispered words, a monologue of where I am, what they're doing, prepping me for the pinch of the I.V. I roll in and out; one second we're in the ambulance and in the next the lamps of the emergency room shoot shards of glass through my brain. I'm alone with the nurses and a doctor asking questions. From warm to cold, the blanket is gone as are my clothes, stripped bare but for the murmurs floating over me.

I can't look.

It's easier to stay tucked away and let them poke, prod, scrape my nails, take my blood, and scan my head. What felt like a minute must have been hours when I hear him again, agitated and insisting on holding my hand as they send me off to a private hospital room. Warm, solid, and comforting with the tickle of recognition that stalls the anxiety simmering under my skin, and I squeeze when his fingers link with mine. He's what I need.

"I knew you'd find me," I murmur.

"Not fast enough," he grumbles.

Not fast enough. It repeats on a spindle, around and around until it pounds out of my ears. It bothers me, but for now I'm a good patient as I settle in from gurney to bed. I even listen when Dr. Patel introduces herself and tells me my head hurts because of a simple linear skull fracture. I'm not so sure there's anything *simple* about it, but I accept her diagnosis and the pain medication rushing through my veins, thank you very much. It dulls the ache there, in my bruised ribs, and every muscle screaming for relief until she gets serious. My shoulders tense when the nurse leaves, the door is shut, and a stool is pulled over to my shoulder.

"Mrs. McKenna?"

"Yes."

"I need to ask you a few questions. They may be difficult; would you like your husband to stay?"

My heart stumbles. "Go on."

"I understand you have been actively trying to conceive and therefore refraining from any birth control."

I try for the word but it comes out as a mimed *yes.*

"Ma'am, were you conscious the entire time you were held?"

One breath, two . . . I swallow the desert and mumble, "No."

"Did anyone take sexually aggressive action against you? Your pelvic exam produced evidence of trauma and semen. Mrs. McKenna there is no shame . . ."

"Stop." I can't.

I won't.

I'm not talking about this but she keeps going. I've been here before and I can't.

I won't.

I hear you, I want to shout. I hear you and NO! No, he didn't. Please. I have to believe that's true. *But is it?*

"Charlie." Colin's voice sinks like a weight in my stomach, it's rough and worried and it tips me over the edge.

"No." I shake my head and hiss out the pain.

"Mrs. McKenna, I'd like to prescribe you the morning-after regime as a precaution. It would eliminate conception that occurred over the last seventy-two hours," she says.

Three days—anything within the forty-eight hour this-is-the-best-time-to-make-beautiful-babies window.

Oh. I choke on a cry and squash my eyes closed tighter.

I can't look.

Not at her, and not at Colin.

"Thank you, but no. I would like you to leave now," I say, my palms pressed flat so I can only see the starbursts behind my lids that I grind in place.

"Mrs.—"

"No more. *Please!*" My chin crumbles underneath the pressure. "I can't."

The fragile hold I had on self-containment explodes in a rush of memories: Colin and the night filled with just us crushed by Johnson, Sawyer, Joan, and Alex.

And Alex.

Not again. I can't choose again because this time it has to be for the baby: my baby, our baby—*Colin's baby.*

I need him to understand.

I can't destroy what could be a life created by our love. But I won't look at his pain; it will be too much to bear, so I hide behind my hands and break into huge mouth-open, someone-make-it-all-go-away sobs. I've fought so hard to get to this place, a healed mind and body. I will not let Joan and Alex take away the possibility of my baby.

Dr. Patel doesn't know, but I do. *Don't I?* Alex didn't. *He didn't, did he?* "Please." I suck in a breath. "You have to believe me. He didn't."

But I can't say touch me, because he did.

He had his hands on me.

"Charlie." Colin's whisper is ragged and torn, just like my heart. He presses his mouth against my ear. I turn to him, forehead to forehead, and open my eyes to the sun. His eyes shine, full of love and sadness, so much regret. *I only want you to live a life without regret.*

"He didn't." If it's a lie I feel convincing, for him, for me. I need it to be true, for him, for me. But I just don't know.

Squeezing my lids closed against my fear of the truth, I raise my voice for the doctor to hear, for the world, for the nagging thoughts of doubt harping in my mind and for Colin. *For my husband.* "Alex wasn't inside me."

It would kill him. I'd be just like her—Abby.

Oh, God. *My sister*?

It's too much. "Where's Ali?"

I can't do this.

I study my fingers and then my arms, as if I've never seen them before. They're filthy and bruised, purple streaks marring the once pristine ivory landscape.

"It's okay . . ."

Colin moves my hair from my forehead. I'm ripped into my mind, a new kind of hell. Their hands pull me back to a place I don't want to be.

I scream *let go, let go, let go of me!*

"Baby, we're going to give you something to help you rest. Ali will be here. I will be here; you're safe. Sleep now."

Conscious thought drifts away on his reassurance. But I know. I know nothing will ever be the same.

Eighteen

Colin

THE HALL LIGHT SLICES through the dark and points to Charlie's pale form. She's restless and on the verge of waking from her forced sleep.

"You've been standing in the same place for more than an hour. She's not going anywhere," Evan whispers, while walking through the doorway.

A grunt is all I can manage. Not from exhaustion, although it's reaching in and taking hold. My wife kept me up for two nights—the first because she couldn't get enough of me, and the second because I was frantic to find her. I choke on the thought and clutch my chest tighter with the arm stretched across it, the other propped up by the elbow so I can pull my lip. Charlie was right; it is my tell when I'm worried about her. If I don't keep myself occupied, I'll kill Miller myself, finish what she started.

I haven't decided how to feel. A battle of wills wars in my heart. A wave of relief shook me when Kyle rushed her out of the house and I felt her breath on my neck—satisfaction that she fought the bastard and took him to within an inch of his life, yet also a desperate anger, because she was in the position to have to do so. But most of all, I'm afraid. I fear the weeks ahead knowing they could pose as much harm to her as the hours she was held captive.

"Did Sylvia make it in okay?" I ask by way of distraction.

He nods. "She's checked in at the Jefferson, waiting on your schedule. She'll see Mrs. McKenna whenever she's needed."

"How is Brady doing with the press?"

"Fine. He released an overview, touching briefly on actual events. You'll need to assure the public she's okay, and if we can get her up and in front of a camera soon that will help, too."

"Evan."

He spans his fingers and thumb from one side of his forehead to the other, holding both temples. "I know. I'm sorry for mentioning it, but she belongs to the people. They love her. In minutes, the security of the nation was rocked—if Kilpatrick could get to the First Lady he could infiltrate anywhere—and then the strength of your leadership was validated. Taking him down will remain a part of your legacy."

I clench my jaw and let the rancor living in my stomach rise. "I've two issues to clarify: she belongs to me and I will decide what's right for her recovery. And the credit belongs to the teams that went in and got Charlie and slaughtered Kilpatrick."

He nods. "Yes, sir, but don't cut yourself short. You and Sommerton figured out Joan's involvement and that led to confirming Kilpatrick's location."

"History predicts the future."

"What's that?"

Shrugging, I say, "He never strayed from his habit of working closely with someone attached to his target. When Sawyer couldn't be linked directly, it was an easy leap to believe there was a third person involved, and Joan wasn't a stretch. Not after our conversation Wednesday."

"Are you going to tell her?"

"About John?" I sigh and press my palms against my eyes, rubbing. "I've no doubt Joan took care of that last night. She was adamant when I met her that she would do it if I didn't. Goddamn it. I should have known something was off; she was wired."

Evan grunts. "You've met her every year on the anniversary of Sara and Abby's death. Telling her this was the last time could have set her off."

I drop my hands and watch Charlie's chest rise and fall under the thin hospital blanket. Guilt for her being here is a lifelong burden

I'll bear. Admitting my responsibility to the man who knows everything about me and my business, because it's his too, is a twist to the knife in my stomach. "I knew that wasn't it, I felt it Evan, and I ignored my intuition, chalked it up to her newfound knowledge of Charlie's paternity. When she laid out the facts for me, I attributed her mania to some asinine idea she could claim a part of Charlie for her family. Reinvent the piece that was missing after Abby's death. But I couldn't quite understand why it was so important for her to tell me everything right then." I grab my neck to knead some of the tension out of it. "In hindsight, I think she was playing with me, cat to mouse. This whole thing is so fucked-up."

"No arguing that point. Ali will be here any minute; she'll help."

I look him over. His hair is askew, as if his fingers have lived in it for the last twenty-four hours, and a new kind of wear has pulled his mouth tight. I called my parents and the Carters, dispatching Captain Greene to bring them here. Evan called Ali. I can't ask how the conversation went because Charlie moans my name. In the next breath I'm by the bed, bending to whisper in her ear.

"What do you need, baby?" I press my lips to her skin, more for me than her, and I admonish myself for the selfishness.

"Bathroom and a shower," she murmurs, hoarse from the long night. "Please."

"I'll get the nurse."

Her fingers sink into my arm. "No, just you."

"Anything you want. Wrap your arms around my neck."

She weighs a fraction of what I think she should. She was thin when we married, from the weeks following my injury and then the stress of wedding preparation. I squeeze as much as I dare given her ribs, and watch her I.V., careful to pull it along with us.

"Don't let Evan see my ass."

I stop mid-room to quash the emotion flooding my eyes. *God, I love this woman.* I breathe in her scent as I half-laugh, half-cry, "I'll kill him if he looks."

Evan chuckles. "Welcome back, Charlie."

The few more steps I hold her isn't nearly enough time. Once in the bright light and for a long moment, I relish her warmth and her fingers teasing my nape. *She's my life.* "I wish I could go back and take this away from you," I whisper into her hair.

She nods. "I know."

I haven't a clue on how to make this better, so I do the only thing I can—hold her. Through my hands stroking her back and my breath in her curls, my lips murmuring into her forehead, I try to show her how adored she is, as precious as the rarest gem. How I thank God with every heartbeat she is safe. I take in her contented sigh, but know I have to let her down when she starts to squirm.

"Easy now." I set her feet on the tiles, but keep my hands hovering around her waist as she stands, eyes closed to the glare of the florescence. It's a good thing I do when she nearly crumbles. She presses her nose to my neck through the minute it takes to get her settled on the toilet and then as I start the shower water running to heat it before she gets in. "I'll give you a minute of privacy while I speak with the nurse to let her know you're up. Don't move." I hold in my grimace. She's so fragile, sitting with her arms wrapped around a billowing gown, a wild halo of red framing a pale face. "I'll be right back, okay?"

"Not going anywhere," she says, doing her best Stevie Wonder impression, but I see through her good nature to the trembling lip. My Charlie is holding on by a thread.

I close the door on her feelings only to enter into the flood of Ali's. She flies by and uses her momentum to light up Evan's cheek in a slap that can be heard down the hall. His head whips back, the imprint of her hand purple against his shocked expression. Fury rolls off of her in waves as she seethes out her anger in bursts of panted breath. "I will never forgive you for this."

"Ali." He blinks. "I couldn't tell you; it was a matter of national security."

"Fuck you and your security. Sometimes people are more important than goddamn secrets." She steps into the little space between them, her finger to his nose. "This is my sister." Her voice cracks, and Ali closes her eyes to whisper, "This is Charlie." When they open, he flinches. "And you didn't think I needed to know some maniac had her or that maybe she needed me as much as I needed to be there for her?"

Tears break through her anger. Evan reaches as if to stroke her cheek and she bats his hand away. "Don't touch me. You lost that right when you lost your trace of humanity and the little compassion you'd fooled me with. We're done, Daugherty."

On Evan's *you don't mean that* she whips around to stare me down. Eyes wide and fragile, she wrenches her hands in a knot by her stomach. Maybe because I love Charlie as much as she does, I'm forgiven, and she runs into my chest. My hands hover over her shoulders until her hurt pulls me under and I fall apart with her. For one moment I give in to the desperation I've felt for fifteen hours. For just a minute I live through the grief and become weak, when I know I'll need to be strong for the next million. Sixty seconds of Ali's tears flowing with mine in silent regret for what our Charlie must endure once more.

Ali presses away and our eyes meet on a mimicked nod—an unspoken agreement to see Charlie through.

Swiping her cheeks dry, she stands in front of the door and takes a deep breath. She opens it a fraction to slip inside and close me out. I almost break my promise and dissolve on Charlie's fractured "Ali," but instead lean my forehead against the cool wood, listening to her sob. Time is suspended as it goes on. Guilt steals my breath as I wrestle with what was done and who did it. My life choices brought this upon her. I hate myself, the decisions I made, and the job I gave everything. It brought us here, listening to an ocean of her tears.

Evan hasn't moved that I can tell, and I don't until the door is ripped open an inch. It's enough room for me to see beyond Ali, through the steam and into the mirror reflecting Charlie as she steps into the shower.

Ali's words about clean clothes fall away just as the world slides out from beneath my feet. I'm gutted. Pain and rage funnel through me as a sickness when I see what was done to her. To my wife, my love, my Charlie. Her ivory skin is marred by deep purple and black. Bile rises to my throat from the fingertip bruises on her thighs and stomach. I groan and look away, unable to stomach what I did to her. The need to possess, objectify Charlie as mine, take her so hard I leave my mark, is as sickening as the bruises Alex and Sawyer left. And Shane before them. I don't deserve her.

"Focus up, Mr. President." Ali snaps in front of my dazed expression. "Charlie needs clothes, preferably her own—something to sleep in and for tomorrow, too. Can you handle that?"

Attention to the task—this I can do. I nod and get to it. Evan escapes the room and into his own hell. I pace, call Betsy, and wait the thirty minutes for the delivery. Shortly after passing an overnight bag to Ali, Charlie emerges like the finest crystal with a hairline fracture waiting to fall apart. Her eyes stay focused on the floor, arms wrapped around her stomach. I take over for Ali's supportive hand on her elbow and walk her to the raised bed.

"Chef Rene sent over breakfast," I say, rolling the table to her side.

She tries for a smile, a slight bend to her lip when I pull the lid back to blueberry pancakes and ham and everything else she loves. Steam rises, but Charlie picks at the fruit to eat more like a bird than a woman who's been without food or water for nearing twenty-four hours. Sleep is what she needs.

Doctors and nurses come and go; the Carters and Gram arrive. Charlie drifts, one minute awake and the next out cold. My parents appear and with all of the commotion, I'm pushed to the side and eventually out the door to address the nation. Before I go, I kiss Charlie's forehead and whisper, "I'll be back, I won't leave."

I'll never leave her but she sleeps through my reassurance.

Night comes and the hubbub dies down. I lie next to my wife. Relief washes through me when she rolls into my chest as if she's as desperate for me, as I am for her touch and sweet scent. But rest is out of reach. I lie awake petrified about what I'll find when I wake.

FROM DEEP SLEEP TO blinking awake in the hard incandescence of the hospital, I struggle to focus on heaven itself.

"Good morning, Mr. President," Charlie says, as if she's been awake for hours. By her appearance, maybe she has. She slept for the good part of the last twenty-four, and today she's taken advantage of the clothes Betsy had delivered to the hospital. Her delicate frame is covered in a simple long-sleeved black dress and tights. Four-inch heels have her legs seeming limitless. No bruises, no sign of trauma—only my stunning wife. Her hair is brushed into soft curves and pulled over one shoulder, but it's the angry flair of her lips that I find most distracting.

She bites the bottom one, sucking it into her mouth. "Something wrong?"

"No." I shake my head. "I've never seen you wear that color before."

"I liked it today. Is it too dark?"

"Charlie?" I call for her attention because she's moved on, checking her appearance in the small mirror hanging on the wall. She wraps a large beaded necklace around her neck and works to clasp it.

"Hm?"

Her gaze follows me as I stand and walk to her side. "What are you doing?"

"Evan scheduled a press conference for nine. I didn't want to wake you until the last minute because you're so tired. You should shower. A fresh suit is hanging in the closet. Brady put together a brief speech for you and me; yours is on the table." She turns and brushes her hidden anger on my cheek. "Better hurry. We can't be late for the nation."

"You don't have to do this," I say to her reflection, because I can't move. What the hell is going on here? Blinking doesn't bring on reality; I'm stuck in an alternate universe. I've woken up to a Charlie who wasn't kidnapped and beaten, one who smiles with near black lips. She sits and drinks from a mug, so poised her pinky finger is extended as if she's having tea with the Queen of England—but she's not. It's coffee, and Buckingham Palace is across the goddamn Atlantic Ocean.

"Yes, I do." She sips. "It's our job. I'd like to attend Johnson's funeral with you this afternoon as well. I've already spoken to Dr. Patel, and she gave her blessing if I promised to rest when we get home. Hurry now." She gestures me gone. "Breakfast is getting cold."

Our eyes meet in the mirror and for a brief second she cracks. Chin trembling, tears misting, until she blinks them away and turns, unwilling to look at me. "Go," she whispers. "I need some time."

Some time? "What does that mean?"

"It means I don't want to talk about it. Not yet."

I could push her, something I've done before. It's easy for Charlie to get buried in details and overthink until the facts become muddled—lost in her mind and the past. She's survived too much, and now an added tragedy I want to erase. If I went to her right now and begged for her to talk to me she would. If I kissed her she would respond. I could strip her bare and murmur my apologies into her ravaged skin and she would let me, but this is a hard gamble. What if I push too hard? Yet if I don't . . .

Maybe my impulse to move her beyond this is because I'm desperate to see forgiveness in her eyes and feel it in the touch of her hand. Or was I expecting her to need me more?

I grab my hair, torn. This is my torture. "Tell me what to do. I want to be whatever you need to get through this, but I'm not sure what that is."

Looking up, forest green eyes blinking away the mist, she says on a faint whisper, "Wait for me."

The knife living in my gut twists, and I nod. "Promise you'll talk to me when you're ready. Even if it's in anger, promise me."

"One day, I will."

NINETEEN

Colin

CHARLIE HANDLES THE MEDIA like a pro. Confident and smiling with appropriate reassurance, she reads the script as if they're her own words and America falls in love all over again. With her—the damsel rescued, more beautiful than ever before—and with me—the hero who brought down the bad guy.

On the way out, we stop for final instructions from the nurse and a painkiller for her head; a conversation with the doctor calls for a week of rest and she's discharged. The event is closed.

Except it's not; it's not near to over.

Reporters line up outside of the hospital doors. I position myself to shield her from the sea of flashes, yet Charlie stands tall and slides in the back of the presidential limousine with a regal elegance. She presses her dress against her legs, smooth along her thighs and then tucking her fingers under the hem, not once or twice, but over and over, as if wrinkles are against the law.

"Charlie?"

"Yes?" Smooth and tuck, smooth and tuck.

"A Homeland Security representative was assigned to investigate Sawyer and your detail. He's requested to meet with you this afternoon."

Stop, turn and stare. That got her attention. Not in a good way, if her narrowing eyes are any indication. "Isn't it apparent he was involved? The video Sawyer sent you should be proof enough. Or, do they think I hog tied myself to the chair?"

The vehemence in her tone assaults me. I lower my voice in hopes it soothes her anger. "Details, love. And not just about that night. Randy Strickland's job is to find out why there wasn't a hint of this before it happened. Someone had to have suspected something."

"You mean Kyle."

"I didn't say that."

"But that's what's they're thinking."

"Strickland will question him, along with those that remain from the team. Leadership will have to answer for the complete breakdown. To answer your concern, I trust Sommerton. It's why I asked for his help. If he had any doubts about your security, he would have intervened."

She looks out the window. "He would have died trying. I," she whispers. "I'd rather not meet with him today—maybe next week. Could you arrange it for a later date?"

"I will."

"Colin?" Her voice cracks. Vulnerability lives in her eyes when I find them wide. "John . . . and my mother."

My heart sinks. It's hard to take in a breath under the weight of her stare and my racing pulse. I can't swallow away how sorry I am, so I take her hand. "I know."

"Okay." She nods quickly. "That's enough for now."

Guilt balloons in my stomach and I want to expel everything, get it out so I can breathe. But I'm a coward. I keep it to myself as she pulls her hand away and turns to the window. Silence suffocates. The city passes us by and at the last minute Charlie dons a mask. As we pull up to the cemetery curb and then leave the motorcade, she can't help but be stunning with the dark mouth, angry on a pale face, and the pill-box hat, tilted low so the black veil obscures her eyes. Closing herself off to the world.

Standing tall, she walks ahead to face the curious glances with a compassionate smile. She pouts her bottom lip when a baby cries, as if the sound has a direct line to her heart and she needs to make it better. So strong, ethereal as she works her way through the mourners—she's one of them, experienced in pain, yet she won't look me in the eye. For all the appearance of strength, helplessness is a heavy burden on her shoulders, and she knows I'll see it.

I'm baffled. Charlie is a firecracker. When she's mad, I know it. When she wants something, I feel it in her body as she uses it to persuade my decisions. She loves, she stomps and runs, flirts with men to drive me mad, dances naked across the room until I fling her to the bed.

Charlie does not hide. Not with me.

Not until today.

The sky accommodates in somber serenity, gray clouds rolling from the breeze. Red, white and blue cloak the casket, adding the only color amongst the sea of grief. Low sobs drift to us as we're directed to the first row next to the family. Charlie stiffens with respectful sympathy. Shoulders back, nose forward, with arms driven down to her sides and fists clenched. Not one tear falls while the pastor speaks of Johnson completing his duty on earth and how he will live on in the house of the Lord, and with his father who preceded him there.

Through the entire passage, I miss my wife. I miss the simple moments. Her hand in mine, the soft slip of her skin as it slides into place. The curl of her fingers as they stake claim. Her possessive grip and the way I felt knowing I belong to her.

Sommerton appears at the edge of the grass, hollowed out just like Charlie with shadows under his eyes. The two of them drive darts through their connected stare, but when she takes a step forward he withdraws, jogging to a nearby car.

As is my duty, I pay my respects. The bereaved family and friends, colleagues and acquaintances, a hundred people sway to the cadence of my voice, the wind now prefacing a storm on the horizon. I recognize their loss with sincere gratitude. Johnson gave his life to protect mine. The burden of his death is laid at my feet, yet my toughest battle is ahead of me still and standing behind me now.

I finish and retreat to Charlie's side, the solemn notes of Taps play to the beat of my heart. A gust rips from the sky, loosening a red curl, and it lashes my cheek. It tears me open and I want to fall to her knees and beg. *Don't leave me*. Not with a shell of the woman I love. Fight for us. The sentiment vibrates out of me as I glance her way.

These last few days have split me in two. As if hearing my plea, Charlie turns. The delicate lift of her hand sweeps away the tendrils acting as my lifeline, tucking them behind her ear. Then she smiles, a soft lift to her lips as her eyes meet mine. Christ, I'm destroyed by her. This, this is my Charlie, my love that's been locked behind a wall of sorrow.

I almost stumble forward when her pinky brushes mine. It's a whisper of pressure that could be the wind, but I know the stroke of her hand as if it's caged inside me.

I belong to this woman. We may have lost our way, but in this moment of crisp clarity, I vow to find a new path. Whatever cages her in, whatever pulls down the mask, I'll help her see the light. "This is my vow to you."

Charlie's head tilts, but she doesn't have a chance to speak because Fitz is at her shoulder to prompt our farewell condolences. As he leads her away, I fall behind to call the one person who can help me figure this out.

SYLVIA ALLARD DIDN'T HAVE an option to refuse my request. Nor could she decline to discuss Charlie's care. Last year, my then fiancée signed a confidentiality disclaimer to allow my participation in her treatment and I take advantage of it today. With her dark eyes and hair, a flowing colorful skirt, and a wrist full of bracelets, Sylvia looks more gypsy than psychologist. I'll trust her because Charlie does, and since the extensive review Phil completed when I re-engaged her services showed a flawless record.

Charlie exited our den seconds before I slipped in. Scheduling an afternoon appointment worked in both our favors. Staring out at the rumbling clouds, I find Sylvia's gaze in the window's reflection. Flicking her eyes toward the crushed velvet couch, I get the impression she's ready to psychoanalyze, but Lord knows it would take her years to figure me out. I'm here for my wife. I turn, widening my stance with hands pressed in my pants pockets to prevent her from seeing them clench.

"Mr. President, your wife suffers from Post-Traumatic Stress Disorder or in short, PTSD. Any event that threatens one's safety can cause it—rape, kidnapping, assault—these are all situations that left her in a helpless state. In truth, she most likely first suffered from PTSD when she was a child, after the death of her parents. Charlie was never treated, and without coping skills, she found her own mechanism which was to withdraw within her mind. She calls it the 'faraway place'. Have you heard her mention this before?"

I nod, stuck in my own memories of last summer on the campaign trail. Charlie tried to manage the repercussions of Shane Roberts and the Texas shooting by holding her emotions too close to the vest. As a result, she couldn't move past them and agonized over events repeatedly, until as a last resort I sent her away to recover with family. An escape from the rigorous pace of my election bid had been necessary, or so I'd thought.

"It's Charlie's made-up haven; she retreats there so as not to remember and relive any troubling event. We don't want her to use that method to cope."

"Understood, but how do I help her not to?"

"With PTSD, a person's nervous system is failing to recover its equilibrium. Because of this she'll struggle with memories and flashbacks, as real as if she were reliving her kidnapping—nightmares and extreme anxiety are added to the mix. She's wrestling with guilt, self-blame, and mistrust. Doubting herself and others, the foundation of her relationships will come into question. It's all normal."

"And this is happening right now?"

"Yes."

"She's questioning our relationship?" I rub the strain out of my forehead. "But she's so resilient. She looks perfect: poised, articulate. It's as if nothing happened, except her eyes are vacant."

"Mr. President, when you're given an expected task and become unsure if you can accomplish it, what do you do in the face of those asking for it?"

"Reassure that it will be done, and then formulate a plan."

"Exactly, and Charlie is no different. She's not sure she is strong enough so she's pretending to be."

"What you're saying is although by outward appearance everything is fine, in her mind she's grappling with what we just discussed."

"Yes, that's exactly right."

"What do I do?"

If Sylvia's smile is meant to offer reassurance, it fails in the sad downturn of her eyes. "Be aware that Charlie is disconnected right now, even from you, the closest person she's been to in her life. She's stuck, Mr. President, stuck in that night, remembering it day in and day out, trying desperately to put the pieces together and move on. Talking about it with you is not cathartic for her, not right now. My recommendation is to keep her engaged in life, find a normal pattern that involves social and physical activity. She's enjoyed volunteering at the rehabilitation hospital, and I've encouraged her to continue. You should too."

"That's it? In essence throw her back into her life and wait until she's ready to engage with me?"

She nods. "Music and singing are successful techniques to open and stabilize the nervous system; this then lends to accepting social engagement, which aids in recovery. Encourage her to play the guitar and sing; it helped her as a teenager and will be of great assistance to her now. Mr. President, your job is to encourage, and be a soothing influence, open to talking. Don't push, be near—offer the normalcy she had prior to the event and when she's ready, Charlie will let you in. Of course, she and I will continue to meet at least on a bi-weekly basis. I will urge her to think and not ignore the event, explore her feelings. She was very good at 'shelving' them, her explanation for what she did as a child."

"I don't do '*nothing*'. It doesn't work for me."

Folding her hand under her chin, Sylvia leans forward. "I can only imagine. In your position you're expected to take action, make decisions. With Charlie you need to find your patience; her recovery will come with time. Eventually she'll open up to you, and that will be very liberating. Your job when it happens is to listen—don't judge or get angry. Prepare yourself for triggers to memories. It can be anything and the more you learn about the event, the better you'll be able to ascertain what they are to support her through reliving that night. Don't take her withdrawal personally. She has a lot to work through and it may take months, possibly years."

The knowledge that I brought this upon Charlie is a haunting whisper in the back of my mind. My involvement in her life started the avalanche; the enormity of my career put her in the path of Kilpatrick. The road to redemption starts now, with the wind swirling unsteady strokes on the other side of the heavy window. I move to leave, my thumb absently caressing the underside of my wedding band, a symbol of my commitment to her.

"I'll have Fitz see you out. Thank you for taking the time, Sylvia, and for all you've done for my wife. She is . . ." I hesitate and look at the impending storm, the same pent-up energy in the sky rages inside my chest. "She is the very breath of my soul. I'll do whatever is needed to help her be well."

This time the smile reaches Sylvia's eyes. "Charlie's very taken with you, Mr. President, and I can see why. Your love for her is evident in your actions."

Or lack thereof—power, control, decisions, everything comfortable in my world, yet I'm in a waiting game. Charlie is at war with her mind, stuck in replay, questioning everything—including me. Sawyer and Joan took more than her freedom; they took her stability. Her world has flipped one-hundred-and-eighty degrees. I think Joan knew the bomb she dropped would continue to eat at Charlie long after she left Abbott mansion—if she made it out alive. Now she's caged in by the evidence of her paternity. A man she hates, a half-sister who wishes her gone—a connection to a family she despises. And a husband who didn't tell her because I needed more time to care for her, time I didn't have because my job took me away. *My job.*

I failed her. Disgust squeezes the air from my lungs. I can only hope Charlie will forgive me. And that she's strong enough to let go of the past and not worry about the future. She's always lived one day at a time, and I need her to be present in mine.

TWENTY

Charlie—May

EVERYONE HAS SOMETHING THEY try to forget, yet I'm desperate to remember. For weeks I've fought with vague memories, a touch and a mumbled curse that drifts away like fog on a cool spring morning. Quick to burn off from the sun, it's tangible until it slips through my fingers.

Alex Miller had his hands on me, but how far did he go?

It's the million-dollar question without an answer.

I've lived through trauma, more than most, and I know all of my yesterdays are gone. I'll never understand Georgette or how she became embroiled in a campaign and involved with the senate hopeful. Sawyer and Joan aren't coming back, nor is John Montgomery going to take the place of my father. I may miss who I was before that day in April, but I'm more concerned about the collateral damage.

Colin.

I saw how he looked at me in the hospital as I stood naked in the shower—a curled lip that shouted his disgust just as sure as if it was spoken out loud. And I see how he looks at me now. Cautious glances, eyes fragile with concern, and when he thinks I'm not watching, fierce with sorrow. Face to face, he acts as if nothing has changed—but everything is different. *I* am different, and that isn't even the half of it.

I live on the edge—a façade of normalcy stacked against a terrifying possibility. Seeds of the future sprout into thoughts in my mind. The vines wrap around vague images of a life filled with separation—Colin on one side of the forest while I'm caught in the underbrush on the other. The divide seems limitless because I lost consciousness during the moment that holds the key.

If only he had gotten there earlier. *Not fast enough.*

I push the thought to the side.

The days blend together because my nights are long. I'm afraid of the dark. Fear slides between rationale thought and living nightmares where demons are real. With the lights on, I can brush up against sleep and then their hands are in my hair, pulling me under. A new reality keeps me awake—watching Colin's chest rise and fall in his own restless slumber.

During daylight hours, he hovers but not too close, waiting for me to reach out and touch him, or open up about what happened at Abbott mansion. Even though it loops on a replay, I haven't told him anything. I can't.

I won't.

The sheets are rough against my skin, adding to my discomfort. Kicking them free doesn't help. No matter how beautiful my husband is, I can't lie next to him with the edgy energy rushing through my veins. I lean in to his cheek and breathe. His whiskers scratch my lips and for a moment, I let myself dream of waking him with my mouth. Stirring up the cyclone of need I feel to be close to him, to get lost in his kiss and his body. To let his fingers sink into my flesh, recalling the bruises on my hips and confirming that they belong to him and no other.

Not Alex.

But I fear the possibility that they belonged to the man who stole his first wife would break his heart. And then it would break me. I couldn't stand his rejection. So I ease out of bed and into the shower. Hot and scalding, I scrub away the memories I do have for the hundredth time, hating the ivory skin that holds on to the color of April in fading pastels. Numb to the touch, I towel dry and wrap up in Colin's shirt he left in the dressing room. Closing my eyes on a deep inhale, I can pretend he's pressed against me and I drown in sandalwood and him.

My Colin.

Time moves on. I find myself in the kitchen to make tea. Then I tuck away in a wingback to watch the sun breach the horizon and burn a thick streak of gold into the reflection pool as it rises. Washington is peaceful right this second, but in an hour the district will take on a hum of rushing traffic and people. I'll join them in my daily jaunt to the military-rehab center. A place I've found solace in these last weeks.

"Charlie, love?" Colin's voice washes over me and I close my eyes. "Did you sleep?"

Tilting my head back, I catch the fallen brow before he levels his features into the expressionless expression. He stops behind the chair, his hand gripping the edge as if holding back from reaching for my shoulder. I shudder at the thought. An internal war wages—I want his touch so bad I can feel his nails rake down my back, yet I dread it at the same time. In my mind, caring hands turn to thick claws of hate when he finds out what I've done. His look will change from compassion to revulsion as it did that day, and I couldn't live with myself knowing he hated me.

Moving next to my knees, he sinks into a crouch to stare up and into my eyes. I grip his shirt close to my chest, holding it tight so he can't see me or the yellow stains that remain. But my thoughts stumble on him. He's so pretty, even concern can't wipe away the appeal of his chiseled jaw and the dimple softening the center. Or his full lips, his bottom caught by his teeth for just a moment in some form of contemplation. It's me, I'm sure—the need to nibble and contemplate.

I'm tempted to brush a wave from his forehead, but he gets to mine first, tucking a wet curl behind my ear. "You look tired."

I shiver as his finger brushes my cheekbone. "I'm not, really. I just got up early and didn't want to wake you."

"You should have."

"Then you would be crabby."

"Crabby?" His mood lightens with a grin. "Not when you're my wake-up call."

"I took my chances. You've got a long flight tonight and I know you won't sleep well."

He turns away and his jaw clenches so hard I fear for his molars. Muscles bulge up and down as if he's chewing on their broken pieces. "Come with me." It's a statement drilled into the air. "You belong by my side, not withering away in this staid room staring out the window. I won't let anyone hurt you, not again. We'll stay an extra day in Paris and I'll make you fall in love with me all over again—be with me."

I close my eyes against his plea. He's asking for more than I can give, because if I go, I'll give in to him and tell him everything. I'll lose my secrets, and then we'll be done. He'll know his worst nightmare lives next to him every minute of every day.

I need a little more time with Colin before I tell him the truth.

"I can't," I whisper, and tear up because he wants me. In this moment he wants me.

The weight of his stare is heavy as he sighs. "I love you, Charlie. More than whatever happened in that house—more than whatever burden you carry. I'll keep asking and one day we'll walk this line together." Leaning in, his breath brushes against my ear when he says, "You belong to me."

And then he's gone.

Oh, God. Every word tears a hole in my heart. How I want that to be true for all of time. I can't fathom the contrary without getting sick, so I get lost in the sun. My thoughts flitter away with the birds in the sky. Better to fly with them than sink into the madness that's knocked on my door since the moment my world changed and Johnson died. For the three thousandth time I let the loop begin: *pop, pop, and silence*—Johnson, Sawyer, Joan, and Alex.

And Alex.

Somewhere in the midst of the chaos Colin says his goodbyes, a promise to call at lunch and a brush of his lips against my hair, and then he walks out the door.

I'm not so far gone that I forget my responsibilities. Dressing is harder than my second shower. Finding the right tank to cover the marks on my chest, a white blazer to hide my arms, slim jeans to conceal my legs, and now no one will know. America will never really know what happened—secrets.

Pop, pop, and silence. I work on remembering the entire way down the steps and into the waiting ride. The larger motorcade may reassure Colin, yet travel in the car tests my sanity every time I slip in the backseat. But it's what I do Monday through Friday. Working at the rehab center has kept me sane.

Kyle hasn't, because he'd gone on forced leave minutes after dropping me in Colin's arms. I miss him and the normalcy of our banter, the safety I felt with his quirks and James Bond-stealth mode. The agency protocol pulled my entire detail after members of it were proven to have worked with Kilpatrick. For Kyle, the distance is necessary. Who wouldn't need time away when your partner turned psychotic, killed your brother-in-arms and tortured your friend? I'd need a vacation too.

So I stay locked in the loop of Alex's hands and fight for control. It comes with familiar routine: taking the steps of Washington's newest military-rehabilitation center. As I walk from car to door, I wave and smile to the media who are a constant companion.

"Mrs. McKenna." Sandra Burke from *The Post* calls three times for my attention. "How are you feeling? Can you comment on the status of Joan Montgomery's arraignment? Mrs. McKenna."

If I have to work with a reporter, Sandra is normally a favorite; her tenacity is equal to her friendly approach and results in accurate stories. Today I smile and pick up the pace while screaming obscenities and throwing out hand gestures in my mind. *How do you think I feel?* I close my eyes on the anger and let it simmer before hitting the first room. One at a time, I meet with men and women fighting to find a new kind of future. Liam Jacobs—lost his left leg below the knee in a blast outside of Kabul. Freckles map across the bridge of his nose. I read to him as he works through the pain following his morning therapy. Michael Huntley and Ethan Moore have heartbreaking stories that I do little to fix but for listening. Some have girlfriends or moms or brothers, and some have no one but the men they left on the battlefield. They do for me more than I do for them, centering my thoughts on the here and now or in their memories, rescuing me from my own.

Last stop: Navy Seals Special Forces officer Caden Lawless. Never one to sit and wait for the physical therapist, he bends into a stretch as I walk in. The tight red shirt with a blue spider spread across his chest announces him a superhero, but this guy wasn't bitten, and kryptonite isn't going to bring him to his knees. He's the real deal. Graceful, even though he's nearly the size of the Washington Monument, he eases into a half-bound lotus, one of fifty yoga poses he insists I should try to find my inner Zen. The angry scar on his neck and his right leg wrapped beneath athletic shorts are the only indication of his injury.

His dark hair is pushed off his forehead, and he looks up to flash a smile. "Ma'am," he says and then laughs, deep enough that it carries through the room.

"You're asking for trouble today," I reprimand without the conviction from our typical teasing, an ease built after all of the time we spent throwing punches and drilling into real feelings.

The second week post-discharge, Sylvia encouraged me to get back to my normal. I returned to the rehabilitation hospital and rounded on the veterans and read and listened and talked. Every day I used Caden as a verbal punching-bag. He became my replacement Kyle. I missed my friend and I needed one who wasn't embroiled in the situation or angry like Ali. She hated that I'd been taken and used in some asinine vendetta. Because how does that happen, in real life with loads of intelligence and security, how does it happen? And the truth is hard to swallow—anything is possible. Airplanes are used as bombs; kids are shot at school; what was safe twenty years ago is not—not today. No place, no one person, is immune. Not churches or malls or the workplace or the First Lady.

What Caden lends is a fresh perspective and an ear to my piece of the tragedy. I rely on what turned out to be his sound judgment. He lives by a set of rules, founded by SEAL principles and expanded upon for personal integrity—to live by his truth. We want different things out of life. He thrives on danger and the next deployment—because of that, he remains single when I need a home and family. Yet in the end, fundamental moral values are universal and he reminds me of that. He's worked me through hard days and encouraged me to open up to Colin because he's the one I need to talk to. More than that, I want to. I want to get real and go take the next step but I'm afraid. That day in April doesn't scare me so much as what comes next. I'm obsessed with it and petrified at the same time.

Standing, Caden plays his part, feigning an innocence that washes over his high cheekbones and chiseled jaw. It looks about right. Yet by the shadows lurking behind his chameleon-colored eyes, blue one minute and green the next, I'm certain it's not a word associated with him, ever. "Trouble is about all I find. And many times I bring it upon myself."

I look around at the drab cream walls. The bright and creatively disjointed drawings of his four-year-old niece are missing. As are the balloons his twin sister sends him once a week. The stuffed bag on his bed is my final clue.

"You're leaving."

"I am," he says, tapping his thigh. "Ratcliff gave me my walking papers ten minutes ago. Good as almost new. But I'll come back for the documentary. You just tell me when, and I'll be here."

Rehab for gunshot wounds sustained in Afghanistan may have brought him back to his former physical strength, but months of counseling hasn't lessoned the pain of his last deployment. Setting aside my fractured heart, I find a bright spark of joy that he's about to take the first step to heal his. "When do you leave?"

"Right after we say our goodbyes. I'm hopping in my truck for a ride cross-country to free my mind."

I smile. "When do you plan to arrive in California, next year?" We both look out the window at the 1957 Chevy pick-up that's seen better days.

He shrugs. "Eh, I'm mapping out the itinerary for Monday."

"Seventy-two hours is more miracle than scheduled route when that thing barely pushes fifty-five." No one wants to go home when facing real life is harder than climbing Mount Everest. But he's been hell-bent on scaling to the top since the day I met him.

"Yeah, well I'm due." Hanging his head, he grabs the back of his neck and kneads. "There's a date for everything, and I'm about to hit mine head on." He laughs, a sad chuckle that gets stuck in his throat. "Here's the thing, Charlie. War isn't a testament to a man's strength; finding peace with your part of it is."

Turning my way, he stops my breath with his hard stare. "Bad things happen. I lost my best friend this go round. He was with me since kindergarten. Mrs. Neely never knew what shit she stirred up when she sat Justin Weber next to me that first day. I don't remember not having him around, but he's gone. I'm going to live today and tomorrow because if I don't, I may as well have died on the field with him."

In a thick heartbeat the table is turned, and I know he's including me in that statement. He's told me this before. Just as the loop plays in my head, his reiteration of why he's embracing life is his way of asking me to move on. I break from his gaze and pick at the clips on his camouflage rucksack. I've never followed his statement with a question of my own, but here it is. "Aren't you afraid of what will greet you when you get home?"

"I'm honor-bound to face his family and their grief. Dodging it will only postpone the inevitable."

I nod. “That’s the scary part—not what happened but what will because of it.”

“You’re strong enough.”

“No, I’m not. Not for this. I’m weak when it comes to him.”

I glance at Caden just as he says, “Some people mistake solitude for weakness or arrogance for courage. In truth, one person cannot comment on another’s reaction because it’s their own interpretation of life. What I feel you will not. How I react is different than every other person who may experience what I do. It’s the human filter that makes us unique. There is no right or wrong here.”

“I don’t know how to talk to my husband.”

“Trust him. That’s everything—trust.”

Emotion curls in my stomach, a small knot growing bigger with every breath until I can’t hold it in. It escapes at first as a small cry and then funnels up into a wet wail of tears that I can do nothing but release as my knees wobble under the weight of the last month. One hand grips the bed, the other his shirt. He lets me go on without a word: standing as still as a statue while I mourn who I was, and grapple with what I am today and will be tomorrow.

So close to Colin’s past that I’m petrified we won’t have a future.

TWENTY-ONE

Colin

THE WOMAN I LIVE with is not my wife. To the naked eye she's a perfect replica, yet the spark is gone from her eyes, the sway has stilled in her hips, and her laugh is silent. I miss her.

Charlie has done everything with precision. The doctor told her to rest for a week, and so she slept. With her parents, Gram and Ali doting on her every need, it left me to tend to the nation and the demands that followed her ordeal. Sylvia insisted on meeting with her every third day, and so she has. Easter rolled in and she stood next to me at mass, played with children as they searched for eggs, and cleared her plate at brunch. She smiles for the camera, waves to the public, and sits in that damn chair staring out the window when she thinks no one is watching.

But I am—from afar. At first because of the Carter invasion, and it wasn't because I resented them or her father's stern glances—I resented that she didn't need me.

For the first time in my life, I hate my job, the media, and the people who invade my privacy and hers. The limited details in her statement to Strickland grate my nerves. I've read it repeatedly. After each review, my loathing grows for her daily visit to the hospital and the man whose teachings saved her when I couldn't. My mood swings violently from fear to anger to panic that although she was returned to me, I lost her in that house after all.

And then the guilt crashes down in an avalanche of self-deprecation. It's my fault. I'm responsible for the bruises to her mind and body; I failed to keep her safe in so many ways. It's no wonder she's sought solace in the arms of anyone but me.

For weeks I've let the distance grow; I've accepted the silence and furtive looks. But a simple desperation has stalked its way inside.

I can't lose her.

Not Charlie. I can't

I won't let it happen.

Not my wife. I won't.

I've guarded her feelings, allowing her time to adjust as I was advised to do by Sylvia. I don't ask; I wait and worry the flood of emotions will come, and she'll drown in them while I'm away on the ten-day European tour that begins in the morning.

Every night, I fall asleep before her and wake without her. Charlie slips into bed, kisses my cheek and feigns rest. But if the lights go out she stiffens, and the scream waiting for release radiates from her in a tremor. I find her on the couch in the morning, staring at the sunrise over the Washington Monument. For every question I ask she smiles and waves it away with an '*I'm fine*' or a '*just thinking*'.

I miss her everywhere, and right now it's in the shower soaping my back when we both know she does it just to feel me tremble under her touch. I want her hands and mouth working me to release when my quick jerk in the hot water leaves me cold and just as needy as I was before. There are no antics to brighten my mood as I towel off and dress. My suit hangs in wait for an evening sure to test my ability to concentrate as I charm former President Winslow and his wife. I should have insisted the dinner be rescheduled, but his anti-terrorism work is a priority.

As I curse my tie, Charlie rounds the corner, frustratingly elegant in a form-fitting black gown. It covers from her neck to her toes, caressing every curve my hands itch to touch. I close my eyes against her stare and listen to the rustling of silk on the floor as she draws near.

"May I, Mr. President?"

The unrequited need I felt moments ago returns with a forcefulness I didn't anticipate from her breathless voice.

"Charlie."

Her name hangs between us as her fingers take over for mine. Years fall away and I'm suddenly a boy on a first date, anxious and reeling from the possibilities. My heart runs ahead too fast and I fist my hands to keep them from roaming. I want my wife. More than anything, I want to hold her.

I'm lying—I want to get lost in her until we both let loose our demons to find forgiveness and heal in what remains. We've relied on honesty, so I ask her, "Can I kiss you?"

I swallow when she fumbles. And then smile in relief at her just as breathless "please do."

The spark I was missing is there when I open to find her. Just a quick sparkle of intense green, but it's a hope I haven't felt in a long while. Seconds pass and my lips press to hers, at first soft and then greedier when they part in hopes she'll invite me in.

She does. *Christ.* I groan in my tentative approach and step into it, leaning in to align her body to mine. Electricity sparks from my mouth and through every nerve ending as I take in her small mewling cry. It grows more desperate when she melts against me. Being close feels so good. I wait for her response to my hands on her hips and groan again when her fingers find my hair and play. *Charlie.* I chant her name in my mind and tease her tongue into a game we abandoned weeks ago.

It's perfect, she's perfect, and I take my time lighting my hand up her spine and into the bun wrapped loosely at her nape. My world tips back onto its rightful axis, and relief streams through me in a sigh.

She tenses.

Her fists find my chest as a heaving cry breaks free and rolls into a gut-wrenching scream. Pushing away, she whips around.

“What?” I pant, watching helpless as she races from the dressing room in a black blur out the door. Minutes pass, and I stare. What went wrong? I’ve held her that way countless times before.

Before.

We’re four weeks post-apocalypse, and everything has changed. Charlie’s world was shattered at its foundation, and she’s only a month out from the tragedy I should have prevented.

When I walk into the great room she’s at the front, head bent, fingers worrying the beads on her clutch. I slow down three feet away. She looks up, and my heart breaks from the tears welling near the breaking point over her lids.

“I’m sorry.”

“Baby, I don’t want you sorry. I want you happy and whole. My regret is that you won’t talk to me about why you feel this way.”

“I can’t.” She shakes her head so fast the water falls.

“Please don’t cry,” I say, stepping forward only to have her step back. *Fuck*. I hold my hands up. So this is how it is.

She sniffs. “Can we just forget this happened and have a nice dinner?”

I try to tame my sudden flash of anger in the clench of my jaw. It shouldn’t be directed at her, yet I can’t kill Alex, Joan is in jail, and Sawyer and Kilpatrick are already dead. The two players left to ferret through the aftermath are husband and wife, and she can’t stand my touch.

“Sure.” *Dinner, exactly what I want*. Tonight marks a new road for Charlie and Colin—one with boundaries, where my advances aren’t welcome, nor is my hand on her lower back. I offer my elbow instead and on her terms, she wraps an arm through mine. We take the steps together but we’re on separate continents.

She dons the mask as our guests walk in. Every minute that passes with her faceless smile and dull eyes drives another scotch in my hand. I slam it back with each foreign laugh. It’s my turn to pick at my food, more interested in drink than the nutrition she seems hell-bent on proving she can stomach. I can’t bear her concerned glances.

As soon as it's reasonable, I say goodnight to the former first couple and walk Charlie to the residence. Following her stiff spine into our dressing room, I stop to help as she fumbles with the zipper at the neck of her gown.

"No," she says on a quick turn, hiding her eyes from me. "I . . . I've got it, thanks."

I swallow the scotch rising into nausea and rip the tie from my neck, relaying a sloppy bow to the wife who wishes me far from sight. At least there is one thing I can accommodate: space.

"Don't wait up, work to do," I mumble, and slip away.

If I can't lose myself in Charlie, I'll do it in alcohol. I'm scheduled to leave in three hours for two weeks. Enough time for this gap to grow into a canyon. I can fix anything; I've proven it in my career, yet I've no clue on how to help my wife.

The house is quiet, with few staff clearing away remnants of the dinner party. The West Wing is just as still, an office lamp here and there casting a dull glow on the checkered tile. I bypass all of them.

Only the best for the President. I snag the hundred-year-old scotch and a glass from the Oval Office, mumbling a hello to the guards on duty as I break through the back door. The chill in the air is not so different than Charlie's cold shoulder.

Another wave of guilt stabs my gut for even thinking the thought. I moan my misery and heave my sorry ass on a bench in the garden, cursing the sweet smell of budding roses. How dare life go on when mine is falling apart in the house behind me?

"Care to share?"

I swallow and welcome the burn down my esophagus. "Misery loves company. Isn't that what they say?"

Evan chuckles as he sits. "Don't hog that shit, Mr. President. Seems as if you've gotten a head start and I'd like to catch up." He holds out a glass I hadn't seen.

"Resourceful. I like that about you."

"Charlie kick you out?"

I shrug and pour him a hefty dose. "I removed myself so she didn't have to say the words. And you? Ali have a change of heart?"

"I'm not sure that'll ever happen. She's tenacious to begin with; add her sister to the mix and she's downright obstinate. I'm not sure how I did the right thing for the country and fucked up so badly with her at the same time."

I stare at the sky as if the lightning splitting it in two has all the answers. We're in for a spring rain; the humidity is thick with the promise of it.

"A better option would have been to stick me with the decision. It's not as if she could divorce me." But her sister could. The word is bitter on my tongue, and I wash it down with a heavy swallow.

"In all honesty, I had no idea withholding the information would annihilate her trust in me and that, my friend, is why I've been single my entire life. Understanding the female mind should be a course taught in grade school right along with sex education." Evan holds up his glass to draw a line in the sky. "Think about the number of relationships we could save if we added that to the mandatories necessary to graduate high school."

"Let that be my legacy."

We contemplate it and listen to D.C. find its level of peace in the early morning hours. It's easier than grappling with the monsters inside our minds, but mine won't stay silent any longer.

"How did I miss it?"

"Miss what?"

"Everything: Charlie's paternity, John and Georgette, Alex and Joan—the big picture, Evan. I pride myself on picking apart the pieces to understand what I'm working with. I ignored even the most obvious—she looks just like Abby." I choke on my oversight. "I should have looked harder, but maybe I didn't want to know."

"If you did, would it have changed anything?"

Christ, my heart leaps. I press against my chest as if it's on the verge of leaping out, unable to live next to the truth. "It may have. I don't know that I would have had you invite her to the press conference."

"Why not?"

"How can you ask that knowing how fucked up the family is? Out of compassion I would have let her live in ignorance of her mother's affair, at least giving her a chance to stay away from this." I spread my arms wide. "Look at what's become of her with my interference. She's back to where she was fifteen years ago. I may as well be Shane Roberts."

"Oh, for fuck's sake, you're ignorant, Mr. President. And," he says, pointing his finger with drink in hand, "a real jackass."

"Is that so?"

"Yes, it is. Have you not heard a word your wife has said to you during the last year? In the span of the last thirty days, have you forgotten the depth of your devotion to her? The only Colin McKenna I have ever known drives at adversity head-on and maps that shit into an opportunity. Why is this any different? You didn't know about John. Stop second-guessing why or blaming yourself for not figuring it out before Joan could use it to her advantage. The fact is the best woman for you is upstairs pissed at your ass because you've got your head shoved inside of it." He adds *sir* as an afterthought and smiles.

My gaze falls to the damned pink roses and I think about everything he just said. Charlie is my legacy. The decisions I make for this country will help shape it, and others will come after me to effect change. But she is my family. My wife is my heart. There is no separation, and to think as if there's a difference is steering my course in the wrong direction. I won't allow there to be anyone to come after me with her.

Although our struggles are correlated, we're sitting side by side to work them through when we need to walk the path and heal together. I need to get her out of her mind and living for today and tomorrow and the rest of our life, because I'll be damned if we don't have one.

I've forgotten who I am these last weeks. So focused on Charlie's recovery, I've retreated, followed Sylvia's direction to wait, be patient, and let her open up when she's ready. That's never worked for me. I charge into what I want head-on and I want her healthy, happy, and in my bed straddling my waist. I want her laughter ringing through these hallowed halls, her joy flitting around the rooms and bringing more light than the sun shining through the windows.

I want my wife, and I want her mine. "Well said, I think."

"You're welcome," Evan says, with a smug grin. "Now I suggest you go beg for forgiveness and make the world tip back into its rightful place where Charlie Carter McKenna can't keep her hands off of said ass."

I laugh and stand. The ground shifts beneath my feet. "Don't drive." I point to the bottle next to him on the bench. "Stay in one of the spare rooms upstairs."

"Nah." He shakes his head. "I had a sleeper put in my office because you're so hard to work for."

I walk behind him, dropping my hand to his shoulder. "Take your own advice and call Ali. The best woman for you is across town waiting. From what I know, she's worth the extra effort."

Leaving him to think about it and right my own wrongs, I head back to the residence. It's late but the lights are on. Charlie's on the couch dressed in my old work shirt and wrapped in a blanket, staring at the flameless fireplace. I perch on the far side arm, clearing enough room not to hover but sitting close enough to read the subtle reactions of her expression. Her lip trembles, and ass isn't a strong enough descriptor for her asinine husband.

Anger clings to the edges of my guilt—anger at myself for letting this go on, for losing sight of what she really needs—a firm hand, the voice of reason guiding her through to the other side. With my blinders removed, it's easy to see the stark defeat in her pooling green eyes.

"Charlie . . ." A sad start to everything I need to say, but her name is like living. It pounds with every beat of my heart.

She shakes her head as if knowing that it means more and she wants time to open up to my plea for the connection we've misplaced. Yet she straightens her shoulders into the elegant posture I'd seen all night with the Winslows, a demeanor made into battle gear to protect her from the jagged spikes of feeling.

She picks at non-existent lint on the blanket. "It's my fault."

"God, no it's not, Charlie. None of it is. Not yours or mine. You are not alone; talk to me."

The demand slices through her carefully constructed pretense as her chin quivers. "What I have to say will destroy us."

Heart lurching, I slip down to the cushion and take her hand. She's cold. "There isn't the slightest possibility of that happening; my love will last through this life and into our forever. There isn't another way for me. Whatever it is, I'm here; let me help you."

I've never seen desperation paint her face with such fear in her round eyes and crumbling brow. "I'm just like her," she whispers.

"What are you talking about?"

"Abby. It's happening all over again and I can't stop it. I won't." The first tear is gut-wrenching. When she chokes on a sob, a similar lump forms in my throat.

"I'm pregnant, and there's a good possibility the baby belongs to Alex Miller."

Twenty-Two

Charlie

I SHATTERED THE EXPRESSIONLESS expression with one sentence. As I fill in some of the blanks, Colin falls into hopelessness one word at a time—pale and unresponsive—ruined by his wife.

The truth didn't set us free; it nailed our coffin. Dead are the Charlie and Colin who existed before a spring day in April killed their future. Although I never wanted Alex Miller's hands on me, they were there, and his intentions clear. I may not remember the act itself—a gift from God—but I've convinced myself it happened. Now Colin faces the exact consequences he did seven years ago. There's no denying I'm a replica of his dead wife, the one who cheated and gave birth to another man's child.

His love will never be the same. Not with this new truth. The scattered pieces of his heart lie on the rug at our feet, a puzzle too complicated for either one of us to renew.

He hasn't let go of my hand. For an hour our fingers lay entwined. I can't remove myself from him fully, although a deep responsibility for where we are weighs down my body and mind. If I had allowed the doctor to run the course of drugs to end the possibility of pregnancy, we wouldn't be here. I wouldn't have had to tell him about Alex, or his hands pulling his belt and pants free, or my loss of consciousness when he ripped my panties away.

Now he knows.

History does repeat itself.

I'm his nightmare reincarnated. *An unfaithful wife.*

"When did you find out about John and Georgette?"

He jerks at the sound of my voice, jarring against the stillness of the room. "Kyle figured it out . . ." he says, and then swallows. "I wanted to tell you when I had more time to help you through the shock of knowing. I planned to that night at Camp David and then you were taken. Charlie." I turn and as soon as he comes into focus I wish I could look away, but I'm stuck on the wild pace of his eyes as he searches my face. "I never wanted it to end this way."

Tears sting against the reality of that statement. I nod, biting my lip to hold in the cry that goes along with them. *We were good together* is what I hear. We were. We are, we can be, but I can't expect him to live through it again. I disengage, leaving his palm up on the couch so I can push my hands in my hair to hold myself together and to keep from throwing myself at him to beg. *Please don't do this.*

"And I want you to know that I was drawn to you not because you looked like her, but because you're you. Beautiful, yes, but smart and confident and sometimes silly, too—everything that made me hope for more than I had."

I close my eyes against the sorrow in his. It's too much. I would do anything for him yet I can't change who I am.

One day altered everything. I fight so hard with my heart and the emotions shredding through my chest. I slip into the faraway place and tune out the rest of his platitudes. Nothing else matters. I made my choice and I'll live with it—without Colin. The magnitude of that stops time. Stringing thoughts together is an impossible feat turned blessing as a cool numbness takes over.

"Charlie, baby, did you hear me?" he asks, but his frantic gaze swings to the foyer and the knock that sounds. His job calls for what I'm sure is a welcomed reprieve. "I have to go. I . . ."

Hanging his head, he says it again and again as if he's created his own mantra to help him out the door.

"It's okay." I reach for his clenched fist resting on his thigh, and the electricity that always hums between us tickles my hand. "I understand."

A silence falls, broken only by our heightened breath rushing together one last time. Charlie and Colin, and the brief glimpse of what we were and what we could have been. He feels it, too. I know he does when his brow draws down and his lip trembles as he tries to speak.

There's nothing left to say.

Standing, he bends to press a kiss into my hair.

One breath, two. *I will always love you.*

It becomes my mantra and I mumble it over and over again through his tortured parting look. When he rips his eyes from mine, I speak to the broad lines of his back and as he stops at the door in his rumpled shirt. When he grabs the frame as if he needs the support, I whisper it so it sits in the air between us. He blurs, and I say it out loud and in my head when he walks away. Louder, so the walls know my truth and it won't destroy my heart that already screams and now so am I.

I hold my belly and look down, remembering this new heartbeat. A new life that this time I gave up everything to keep safe.

With uncontrolled fury, I sob for what we had, what we lost, and for the child I already love.

Thunder melds with the tortured music of my soul, splitting it open one drumbeat at a time. It jars me into motion. I can't stay here, not drowning in a suite I designed to remind me of him: the color of his eyes on our bedroom walls, pictures of us everywhere, and the vintage vase he bought me on our honeymoon filled with flowers on the table. It's a new torment that I flee, running through the house to the back staircase, down and out the door to the yard.

The rain starts as a mist, soothing my ravaged cheeks. It picks up into a tapping beat and washes away my tears. Colin's helicopter lifts and turns to race off in the distance. At the same time, the sky opens as if it is my breaking heart heaving its sorrow toward the earth.

Throwing my head back, I let it take me, welcoming the angry torrent that is no longer a whisper but a howl lashing against the pain and releasing me from its grip.

Each drop taps and blends with the next as it hits the ground, the patio, and chairs, falling with irreverence to my sorrow. And so I join in the mockery, allowing Colin's shirt to part at the neck and slide from my shoulder without care of the guards by the door. The downpour soaks the cotton, sure to color me indecent for prying eyes, yet the beauty within nature is more cleansing than one hundred showers, and it washes the sin from my skin. I let the memories flood my mind—Colin when he was mine, Alex, Joan, and John. I give them up to God and beg for his help but all that comes is the cold morning air.

"There has to be something meant just for me," I say to the rolling clouds as a shiver trembles through my shoulders.

"You know it's my heart."

Colin. I sink into incredulity from the rough gravel in his voice. With my eyes closed, I can hear his soft steps squish in the wet grass as he comes to stand behind me.

"It does, and always has belonged to you.

I choke on a cry. "What are you doing here?"

"Why would you think I could leave? An hour ago you broke my world open, and laid fate at my feet with a miracle. Of course I would stay." One more step and the heat of his chest warms my back. "Europe can wait, or they can meet with Parker; I gave them the choice. Nothing is more important than you and our child—my family."

Hope is a pinprick in the distance, a light I latch onto as an answered prayer. "But work? Munduozzi and Aguillard, the tour? Alex? John? And Alex," I say, as if an echo pounds through the yard. I can't forget about them—how can he?

"Look at me, Charlie." His tone leaves little room for argument so I turn, staring at the grass until the last second when I glance up and get caught in a new storm. Emotion churns in his eyes. His jaw is set, hard and unforgiving. "It's been too long since I've had my hands on you, and I think you've overlooked a very important fact." As if on cue, they rise to cradle my cheeks, slow and deliberate gentleness that I lean into. "You belong to me."

My pulse speeds as he studies my face and then my soaking hair. His fingers follow the path. I whimper when they sink in and instinct has me step away, but he tugs, holding me in place.

"Who am I, Charlie?" He punches the words into the night on a dare, spraying water from his lips. "Say it," he says so loud it volleys with the thunder crashing overhead.

"Colin." My voice is too weak to be heard over the rain.

"Who am I?" He clenches harder and pulls until my hips meet his. A hot, rolling pulse starts in my groin as we're mashed together.

"My husband."

He growls and asks again and again until I'm bent backward with his heaving breath crashing against my mouth. "Who am I?"

I crack with the lightning and scream, "Mine, you're mine, always mine!"

And then he's there, sealing the words in like a promise.

Colin

I'VE HAD ENOUGH. DANCING around what I want has never worked for me. My willpower has slipped and so have my hands—to her hips. I'm not asking for permission. Not from Charlie. She's my wife, and it's time she remembers my fingers as they dig into her flesh.

Marking her as mine has never felt so good.

I push as far as she can go. When her hands struggle for purchase in my hair and she moans into my mouth, sliding her tongue against mine in urgent lashes for more, I know we're okay. We'll get through this together. Unwilling to give up her lips, I pick her up and cradle her against my chest. I retreat through the south portico doors.

White House employees are sworn to confidentiality, but they also know when to disappear. The sun is about to break over the horizon, yet no one is in sight as I rush her upstairs and into our bathroom.

"I love you," I murmur into her mouth as I set her down to start the water. A twinge hurts my heart when she starts to cry, but I say it again and then again, wrapping her in my arms until she sobs into my neck.

Minutes pass and I hold her. I hold my Charlie, welcoming her breath on my skin. When she calms, I strip us bare. Everything is gone, my shirt, her panties, all the way down to her doubts. She tries to hide behind her hands, covering the seeping yellow bruises that are the last physical reminders of the night that separated us. I press her arms out, open, naked, and vulnerable. I feast on her, hungry for every curve, starved for the slope of her breasts that bud into tight pink nipples that beg for my touch. The flat surface of her stomach holds the promise to round with a life beyond ours, something she feared couldn't happen. Arms, legs, thighs—I score every inch of her with my eyes and swallow my grief for the pain she's endured.

"You're beautiful." I pull her into my chest. As much as I've struggled with guilt during the last month, she's fallen victim to self-recrimination and skepticism. As if I could ever think of her differently because of biology or another man's forceful touch. Had I known missing time and what Alex may have done had fueled her distance, I would have worked harder to put the pieces together. It was enough for me to know Sawyer and Kilpatrick were dead, along with countless others who'd guarded the house. I didn't seek out specifics from Joan or Miller because I didn't need them to move on, but Charlie does. I'll find the facts for her, and the outcome won't change my love.

Even with the wash of tears on my shoulder, I smile when thoughts of spanking the truth into her darts through my mind. I've not had the impulse to take her over my knee before now, but that she believed I would abandon her brings out the itch in my palm to connect with her ass. I press my grin into her neck and maneuver us under the hot water. "Shush," I say to her started hiss. "It's not too hot; you're too cold. Let me warm you up."

She nods as the spray hits her back, and lifts her face in search for my mouth. I start slow as she watches me lick her lips, then bite at the bottom one and press mine against hers, chaste. A spark flashes in her eyes. She groans and fists my hair. *There's my girl.*

"No more silence." I brush a kiss across her cheek and then mouth. "You'll talk to me and tell me everything. As your husband I have the right to fight for us, and it's only fair for me to know what I'm battling. I'll win, too. I promise you that. I'll never fight fair where you're concerned because I want you, baby, too much to ever let you go."

A broken smile pulls up her pout. "So much happened I forgot how to just let you love me."

"Then I'll remind you how it's done. I'm going to start here," I say, pulling the shampoo from the shelf. "It's my hands, Charlie. This is me; I belong to you." With each word, my fingers become bolder, sinking in to the thick silk and massaging her fear into pleasure. When I pull the suds through to the ends, her eyes flare and anxiety comes to life as if it's a presence between us. "Say my name."

Tears well and fall in heavy drops until they disappear into the stream flowing down her chest. I prompt her again as I tug and rub, soft caresses that have her moaning seconds after she calls out to me.

"I'm washing away every unwanted touch. You'll remember mine, my love."

I flinch from her sob, and as she throws herself at me. "Get it out, all of it," I say, and she does. In a rush of sobs that turn painful, loud, from-the-gut cries. Her once soft hands turn to fists, pummeling my chest.

"I waited for you to come," she howls, and the words wound me and her. "I needed you, Colin; they hurt me so bad. I needed you and you didn't come."

Guilt strikes harder than her jab to my kidney. We face our demons locked together, at once struggling with the pure force of feeling, and then as the emotions are spent and we sink one into the other. Charlie clings to me, now whispering apologies into my neck, and mine are pressed into her ear.

When exhaustion wins, I get us out and dry, careful as the terrycloth passes over her breasts and between her legs. "New memories," I whisper, fearing another bout of tears. She's not only fighting with a newfound reality, but working with the range of hormones that strike in early pregnancy.

She nods. Her chin trembles as I let my finger skim over her folds—something to think about, something to recharge her need for me.

I smile and tilt her face to mine with a thumb pulling her bottom lip. It's so full, lush from crying and the burn of my whiskers she hasn't felt in weeks. "All is fair in love. I'm fighting for us, sweet girl. I'll do anything to win you back."

In the second her mouth parts to reply, I crash mine to hers. This kiss is deep, filled with love and lust, and everything else bottled up within me for the last month. I bend over her, tasting and taking the sweetness that is Charlie, and when she teases me with a vibrating moan, I break away. Just as fast as I'd taken her, I stop and whisper against her whimper, "Come to bed."

Tugging her behind me, I bring her to our king-size mattress and wait, looking to her for the first move. Our eyes connect, and hers sparkle with understanding.

"Lie down," she commands.

I pull the sheets open and fall in. The heavy thud of my heart is loud in my ears as her gaze rakes over my chest and stops at my cock that's been semi-hard since I saw her practically naked in the yard. I grow thick and rigid under her appraisal. Need burns like a fire in her eyes, a promise for another night, an invitation to keep going, keep pushing, because each time I do, there's a crack in her armor.

"Don't move," she whispers and crawls over me. Breasts heavy, peaked with her own arousal, her breath scrapes my aching erection and then she moves up to settle in the crook of my neck. She wraps her limbs around and between my legs and arms, and I sigh into the feel of her skin, smooth, hot, and exactly how I remember it. *Mine*.

I reach for a blanket, tucking it around us, and before I'm done her steady exhales fan over my skin. "Give me another day, baby. One more day to prove I'm good enough to be yours."

TWENTY-THREE

Charlie

LIVING WITH UNCERTAINTY IS exhausting. The sun has come out and breaks through the drapes in our room when I wake more rested than I've felt in weeks. The night rushes through my mind at the same speed as my accelerated pulse. In the few hours sleep held us captive, we haven't moved other than to become more entwined. One of Colin's knees is kicked out to the side, his foot woven through my legs, and I snuggle against his bare skin. Heat burns into my cheeks as his body stirs to life beneath me, poking my belly. I press a smile into his chest and inhale pure love. I'm not sure how much we resolved in the early morning hours, but I do know Colin McKenna adores me. He placed me and our relationship above a long planned European tour. The President of the United States doesn't do that, but my husband did.

I hate that my inclination is to stiffen when his hand tightens around me, and one finds its way into my hair. Months ago it was as natural as the sun setting, but it's hard to forget the pain and how it was used to hold me back from freedom.

"Only me," he whispers, giving it a soft tug.

I don't respond, just let him hold me through the anxiety, and every few minutes his grip closes in. Our breath finds the same pace. It's beautiful and before I can stop them, tears squeeze past my eyes. One second I'm bursting with joy over our connection, his touch, and in the next, I whimper as peace fades to pain. Alex drags me up each step and back to the room from hell. The burn, my head, my hair—he's scalping me. *"Please."*

Shaking, I scramble from underneath the covers and to my knees, gulping for air. Wild with panic as it lights up my spine, I stare at Colin. His expression hasn't changed—smooth forehead, a subtle upturn to the corner of his mouth. He pulls a pillow behind his head and lays an arm out to his side, reaching toward me. I watch him watching me, and as the minutes tick by on the grandfather clock in the great room, my heart rate slows.

I swallow past the lump in my throat to say, "That came out of nowhere."

"Patience, my love. I have enough for the both of us. We'll get you to the other side of this together. Hold my hand."

That voice commands and takes away any other option but to comply. It brings about my smile and a natural "yes, sir" that lifts his own grin.

Ridiculous tears spring to my eyes again, and I've about had it with the rollercoaster that's decided to play with my emotions on this bright morning. I need him to talk and take my mind off of the loop that still likes to play in my brain: *pop, pop, and silence*.

"When will you leave for Europe?"

His smile gets bigger. "I'm not going anywhere but to Camp David with you. Although I do have to make a stop in the press room, as the public deserves to know about the change to my plans."

"I'm sorry to lay everything on you as you were leaving."

"Charlie." He sighs, sitting up to look me in the eye. "I'm thrilled with where we are today—it's a million miles ahead of where we were yesterday and the day before. I've failed you as a husband in so many ways, and I will spend the rest of my life making it up to you." Combing a hand through his hair, he sets it on end. "And the first thing I'm going to do is take you out of Washington. Canceling the tour has left two weeks open. I can't promise I won't have to work, but I plan to spend every possible minute with you and for those times when business calls, you'll sit with me. We'll stay together. How does that sound?"

More tears—I know, it's so crazy that they're back—and I blink them away and nod. "I thought you left me."

"Baby, I know you did, but I promise it was only to call Munduozzi and Aguillard. Trust me when I say the world is on our side right now. They both know what you went through and neither were surprised that I was needed at home more than in Europe. Everything is fine. I sent Parker, who was more than happy to travel in my steed." Tipping my chin so our eyes connect, he says, "It may have taken many life lessons, but I've learned family is more important than politics. I won't always be in this position, but you will always be my wife."

I struggle against a full-out cry and tip forward to rest my forehead on his leg, the hair tickling my nose. "What about the baby?" I whisper and clutch my stomach, both out of protection and because I'm hungry, so hungry. His meaty thigh looks appetizing. My sick sense of humor strangles out a laugh even when I want to wail in fear of his answer. *Ugh, hormones, and this is just the beginning.*

His hand is in my hair, a soothing caress, and this time I'd purr like a kitten if I had the skills to do it. I hum instead, waiting and waiting, until I have to look up to prompt him to speak. Starting with his bare abdomen and chest, defined by muscle, I find he's turned his head, his chin resting on his shoulder so his face is hidden in shadow. Throwing away my apprehension, I climb on top of him, straddling his legs and turn him toward me until I stare into his eyes. They're bright, shining with his own emotion and so damn beautiful, just as I remember them when he looks at me with pure, unadulterated love.

He cradles my cheeks in his hands and I find myself doing the same to him. "I . . ." he starts, and then has to stop to drag in air. "Charlie, I had no idea you thought it possible Alex raped you. I should have dug through the details. Had I known it was your fear, I would have sought out answers, and they do exist. They do," he says, when I shake my head. "We'll get the results of the tests performed in the emergency room. I'll read through every transcript of Miller's interrogations. Fuck, I will order him tortured until he spills the truth so you will know for sure. We'll have a paternity test, but baby, the answer will never, never change how I feel about you or our child."

Leaning in, he brushes his lips against mine, and then the tears overflow from my lids. I slip my arms around his waist and hold on. "You are mine," he whispers over and over as he kisses every inch of my face, resting his mouth on my forehead and breathing into my hair. "This is and always will be my child. I will love him with every fiber of my soul, as I do you. Never doubt me."

My fingers drag along his back, over the sinew and the strength in which he holds me, and into his hair, clutching him as I gasp out my relief. I drag in the sweet scent of sandalwood, drowning in the comfort it brings. In a minute I need more, more Colin. I tug hard, baring his neck to lick and suck away the saltiness of his skin until he moans and presses me into the mattress. Skin against skin we roll together, kissing wildly in needy scrapes, lips, tongue, and teeth. I cry out when he says my name just before squeezing my breast and sucking my nipple all the way to the back of his throat. Oh my God, so sensitive. An electric sting sparks and travels to my clit with an insistent beat: *take me, love me, use me, fuck me*. I want it all. Arching into him, I open my eyes to blue wallpaper peeling at the corners.

I whimper—arms and legs disengage and lie limp by my sides as the reel starts again. *Pop, pop, and silence*.

For how long I'm lost in history, I'll never know. When I come out of the replay it's to Colin's eyes, steady, worry pushed to the rear so I can focus on compassion. He pets my cheek and whispers unintelligible words, soothing in his deep caramel, smooth baritone.

"I'm sorry." Heat creeps up my chest. "We were—on our way to—and then I—I'm embarrassed." I try to look away, but he clutches my chin.

"Never be sorry with me. Explain, so I know what happened."

Panic sets in. I never wanted him to know the specifics, as I thought it'd make me feel worse. Sylvia is the only one who knows most of what occurred. Last night, I went through the basics, mostly about Alex, but Colin won't let go so I start with my mother's old photos and then get to the motorcade, my head crashing into the window. And then Sawyer.

The expressionless expression fails more than once when anger or urgent sorrow break through, but he lets me tell the story. In a bizarre twist, it's freeing. Details rush out of my mouth: Joan and John, her hatred toward him, my mother and me, Alex, her companion since Abby died, and his sickness.

"He wanted me to be her. He pretended I was, but I'm not sure he really believed it because in the end he was angry." Colin growls when I break down the particulars of each of his visits. His hand clenches in the sheet next to my hip so hard I fear he'll shred the cotton, but I go on until the moment I was saved by my friend. My *missing* friend.

"Where's Kyle? Why did they remove him from my detail? I want him back, Colin. I don't care if half my unit and his partner turned psycho; he's the right agent for me. And he's my friend."

He takes my hand. "Sommerton asked for another assignment; he'll be reinstated next week with a new team."

"What? Why?" Those damn tears. I bat them away with my fingers and indignant anger. *How dare he leave me!*

"Guilt, mostly. I think you should talk to him to get a full understanding of the reasons, but go into the conversation knowing he's been aware of your biological relationship to John for months. He chose to keep it hidden from you and me because he thought it would be more harmful than helpful. I've had words with him about it already," Colin says, when my mouth pops open. "He told me two days prior to when you were taken because Joan's behavior had become erratic. She made great effort to be where you were scheduled to speak or at any event you were attending. Sommerton found it strange, and then she called to have lunch with me. You know the rest."

I bury my eyes in my hands, rubbing the recent revelation out of them. "That doesn't amount to cutting ties."

"We can stop by for a visit this afternoon, and then leave from there. Don't you owe him a cake?"

I nod, and we both turn to Colin's ringing phone. He picks it up, and there's not much said other than a commitment to be downstairs in thirty minutes.

"I've got to go to the office for a couple of hours to tie things up. Will that give you enough time to get ready?"

I nod again. He leans in to brush his lips across mine and then he pops out of bed in all of his naked glory. It's hard not to sigh and get dopey-eyed when godly perfection stretches three feet away. Seriously, he could be the deity of procreation because just looking at him causes wombs to quiver with want. I could watch him all day, and I think it's exactly what he'd hoped I'd do as I catch him checking on my response from the corner of his eye. I have to get my mind to match my body's pulsing responses and we'll be all set. This internal war of wanting him and fearing it at the same time is too much for my hormonal imbalance.

He chuckles when I fan myself. "Patience, baby. We've got all the time in the world."

THIRTY DAYS, FOUR WEEKS, one month—a long time for things to change, and it has. I lost a friend and confidant, one I trusted with my life. But as my equilibrium returns, I'm hell-bent on getting my world straightened out as well. Colin has my hand as we weave through the Maryland neighborhood where Kyle bought a house after learning Faith was pregnant. We pull up to a yellow two-story with a wraparound porch—the perfect place to raise a family.

Neighbors have stumbled onto their lawns as the caravan carrying the President bombards their street with flashing lights, motorcycles, and an explosion of Secret Service agents that spread out in an instant. It's a good thing I called ahead in warning. It doesn't take long to walk up the cobbled path to the door where Faith waits with her hand resting on a little bowling-ball belly.

Shoving the cake at Colin, I rush forward and throw my arms around her shoulders. I don't know what comes over me—nostalgia, missing my people, or the normalcy of friends and living in a neighborhood with picket fences and children, not the stuffy head-bobs of Washington wives. "It's so good to see you," I breathe into Faith's hair as she squeezes me with the same strength I do her.

"I'm glad you're here."

I pull away to catch her eyes, and then drop mine to her stomach. "How's my baby?" I ask, itching to touch.

She takes my hand and places it to the side. Faith's T-shirt stretches tight and offers little barrier against the jab to my palm. "Crazy, just like her daddy."

"Her?"

She nods, smiling. "We had the ultrasound a few weeks ago. Everything is perfect. Come in, please."

Stepping aside, she motions us into a front room that transitions directly into the kitchen, one wide, open space. It smells new and of sawdust, as if Kyle just finished the natural oak wood floors this morning. "It's beautiful. So different from the pictures when you moved in."

"Kyle has had a lot of time on his hands to get things done."

"My fault for that."

"No, I didn't mean . . ."

"It's okay." I wave away her apology. "Is he here?"

"In the back with his power tools." She points to the far door next to the fridge. "I didn't tell him you were coming, Charlie. He's pretty broken up about everything, and I wasn't sure if he'd try to avoid talking with you."

"Thanks for the warning."

I look to Colin and he bends to my ear. "It'll be fine. Go get him, tiger," he says with a smack to my ass, one more stride toward the normalcy I crave. He kisses my cheek then turns a disarming smile to Faith. I should remind him that if he's trying to make wombs quiver, Faith's is already full. "Cake?" he asks. "It's famous for placing people into sugar comas."

On her relaxed laugh, I step down to the one-car garage made into Kyle's workshop. I glance first beyond the solid wood door. Other than the lamp overhead, the room is devoid of light. It's dark and so is Kyle. Black T-shirt and jeans are covered in a fine layer of dust, as are the crib spindles he sands one at a time.

"Did you make that?" I ask, stepping in at the same time I'm surprised by how much he knows about woodwork and home improvement.

A string of colorful expletives and a hanging head is my answer. "You better clean up the potty mouth, cowboy. Can you believe she'll be here in three months?"

"What are you doing?"

"Visiting a friend before I go on vacation."

Kyle doesn't look at me; instead, he stands and walks to the far wall to grab a new piece of paper. It's on his way back that he says, "You must have the wrong house then."

"Stop being stupid."

His laugh is jagged, as if he hasn't used it in a while. I hate his hollow eyes when he finally brings them to meet mine. "I wasn't a good friend to you, Mrs. McKenna, and I provided even worse protection. I apologize on both accounts."

My hip juts out, a natural reaction when my mother hen starts waging her finger. As if I would ever let him get away with this nonsense. "Let's start at the beginning, shall we? First off, the name's Charlie. I haven't heard you're suffering from amnesia, so I expect you'll use it. If not, I will use my newfound defensive techniques to torture you into good behavior. Second, you've been one of my best friends." Tears, here they come. *Oh, shit.* "I don't have that many, so when I make one I tend to keep them around. Shy of death, you're stuck with me—got it? Next, I will not ever, listen to me when I say never, accept your resignation unless the aliens that birthed you return to claim their crazy-ass offspring. Am I making myself clear?"

"Charlie," he says my name, and it's rough like the sandpaper in his hand. "I knew about Montgomery and didn't tell you—even after I prom—"

I cut him off with a raised hand. "I don't care. If I was in your position, I'd have done the same thing. It's shitty, Kyle; I really hate being attached to that family. It's like Luke learning Darth Vader is his father, except for me there's no return from the dark side. I'm not even trying to process that news right now; honestly, there are more pressing issues taking up space in here." I tap my head.

"God, I'm sorry. Fuck," he says, as his lip draws up in disgust. "I should have been there."

"I'm glad you weren't. You could've been killed." *Pop, pop, and silence*. The moment Johnson had died. I live his death in my mind over and over. It could have been Kyle. I'm so glad it wasn't, and that makes me a monster because Johnson had a family, too.

"I could have stopped it."

My heart sinks, even as frustration bubbles up and I let him know it with my lets-get-serious tone. "Half the unit had been bought out by Kilpatrick. You'd be dead, just like Johnson, and your little girl would have grown up without a father. We both know how difficult that is, so just be thankful."

"Thankful." He shakes his head and whips the sanding tool so hard it hits the far wall and boomerangs back at him, skidding to a stop at his feet. "I failed you. Sawyer, the fucking bastard—I missed it, didn't suspect a thing. He was always an asshole, but I never thought he'd go there—not with Kilpatrick and Joan. Here's the thing—I should have known his brother was killed and his reaction to it. I should have known he flipped sides because I was with him every damn day."

"That's Randy Strickland talking—his voice, not yours. Why are you buying in to his bullshit?"

He takes a deep breath and shakes his head. "Even if you're blind to it, I'm not. I'm not fit to provide protection to the First Lady of the United States. I can see it, and it's time you do, too. I regret to inform you that my service with your detail has ended."

TWENTY-FOUR

Charlie

"LIKE HELL IT HAS." I round on him and smack him upside the head—someone has to drive some sense into him. I've heard the stories, I know he's gotten worse from his sisters, and I fall close to that category so I feel in the right to tap him back into this universe. When my fingers connect with a good thud, he shakes his head but the corner of his lip twitches. "It's not your job to know everything about every member of my detail, nor was Sawyer your responsibility. And if I've got the story straight, you worked with Colin to figure out where I was and then barged into that Godforsaken house to get me. Am I right?"

He runs a hand down his face, and then back up and into his hair. "Yeah."

"So you're running away because you feel bad?"

"I let you down, more than once."

I roll my eyes. "I don't need your guilt, Kyle. I need you to be there. Be my friend, make me laugh, draw your gun because you think it's cool to show me how quick you can dismantle the damn thing—just be you and make my life normal again. That's how you can make me better."

He stares at the crib and then the floor, thinking so hard his jaw is about to crack. Then he looks at me, a hint of a smile pulling at the corner of his mouth. "But I'm Catholic; I do good guilt."

I grab his shoulders, shaking as if I can move a Kyle Sommerton mountain. He doesn't budge. "It's not your fault. None of it. I never blamed you, except for a second when I was pissed you didn't shoot Alex. Other than that, let your conscience be clear."

Finally, he smiles. "You did a pretty good job of it by the time I'd arrived; I didn't want to waste a bullet."

I punch his arm and then lean on my tiptoes to kiss his cheek. "Thank you for coming to get me. I'm really glad it was you."

Our eyes lock. My tears must be catchy because his clear irises swim in water.

"I can't tell you how sorry I am." He wraps me in a hug. "I'm so damn sorry."

"I know. Just come back, okay?"

He sighs. "If that's what you want."

"It is."

"Then you got it, boss-lady."

I squeeze and then release. "Excellent. Now let's go. Colin and Faith have a head start on the chocolate cake."

His eyes flare. "You brought it?"

"It was my back-up plan. If reason failed, I was going to bribe you with sugar."

"Good call. I would have caved in a second," he says, as we head back to the kitchen. "You want one piece or two?"

Oh, Lord. The same wave of nausea that crashed in like a tsunami when I baked the damn thing has me stop in my tracks. I hold my stomach and cringe as the churning slows.

"Fuck, you're green." Kyle says from somewhere in the distance, ignoring my raised finger—a clear indication I need a minute. "I've seen that color before."

I swallow it down my throat. *Gross*. "It's not cool. I'll be seven weeks on Tuesday so I've got a while to go before it's over."

"Char," he says, one hand raking through his hair. I smile his fear away. For the very few who know I was alone with Alex, they'll wonder and count weeks.

"It's okay. I'm happy about the baby and Colin and I are solid. Now that you're back I can see my normal on the horizon, and I'm coming to terms with everything else." His sad eyes tell me he's not convinced. "Really, it'll be great; our kids can play Barbies together."

It takes an extra beat, but he gets on board. "Or cops and robbers. How old do you think they have to be before I can teach them how to shoot?"

On our way back to the kitchen, Kyle devises the timeline and birthday presents for the next five years. Cake makes everything better. When he finishes his second piece, the grin on his face is a permanent fixture. With his arm wrapped around Faith's shoulders, he settles into the corner of his counter and tips back a beer.

"Stay for dinner. I was planning to pull out the grill."

"Thanks, but no. We've got to head out," Colin interjects.

They both step forward at the same time, hands clasp. Some silent message passes between them as their eyes lock, and then Colin pulls away. "Give me a minute," he says, and kisses my forehead. He walks to the front of the house, leaving me with enough time to say my goodbyes.

Faith is first, a long hug and a promise to call when I get back in town. Kyle is next. I tuck my head in his neck and squeeze my appreciation around his waist. The loop from that night running in my head always ends with his face and for that I'll be forever grateful.

"I'll see you in two weeks." I point at his smirk and wait for his nod.

"Yes, ma'am. Try not to get into any trouble until then."

I roll my eyes and lean in to Colin's hand on my lower back when he returns. He steers me toward the back door. "Why are we going this way?"

"I have a surprise. Come, I'll show you."

He tugs my hand, and I can do nothing but follow as we're greeted by a dozen agents, some of who are appreciating a shiny, black sports car.

"Do you like it?" Colin asks, beaming as he runs a finger along the hood.

"Um, sure. I didn't know Kyle had it."

"He doesn't. I do," he says, while stripping off his sweater. Underneath is a navy long-sleeved tee stretched so tight across his chest I can see his muscles and the points of his nipples—*for the love of God.* When he slides on a baseball hat held out by Fitz and brings his finger to his mouth as if to quiet my racing heart, I plop down on the cement stoop, breathless. Colin in a suit is mind-boggling, but this, this is dangerous to the female reproductive organs. He steps forward, hands out to pull me up. "I'm driving."

"You're what?" I point to the race car. "We—but—I don't think—you can drive?"

He throws his back and laughs. "Yes, I can, very well actually."

"But we've never . . ." I forget what I was saying when he tugs off my cardigan, leaving me in my strapless maxi-dress. Again Fitz is there, this time with my favorite leather jacket, the one I've not worn in a very long time. I slide into it, dazed.

"We haven't done a lot of things," Colin says, holding my hair in a loose ponytail so he can slip it through the back of my own cap. "Two weeks, baby. Two weeks of my lips on your neck, your laugh in my ear—time is what we need. Every day we'll uncover secrets and make new memories." Taking my hands, he draws me to the passenger-side door. "I love cars—old ones I can take apart and rebuild. This is a 1968 Shelby Cobra, my first reconstruct I started in high school. I haven't taken her out in years."

"Her?"

"Pretty cars are always girls, baby. Get in."

That grin, holy hell. No more loop, nothing but Colin McKenna's panty-melting smile takes up space in my addled brain. "Keep smiling like that and you may need to pull over before we get there. Does this thing have a backseat?"

He stares at my mouth and I think he might kiss me, right here, with Faith and Kyle looking out the window and half the Secret Service in their driveway. I'd be okay with that, but instead Colin hauls me forward so we're hip to hip, and he tucks his face into my neck. The heat of his breath is like a feather running down my spine, a light, ticklish tease. "Get in, Charlie."

Wait, what? He laughs again as he steps back to open the door. I forget his taunting ways when I sink into the embrace of supple black leather. This car is as decadent as the driver who slides in as if he were born to be behind the wheel. Damn, man.

"Is this legal? Are you allowed to do this?"

He shrugs, and I swear he's glowing. "I'm about to break all the rules."

I giggle as he revs the engine and at my husband who in minutes went from refined dignitary to billionaire bad-boy. It's not that we're alone. I can see that as we swing onto the street. The entire entourage is assembled just as it was on our way here, but now in the middle of the pack is a tiny sports car with a giddy driver.

The whole way out of the city, Colin expels an encyclopedia of facts about the Shelby and a Camaro he rehabbed and sold years ago. When we reach the freeway, the top comes down, the motorcade loosens, and he falls silent. Looking out the window I pretend it's just us, Colin and me as we would be if our life was normal. No security, no media—just his car and the wind. I look at him, one hand on the wheel and the other he slides to my knee, his pinky inching up as if it has the right to torment my thigh. Every minute that passes I think I couldn't love him more, and then he surprises me again, and I plummet even deeper. Closing my eyes, I lean against the window and press my fingers against his, searing them into my flesh and erasing a part of the loop.

Colin

IT SHOULDN'T BE POSSIBLE that a ninety-minute drive could top the list of highs in a lifetime that has seen so many, but the simplicity of it—the miles falling away with Charlie by my side, relaxed and smiling, one hand holding mine and the other lying protective against her stomach and our child. It's perfection.

She fell asleep halfway through and I try my damnedest not to wake her as I carry her inside. But she's out cold, a splash of red curls flaring into flames on the white pillows. I strip her down to lace lingerie and struggle not to remember Abby in her first trimester. It's my only point of reference for pregnancy, and I keep going back to it. Every time my thoughts drift in that direction guilt washes in, as if I'm disrespecting our marriage or Charlie herself. Not only because it was a prior relationship, but because it was technically with her half-sister.

That truth burns sour in my stomach as I look at hers. She's about to begin her seventh week with few changes to the body I know better than my own. Yet the mood swings are new, and she'll be hungry when she wakes up. Tucking the quilt around her, I press my smile into her forehead and then head out to make dinner. It's been a while, but I think I can manage steaks on the grill and a salad. I could cheat and have the chef drop off a full meal, but I want this time to be as free from presidential hoopla as possible—back to basics, as she would say.

Removing Charlie from Washington was the start of what I hope will be a reprieve from the pressure to perform. Standing in a fishbowl twenty-four/seven is exhausting. Add to it the curiosity to know what happened to her, and the media has been more relentless than is usual. She can let her guard down here. Hell, Camp David has been called the safest place on earth, so even my shoulders are relaxed.

At my direction, the staff stocked more than essentials in the kitchen. It's easy to find everything needed for a quick meal in the fridge. Dinner prep complete, I grab a beer and my phone. I tap into my voicemail and the expected call from Evan is there, indicating he has news for me on the records I requested this morning.

With my feet on the ottoman and my head back, I drain half the bottle and then breathe for a minute. The pine-paneled walls are pitched in shadows and a timed lamp in the corner pops on as the sun prepares to set.

A baby. Charlie is having a baby. I'm going to be a father again. A piercing joy stabs my heart at the same time as revulsion creeps in to steal away the happiness. I close my eyes, as if I can banish thoughts of Alex Miller with the darkness. I have half a mind to strangle the truth out of him myself, much like I did with Roberts, but this time I'd kill the worthless piece of shit. During the last month, rage and guilt have been constant companions, but for now I shove them aside to call Evan.

"Make it okay?" he asks in greeting.

"Faster than I would have if you were driving."

"Well, I'll be sure to tell Director Simmons how much you enjoyed the ride. His coronary bypass is scheduled tomorrow at eight. You should be proud, Mr. President; your stunt singlehandedly felled the leader of the Secret Service."

"You're a comedian; we were perfectly safe. What have you got for me?"

He sucks in a breath. "Mrs. McKenna's hospitalization records and each subsequent visit to her physician have been sent confidentially to your personal e-mail for reference, including test results. You'll have transcripts from Miller's interviews in the morning. I'm working on Joan; her lawyer has an absurd injunction in place that I've got to go around for the records, but there's not going to be much anyway. She's pled the fifth at every hearing. If you tell me what you're looking for I can shorten your search."

"Charlie's pregnant."

"Christ." A sickening silence hangs between us, and I know he's contemplating the timing. "Did Miller . . .?"

"Instinct tells me he didn't rape her." The words taste like filth coming out of my mouth. I would know it, feel it if he had taken her in that way, and the voice of reason I rely on is swift with a resounding *no*. If I'm wrong and Alex did assault my wife, if the child she carries is only mine through the love I'll shower on him, then so be it. My devotion is not tied to genetics. But my gut reaction on the baby's paternity will not relieve Charlie's burden, nor will it repair the security Alex has stolen from her, or free her from the violation of his hands. "Charlie blacked out for much of the night so she thinks it's possible. For her sake, I need to find the truth. Don't waste your time with Joan; the medical records should be sufficient, but I'll let you know if I need more."

"I'm not sure what to say."

"Save it. You can congratulate me when I see you next week."

"Yeah, yes of cour—"

My heart misses a beat from the blood-curdling scream bouncing off the walls. The same one Charlie lets loose on most nights. "I'll call you later." I throw the phone as I lunge for our room.

The unfamiliar floorplan slows me down. So does the darkness that has fallen with the sun. Up the stairs and two doors down, I snap on the light. Charlie moans when I make it to her, curled in a ball, rocking with her hands over her ears as she mumbles *no more* and *don't touch me*. I clutch my chest when she starts to chant *only Colin.*

"I'm here, baby. It's me, my hands," I say, as I lay them on her shoulders to roll her toward me.

Wild eyes find mine, erratic while she searches my face. Recognition is slow to come. "Colin?"

"Right here. I'm going to pick you up." I wait for her nod of acknowledgement. Closing my eyes, I bury my nose in her curls when she's in my lap. Her fingers dig in, clinging to my neck. "Deep breaths," I say, encouraging her with the steady rise and fall of my own.

In time, her grip loosens and she sits up, licking her lips. "I'm afraid of the dark . . ."

She stops and we both stare at her stomach as an enormous growl resonates through the silence. A healthy pink paints her cheeks with the color she was missing a moment ago.

She giggles, and it happens again. Charlie's laugh is the most beautiful sound, a light and airy melody. I run my fingers down her side, just under her bra strap, knowing full well it's her most ticklish spot. She bucks against my hands, shrieking in laughter that melds with mine. When she straightens, I do it once more to ensure any residual fear is gone and maybe because I love to see her so carefree.

"Dinner?" I ask, when she begs for a reprieve.

"God, if you don't feed me now I might have to gnaw on your ribs."

I've got something else for that sweet mouth, I want to say, but the warning bells go off in my brain. This is about Charlie and her recovery, not my constantly hard cock. "I have something much more appetizing downstairs."

"Really? You're cooking?"

"If salad and turning on the grill fall within the category, then yes, I am."

She pops off my lap and reaches for her dress I laid out on the chair earlier. "Ah, baby, I'm impressed. I didn't know you could use a knife or a grill. You're full of surprises."

"Take that back, Charlie."

I love that smile, broad, stunning, and the playful sway of her hips. "Or what? What will you do?"

"Use these." I hold up my hands and laugh as she shrieks, running for the door. I'm too close for her to slip away—as if I would ever let that happen.

TWENTY-FIVE

Charlie

COLIN CATCHES ME BEFORE I make it to the stairs. A moment of panic threatens to overtake our fun, but then his fingers caress my hips and his mouth murmurs the most delicious words in my ear. Some are lovely and others are downright dirty. He's stepped up his game. And I like this wicked side. Oh God, I like every side of Colin McKenna, especially his backside, but this might be my new favorite.

All of them keep me grounded and focused on him, the cabin, and the steps he walks down with me one foot at a time. He's always there, always touching and soothing away my fear.

He doesn't let me go until we're in the kitchen. "Sit," he says, pointing to the stool by the island. I'm not in the mood to argue and in fact, I love the view. Out of the open sliding-glass doors is a ginormous in-ground pool. It glows as water laps at the blue tile from a slight breeze, and the tallest trees I've ever seen line the rolling campus of the yard with the sky brightened by a full moon above them. But it's my husband who I can't stop staring at as he pushes his sleeves to his elbows. A stern frown pulls in three lines between his eyes as he contemplates the wine in one hand while jerking a glance in my direction.

"Ah." A flicker lights his face. He digs in the fridge and presents to me a bottle of sparkling cider. "I'm afraid it will have to do for the next nine months or so." He pours me a glass. "When is your pre-natal appointment? I'd like to go."

I bite my lip, partly because anything sweet he does has my eyes welling, but mostly because I plain ol' love him. "Not for a few weeks; I'll have Betsy add it to your schedule. We should call it something so no one can figure out I'm pregnant, like a code name: Arnie Abrams."

"No," he says, choking on his wine. "Not Arnie; maybe Clark or Thor, but why the secret?"

I giggle at his hero reference—he is, after all, my very own superman. And then I watch, fascinated, as Colin turns more Martha Stewart than super-anything, setting out cheese and grapes, and crackers, too. "Maybe I'll make the appointment under my name. And twelve weeks is the safe point to let everyone know. Besides, Brady and his public relations team will probably want to put together a press tour or something."

"Hey." He reaches across the island counter to take my hand. "This is our baby. Not Brady's or the nation's; we can do whatever works for us. You decide."

Sweet again, that damn man. "Okay. We should call our parents soon. You never know when the rumor mill will start, and I don't want them to read about it on the internet."

"We'll do it tonight. Everything's going to be great, Charlie. I don't want you to worry about anything."

Kissing my palm, he lets it go to head out to the grill. Meat, oh God, I gag, but keep my thoughts to myself, because he's so proud of his accomplishment.

A minute later he's on break from dinner duty. Stopping at the microwave, he sets a timer to know when to flip the steaks and then moves my way. A thanks-be-to-God zips from my lips to the heavens. Not because he's hot as sin with a hundred different looks from the boardroom to the bedroom, but because with his guidance, I can be anyone I need to be—happy, sad, needy, sassy—the list is long. Maybe that's why we fit. Within our bubble, we can explore every facet of ourselves and stretch our wings.

He turns my stool so he can squeeze between my thighs. "I love you." His voice is thick, husky, as if he's not only declaring his feelings, but engraving them in stone or branding my skin. A permanent marker so I'll never forget they came from him.

I wrap my arms around his neck to pull him down to my mouth. Just lips, brushing back and forth in a tickle of temptation. He presses in and murmurs, "I'm going to find a thousand different ways to kiss you."

Groaning, I pull him closer so the tips of my breasts brush against his chest. "You don't have to seduce me. I'm already there. Make me scream."

His hand slips from the back of the chair and his tongue is in my mouth. *That's more like it.* What was innocent becomes deep, and in its' own dirty way, a declaration of devotion. He may want to take it slow but I've got other plans. It's a matter of who's going to make it out on top. *Oh, on top—that sounds fun.*

The damn buzzer drills over our panted breath and he stops, almost shoving me away as if I'm the forbidden fruit and he's shocked by his will to sin.

I conjure my most devilish grin and bat my lashes.

"Wicked, wicked, woman," he says, touching his red, swollen mouth.

"Game on, Mr. President—may the best spouse win."

He turns, shaking his head as he walks out the door and mumbles to a squirrel while it demolishes an acorn on the patio. I laugh when he flips the steaks and then stays there, sitting down on a bench to talk with his furry friend—safer outside than in the house with his wife.

In that case, I'll finish the table prep. Plates, napkins, silverware. Steak knives are a must, so I search the drawers and come across one that's too familiar. The handle as it sits in my grip, the blade reflecting the overhead light and catching on the image of my eye—round, green and scared. And just like that I'm right back where I was weeks ago. The moment flashes, and in an instant I'm in the mansion. Stale air stutters through the register with a whir. Palm to hilt, edge up, I swing to drive it through muscle, past bone and into organs—once, twice, until Alex is limp and falls to the floor.

"Charlie, let go."

Pop, pop, and silence.

"Baby, give it to me."

I drop the knife and turn into Colin's shirt. The fog has me, so thick I can't see, can't breathe. Pain flashes in my chest, on my hips—everywhere. Time seems suspended and although I recognize movement, and sitting, it's as if I'm watching it happen versus living the actions.

When the haze clears, I'm lying on the couch with Colin. He's built a fire. Wrapped in a blanket and snug between his thighs, I'm tangled up in him. The deep cadence of his voice is a melody, and as his words form a pattern, it clicks he's reading *The Great Gatsby* out loud.

"I don't want to be like her." The thought registers in my brain one second and slips from my tongue in the next. The hand in my hair stops stroking. I've not spent much time thinking about John Montgomery and biology, but I knew it would catch up to me. Apparently, now is the moment of no return.

Joan's bomb didn't rock my world. There is no fear, no sadness, no hole greater than losing those closest to you. My parents' death crushed me, altered my future into a frightening direction. After seven years of foster-care horror, Shane Roberts and then the joy of joining a family, learning how to love and finding Colin, I couldn't think of much that can top those highs and lows. Her weapon has landed a superficial wound. It hurts, but I'm not comatose with devastation.

"What do I see when I look at you?" He breaks up my thoughts and the rhythmic strokes begin again.

"Red." It's the first thing to cross my mind and he chuckles, a rumble under my ear.

"Passion, yes, and strength. You're courageous, Charlie, proud and beautiful. You love with your whole heart. I see you for who you are—no one else."

"Even when we first met?"

Setting the book on the distressed pine coffee table, he tips my chin until we're eye to eye. "I have never thought of you as Abby, not one time. There may be similarities in appearance, but you don't resemble her in the least. You're very different."

I grab his fingers and wind them through mine. "How? I need to know."

His smile is thoughtful as he remembers. "She loved attention, from men, women, the press—she liked to be at the center of everything going on. Where you want my attention. My Charlie likes to be wherever I am, and if it's within a media storm you'll enter the fray for me." He tucks a stray curl behind my ear as he looks it over. A sadness I haven't seen from him in a long while stings his eyes. "Abby walked with an air of condescension, a product of her upbringing—arrogance that is a side-effect of affluence. Your approach is more humble, and then the fire flares and something unexpected happens."

A calm I haven't known for weeks settles within me, as if the storm raging since that day in April is on its last leg. Breathing is a little easier, not because Colin knows me, or can differentiate between Abby and me, but because I can. I'm Charlie Carter McKenna, sister, daughter, a pseudo-journalist from a small town with growing experience, a wife and soon-to-be mother. Whoever Abby was, she wasn't me.

"I loved her." My blurred vision narrows in on Colin, his square jaw rough with stubble. "In a very different way than I do you. I'm not sure how to describe it other than she should have been the perfect woman for me. But the moment we met, I knew you were my beginning and the end. My forever began with you, Charlie."

Reaching below my shoulders, he pulls me so my nose rests in the crook of his neck. My favorite place smells exactly as it should—

of sandalwood and Colin. I snuggle in and let him wash away any remaining doubt. "We fit so well, I don't have to try or second guess each step forward. At first I stayed away because I was afraid of falling in love, and I knew it was possible with you. The way you look at the world, the simplicity of it, the light you bring . . . Before I met you it was as if my days were clipped together in black-and-white slides, clicking into place one at a time to frame a silent movie. Now it's animated and so bright."

He swallows. "I thought you were lost to me forever," he says with such emotion I can feel it in the fingers digging into my back. "If that ever happens, my candle will burn out and my light will fade. I'm but half a man without you."

I know who I am, and why my life journey brought me to Colin. We're meant to love each other, provide solace and an ease to our troubled souls. I look up at the same time as he tips his head down to capture my mouth with his. He tries for soft, but we're too hungry for slow. We bite away at the horror of it all and in the depth of this kiss is our pledge. Our flawed fairytale from front to back is full of happy and sad, good and bad, and through it all we'll stay together. There is no other end for us.

Breaking away, he drags his lips to my forehead to murmur, "Your beauty lives in your soul, not in who created the masterpiece."

I close my eyes with his hand in my hair, the fire crackling, until the love I feel turns into a dream without Johnson, or Sawyer, or Joan, and it ends without Alex. The wish comes true for peaceful silence and a break from the never-ending loop.

At some point I wake as Colin carries me to bed. He's gentle as he forces food in my belly with sweet words of encouragement. I think he may even help me brush my teeth because I've never been this tired before. Finally, he strips us down to nothing, and I fall into la-la-land with his heat to my back, his fingers stroking up and down my skin.

SINGING BIRDS, THEIR CHIRPING rouses me from sleep. With my eyes closed, I accept the flood of memories from yesterday: my confession, Colin's canceled trip, Kyle and Camp David—*the baby*. I blink open my heavy lids to find a large window, cracked at the bottom to allow the sweet, yet heady scent of honeysuckle to wash through the room. White lace curtains ripple with the mild draft. Colin's gentle murmur mingles with the singsong chirping, but it's not in my ear as it is so often. He's moved low in the bed, his head resting on my stomach. Stripped bare, he has the soft plane of skin to draw on and talk to.

"I fell in love when she scolded me in front of thousands of people." He chuckles and then peppers me with kisses, his tongue tasting me as he does. "You'll know why when you meet her. It's hard to describe because it's more of an ethereal feeling that can't be held down, like the very essence of living. She's more beautiful than the brightest star in the sky, my Charlie; she's radiant like a sun that never sets." Pausing, he spreads his hand across the expanse of my stomach and whispers in a light breath I feel against my skin, "A blend of Heaven and Earth, she paints life with her own colors. She's the midnight sun, twilight and dawn all at once, creating a day that is never-ending."

The rest is lost in a rush of my tears, but it's not just a coating—this is a full-fledged cry, and I bring my hands to my eyes to hide them. It's not as if he's going to miss the heaving wails or snot. It's big and out there, but he lets me finish without a word. He moves away and when I've got it together, I open my eyes to him on his elbow, staring down at me with a half-grin, tissue in hand. He's grabbed the whole box from the side table and it's cradled in his arm. I snatch the tissue and blow and wipe and start all over again because I'm such a mess.

"I—" My breath hitches. "I'm s . . . sorry."

"I'm not. You're making a baby, Charlie. Lots of changes are in the works, not to mention everything else you're dealing with. I'm not afraid of your tears, or the lion living in your stomach. I swear, he gets louder and louder each time he roars for food."

"He?"

Colin shrugs and runs a hand over my belly. "I just have a feeling."

"Did you when Abby was pregnant with Sara?"

His gaze flies to mine.

"You can talk about them; it doesn't hurt my feelings." I point to my face. "God knows, if it does you'll see the evidence."

He presses a kiss to my forehead. "I did, and my guess was correct."

"A boy." I fall into the vision of a little man, exactly like Colin. Chestnut curls and midnight blue eyes, a baby jaw that could cut glass and make his play-dates swoon. He'll probably wear a tie at his first-birthday party. My smile dissolves into a fresh bout of hitching cries. "I want him to be yours so bad."

"Oh, baby. He is, I know he is."

"How can you be so sure?"

Tossing the tissues aside, he grabs me and rolls to his back. Hot and hard beneath me, I revel in his body and feeling all of my parts pressed so deliciously to his. I need this, I need him, and so I play with the hair on his chest and circle his nipple with my nails. He growls and grips my hand, smashing it flat.

"I have your emergency room records."

"What?" I fly up to my knees, holding my heart so it doesn't explode through my ribs. "You looked?"

"No, not until you're ready." He takes my hand and clenches it between both of his. "In the hospital, when I saw, I . . . I couldn't stand what I did to you. It made me sick."

"I don't know what you mean."

"I'm a monster, Charlie. I lose control with you. I get off on marking you so everyone will know you're mine. The bruises on your thighs, the vaginal trauma Dr. Patel found—I think they were from me. I took you so hard that night. I . . ." His eyes search my face, driven by a frantic storm of self-loathing. "Alex didn't use you; I did. I came home from Chicago frustrated with how I left, and then I saw the test results—I knew it was our window to try. It was all I could think of, giving you what you wanted, what I wanted, so I just kept going until I was sure a baby was growing inside you. The next morning when you opened your legs, the scrapes and bruises were already forming. You were raw and even then I felt this depraved satisfaction that I marked you as mine."

A puzzle piece clicks into place.

I can't look at you.

"Alex saw them, the marks. He must have," I whisper, staring unfocused at my thighs and remembering that night and how Alex must have seen me. Visibly used by my husband.

I can't look at you.

"Alex knew they were from you." A pinprick of hope sprouts into the size of the sun. *He knew.* Joy bursts through me, and I throw my head back to laugh, my hands in the air. He couldn't do it. Alex couldn't do it because I belonged to Colin—the evidence was there for him to see. It was why he left the lights off the last time, but even then he knew. *He knew.*

"You did save me, you did." I fall over Colin, rubbing and kissing happy tears against his cheeks and chin, down his neck and chest, up his arm to his mouth.

I stop because of his narrow-eyed expression. "I'm not crazy, I promise," I say, taming my manic smile. "It makes sense now. Alex and his behavior—he was pissed, like he wanted to believe I was Abby but he couldn't quite buy into his fantasy. He saw the marks, your hands—your wife. I kept telling him that, and he saw the evidence, too. He even tried to take off my rings. I don't think he could rape me."

The expressionless expression is in place as he tucks a wayward curl behind my ear. "You tell me when you're ready for the results to confirm it. We'll do it together."

"Okay." The grin is back, and I press it to his lips. He takes my shoulders and tries to push away. "Don't," I mumble into him. "Don't, please. I need this, I need you."

He groans and gives in with the crush of his mouth against mine. The restless energy that has followed me from the night in April simmers under my skin. Colin's touch, his hand wrapping around my thigh and then up to my ass, clenching it, is the wick dosed in fuel. And his tongue, when it reaches mine, just the tip lighting against my lips, it flares the match. I explode. I'm a phoenix reborn from the ashes. It may be insane, but the same surety Colin experiences showers over me and freedom winds through my limbs, releasing me from Alex Miller's grip.

We wrestle on the bed, a good WWE smackdown. Rolling, limbs and tongues entwined, we fight with teeth and lips, sucking and biting and inviting groans to join the melody of nature. God, it feels good to be this close to him. But as soon as I rear up and take his erection in hand, he has me on my back, arms held above my head.

"Why are you stopping?" I ask. It's hard to keep my pout in place when I can barely breathe, but I manage through the challenge.

Colin looms over me, blocking the light with his shoulders. Intense blue eyes pin me down with the same strength as his grip. "You're not ready."

My growl puts his to shame. "I am."

"I'm not," he says, flipping off of me to sit on the side of the bed, rubbing his face in his hand.

I climb on his back to rest my chin on his shoulder. "You've never hurt me. Not once." He allows me to hold him, kissing and licking the sweet salt from his skin. I poke his side after a minute, just below his last rib in the one spot that makes him smile. "What's going on in that head of yours? I need to know."

He sighs. Faster than I can take a breath, he has me cradled in front of him, and he pierces me with his stare. "Listen to everything I have to say. Do not go half-cocked after the first word."

I nod. "Promise."

"I don't trust us."

Tears. *Oh crap.* I hold them in with a hand to my mouth, but he must see the hurt breaking my heart.

"Charlie," he says in that voice, the tone that has my spine straighten and a salute forms without any indication to my brain. "The memories are too real for you. Anything can set them off and then I lose you, sometimes for hours. What if I do something that reminds you of him or that night? I can't chance it, baby. I won't have you cower away; it would kill me."

"I won't. I couldn't."

"We both know that's not true."

I hate that he's right. The slightest memory or touch sends me off into never-never-land. The last thing I want to do is hurt him in the process of healing myself. Losing the argument to the truth, I snuggle into his neck. "For how long?"

Breath expels from his lungs in a rush. "For as long as it takes to be sure you're not terrified and I'm not afraid of breaking you. I love you, Charlie, and I'll show you just how much by caring for you with a simple touch, or a word."

My heart flutters. I love him too, so much, and I want to show him how deeply I'm devoted. Now I have a restriction. "But I can kiss you?"

"Anytime you want."

"This is going to be hard."

I like his smile, mischievous. He's a naughty plaything I was about to take for a ride. "Not this," I say, wrapping my fingers around his semi. He's always at the ready now that I think about it, so I squeeze harder, making him gasp and flex into my hand.

"Charlie," he says, clenching his teeth around my name.

Popping off his lap, I turn and throw a look over my shoulder. With my hip curving out, I pretend to cover my breasts but let him see just enough to drive him crazy. This is where Brigitte Bardot meets Marilyn. "What are you going to do? Spank me?"

I giggle at the growl to beat all growls. He's so fast. Before I can sidestep his reach he has me and tosses me on the bed, cradling my fall with his arms.

"Why do you do this?" he asks, staring at my mouth. At the same time, he flexes against me, sliding the delicious ridges of his erection through my folds and into my clit.

"Because I can."

"Hm," he murmurs and does that hip thing again while he watches my parting lips and the gasp I drag in.

"Aren't you going to kiss me?"

He leans in, so close we're breathing the same air. "No, I'm not."

Wait, what? "Come back here," I cry as he pushes off the bed.

"Shower and breakfast, Carter."

From sex god to drill sergeant. I'm left to watch the sculpted lines of his retreating ass and try desperately to form a plan on how to seduce my husband.

TWENTY-SIX

Charlie

I TRY EVERYTHING. THE first day it's a lingerie fashion show after we go for a hike. I pull out the pieces I brought and go so far as to have a personal shopper in town bring me more. Nothing, no go—he's stoic yet quite responsive to the barest of lace. My breasts are full, sensitive, darker at the tips, and I beg him to massage them. It's equal parts pain and exquisite pleasure, but the mood is ruined when I turn green and vomit in the toilet.

It's cloudy and damp on day two. Nausea has me sidelined in the morning. I experience a slight set-back with a *pop-flash* memory, and then Colin finishes off *The Great Gatsby* while I nap next to him. Later we work side by side in the kitchen to make dinner, vegetarian lasagna because meat isn't sitting well with me. While it's in the oven, I slip away to get dressed in a gown way too fancy for a weekday meal, but it's sexy and clingy satin that plunges to my belly button.

I pass by his shoulder to whisper that I'm sans bra and panties. Steam may come out of his ears, but instead of throwing me down on the counter and having me for dinner, he turns me in a twirl. There is no music, only his voice as this time he sings to me. The tables are turned with his breath on my neck and his hands scraping down my back. I can feel every line of his body, the ridges of his chest and stomach, and the not-so-subtle signs of his own desire that has turned into a constant rubbing terror. *Oh, for the love of all that's holy.* I'm burning up. He must see it in my eyes, as he swings us outside while the sky opens. We dance, or at this point sway, pressed together in the rain until we're soaked and I'm putting on my own dirty show. It ends with a low dip and his tongue streaking down my chest. That's it—nothing else.

The rest of our vacation is more of the same. Flashbacks take a backseat to vomiting. In my mind, this is progress. For Colin, he watches with a cautious eye and forces food and drink when I can keep it down. He works a few hours each day and I play the guitar, singing until I'm hoarse. Hiking, swimming, golf—they're all on the agenda. We've finished relentless bouts of Scrabble and Monopoly, but he always wins so I'm intent on victory with my own game.

Tuesday and every day thereafter, when morning sickness passes and he tries to wear me out mentally and physically, I bring out *Cosmo* and implement my tactics. I even leave the magazine open to the best articles, hoping that's what we'll read at naptime. I get significant use out of my highest heels—five-inch black platforms—with no clothes on, of course—eat a ton of bananas, and still face nothing but furtive looks and low grumbles.

Day twelve and I take on a new tactic—kissing. Oh, dear sweet baby Jesus, I love kissing Colin McKenna. And so I do it. Every chance I get my tongue is in his mouth.

It's a game between us. Who can make the other more desperate and needy? He stops me in the hall before lunch to grab me. A quick, passionate kiss leaves me breathless with delayed desire—a gift that keeps on giving. He moves on to do God-knows-what and I'm stuck against the wall, shifting restlessly for any kind of friction to alleviate the constant ache between my thighs. I start the laundry with an attitude and a huff, and then I stalk into the kitchen and jump him. Hands in his hair, I wrap my legs around his waist and kiss him until I'm on the verge of finding Shangri-La. But he pushes me away, mumbling something about me not being ready.

My response lies in our bedroom, drawer number two in the dresser to be exact, and it barely takes up space. The skimpiest bikini known to man looks good on me, really, really good. It's white against my newfound tan with triangles that barely cover all my good parts, and I strut out to the pool. I walk by Colin with a cool air of confidence and a tap to his backside. When he retreats, I dive in the pool for relief. The man makes me hot.

He returns, sexy as sin in his own Lycra suit that hugs his glutes and quads, I start my backstroke and mumble about the weather, the trees, the sweet birds to steer my thoughts away from my husband. *My husband,* I want to scream. The man who *must* satisfy all my desires.

But when he starts critiquing my backstroke, arms behind his head, legs out and crossed at the ankle on a lounger, I can't stop. I tell myself I should, but he's so tempting, so distracting, I end my midday swim and leap at him. He catches me with a grunt and darkening eyes. Our mouths connect and the angels sing *Hallelujah*. Or maybe it's me humming my praise. Straddling him, I claw my way up his bare chest, my nails scraping his skin now wet from mine, with the oh-so-thin fabric of our swimsuits as the only thing keeping his thing from sinking into my thing. I've lost track of where he ends and I begin. Is that my heartbeat or his? His groan or mine?

I don't know how I could be more ready. The pool of natural resources collecting on his upper thigh is a sure indicator I'm well prepared and that is only a slight exaggeration. If he doesn't touch me, really touch me, I'm going to self-combust. What kind of husband would let his pregnant wife expire from want?

His grip loosens and the pressure of his mouth fades. Oh, God. "Don't slow down. No, please," I beg, but he does, releasing the hold his teeth had on my bottom lip and rubbing his nose over mine, all the while his eyes stay stuck on my parted mouth. His expression is rigid, fighting for control in the flex of his jaw. I bite the tip of his finger when it nears my lips, then I suck on it, and get into a good, deep rhythm.

"That's enough." Colin's voice could grate granite into pebbles. "You win."

Colin

***YOU WIN.* HOW IN** the hell did I ever think I could stay away from her? Two weeks of Charlie Carter McKenna–torture, and on the twelfth day I'll give her anything—national secrets or my cock. I can't take it anymore. I'm so hard for her. I have been, without relief, and need shoots through me in a violent vibration. In a flash of recognition, I think I shouldn't have waited this long.

Her whimper is like a mating call, and before the wild animals living in the mountains around us, seek her out, I stand with Charlie wrapped around me. She does it again. I deepen the kiss, my tongue tasting every part of her mouth as I walk us to the house. I love my wife, I love her sweet and playful side, but I love her dirty and needy, too. Begging is a beautiful thing when it falls from her lips.

Her fingers slip beneath my suit and she grabs my ass, hard, grinding her damn hips against me the whole time I cross the patio. As soon as the screen slams behind us I set her down, giving her the chance to run. Wide green eyes look up into mine as if I've become the big, bad wolf and I'm going to eat her. It's so close to the truth I have to clench my twitching palm to stop from taking her hair.

I step forward.

She backs away.

My plan in bringing her here was to ensure she felt safe and secure, with me and with our life. I adore this woman. Yet every minute since we've arrived, I've warred with fucking the fragmented memories from her mind or easing her back into my bed. By day two, there was nothing easy about me. Day twelve and I'm a goddamn animal.

"Tell me to stop and I will." I give her a chance to end this game, to stop the madness, because she needs more time or maybe I do. "Say no or push me and it'll be done."

Charlie comes to a standstill, reaching forward for my fists and placing them on the very thin strings of her bikini bottoms. Her smile is devious. "I like your hands on me. I like it even more when I can feel them there the next day." On the tip of her toes, she presses her lips to mine, watching me as she does. "Don't be gentle. Be mine."

"Christ." I groan and lean in to devour her mouth. Without hesitation, she opens to let my tongue fight with hers.

There is no thinking, no planning; I want her mouth everywhere, and so it is, sucking my lips, my jaw, my neck, and then she falls to her knees. She trails her hands down my chest as her teeth pull at the waistband of my suit. I warn her with a look, my head tilted with a small shake—*don't do this*.

She smiles.

She fucking smiles and tugs until my dick springs free.

I change my stance, opening my legs so she has access everywhere, and my hands slide into her hair.

"Okay?" I ask, and clench my eyes shut because her answer is to suck on my head, flicking her tongue on the underside of my crown.

She takes me in, sucking so hard that when she pulls away I pop out of her mouth with an audible burst. I growl as she does it again. This time her moan vibrates around my aching shaft, and God help me, before I can stop myself I push to the back of her throat. I don't deserve her and I tell her that as she fists me, pumping with her hand and mouth.

"Charlie," I moan her name in warning. I'm embarrassingly close. It's been five weeks since I've felt her, been this close to her, and the urgent swipes of her tongue, the way she cups my sack and rolls my balls in her fingers has me on edge. Desperation comes out in the punch of my hips and my swelling cock. It's too soon. I tug her hair to move her or push her down harder, one or the other or both. I don't know until finally I step away, and pull her off me. I bend to take her mouth, her tongue, and strip her bare at the same time. Damn barely-there bikini that is more temptation than cloth.

I have her in my arms and our kiss goes on as we stumble through the house. In seconds she's on the wingback, hands above her head, a step up from the floor which is where we nearly landed in our frantic need to touch and lick skin.

My Charlie sighs, as if this is the exact position she's dreamed of for days: naked, spread out on leather that's seen its share of world leaders, with the shredded evidence of her suit thrown to the side.

"Do you ache, baby?" I ask, sinking to my knees as I hook hers over the chair arms—a regal throne for my princess.

She moans and arches, her hand falling from its grip on the chair back to squeeze a breast. "God, yes—all over—everywhere."

"What do you want?"

Her nostrils flare and she sucks on her bottom lip, biting it as she pulls her nipple. "You."

"You already have me."

"No." She drops her hand, making sure my eyes follow it past her belly button and into the lush, bright pink folds of her pussy. Pressing two fingers against her clit, she sinks farther down and into the slick need at her opening. My groan blends with hers as she paints the offering against my bottom lip, and I get drunk on her sweetness. "I don't want mere kisses. I want you to lose yourself. Make me know I belong to you in every way—in this way."

My eyes burn into her and over her decadent body—rounded curves, flushed, ripe and full—trying to hold on to the one thing she's asked me to give up: control. "You're shameless."

"Only with you."

The beast within me shakes in triumph as I let him follow her command. I grip her inner thighs, spread her open with my thumbs, and run the flat line of my tongue from bottom to top, stopping to suck her inflamed bundle of nerves into my mouth. This is not meant to tease or coax a climax to the surface; this is a demand for it. Her cries are not quiet, and I know the men walking the perimeter can hear her. With a sick, prideful satisfaction, I lap and stroke her into a scream. Let them know what this beautiful, impulsive imp sounds like when she rides my face, when I make her come.

I talk into her. *Is this what you want, my sweet, wicked girl?* The vibration pulls out a litany of fragmented pleas, and I do everything to keep building the pressure, anything to push her over the edge.

"Please." *Please*, she says again—as if I would let her suffer with the misery of want. I'd give her anything and I do, my fingers, two of them, stroking through her folds first, and then sinking down to where she's the wettest, where they slide in and twist up into the spot that drives her insane. I find her clit with my mouth and suck, looking up to her flushed chest and cheeks, her eyes bright as she gulps in a breath and reaches her hand to my hair. We move together, finding the rhythm that's unique to us, familiar, hard, and loving at the same time. I missed this, missed her and the honeyed taste of her on my tongue.

"I'm . . . yes, please, please, please," she says, writhing into a jerked cadence. I grab her breast, full, more than it was when last I held it, and tweak her hard extended nipple until she arches into my hand. Pulling my hair and then pressing my head down, she screams with the intensity of the orgasm clenching around my fingers.

I'm so hard. But I have no time to contemplate how I want to take her because Charlie pushes me to the rug, and onto my back to sit on my hungry cock. She's so wet and in a mindless race, she rubs the folds of her pussy all over me, her clit bumping my crown, with her head thrown back and hands in her hair. And then they have her breasts and she squeezes, moaning as she uses me to pleasure herself. It's amazing. I grab her hips to push and pull her faster, harder.

She stops.

Everything is so wet and warm where she sits on me, and before I can take another breath she's on her knees, grabbing my base, and *Oh, Christ*. What have I done to deserve this woman?

So tight, so tight and warm and wet, she sinks down on me in one rough movement, as if the orgasm pulsing through her veins seconds ago was an appetizer to the meal she's about to make out of my cock. *Fuck, fuck, fuck.* The tables are turned, and she commands me. The imp is now the lion, and I'm the sacrificial lamb. She's fierce, intense as she finds a frantic pace, back and forth, brushing her clit against me with each move forward. Finally, she looks down, recognition dancing in her eyes and her spontaneous smile.

"So good," she whispers, and then takes my hands from her waist and forces them to her breasts. "Knead them," she says. "Pull them; they're so sensitive."

It's too much, she's too much—the pace, her hips, the tight, warm, wet clench she has on me, and now her nipples gashing into my palms. It's the sweetest torture that I'm going to give in to too soon—it's too soon, but it builds in my spine.

"Charlie," I pant, pinching in a desperate attempt to get her there before I explode. Throwing my head back, I close my eyes and think about work, the tax and spending package: numbers, words, not wet or warm or tight and Charlie. I groan, and in a last-ditch effort to save my manhood, flip her on her back.

With her ankles on my shoulders, I hold her calves and sink in, slow, deep, long strokes that have me pause when her ass meets my thighs so she feels the full reach of my hold. She's beautiful, flushed and glowing with a light sheen of sweat. Her hands have her breasts again as if she can't stand for them not to be touched, held, soothed. I place my fingers over hers and slow us down.

"There is never an end to us, my sweet Charlie." From the first moment she spoke to me, when I heard the strong rasp of her voice, I knew I would need to hear it for a lifetime.

I need her like I need air to breathe.

The sigh that meets mine and her serene smile belong to me. I won't let the past determine our future. It won't work that way for us. No one, nothing will ever take her away from me.

"Tell me how you feel."

She swallows and shakes her head. "I . . . so full, good. Oh, God." Arching up, she moans. "So good."

I press her knees down and out so she's open and I can play with her clit, stroke it until it swells under the pads of my fingers.

"Colin," she cries, reaching for my shoulders to drag her nails along my arms. "I want to come, please; it's too . . . oh . . . *oh*."

She grabs my neck when I pull out to tease her, dipping in over and over until she growls and tugs my chest against hers, no separation from her mouth to mine. This is love, the freedom to take and demand, work together to come to an end we've both wanted for so long. Placing my elbows on either side of her face, I give her what she wants, sinking in deep and grinding at first. Then the hunger takes over and I rear back, driving into her with quick, snapping thrusts that move her up the rug an inch every time.

Faster.

Harder.

Her breath becomes fragmented, panted out in sharp puffs that abrade my lips.

A blush stains her chest and cheeks. Small, chirping cries escape when my hips catch hers, and then her mouth parts, her eyes widening in surprise. Everything stills: her fingers in my hair, her legs around my ass, and her shoulders and arms stiffen.

She breaks apart.

Arching her neck, she turns her face away as spasms roll through her frame and clench around me in an almost painful grip.

"Oh, Charlie," I moan into her chest, pressing my teeth around her razor-sharp nipple. I move through her orgasm, pulling out every ounce of pleasure I can give her. "Yes, baby. Give me everything, all of you."

When she relaxes, murmuring her appreciation, I lose myself in her body, bucking wild, deep frantic thrusts that drag the heat down my spine and expel it in a rush of hot, desperate satisfaction that tears me apart one jetted stream at a time. I collapse on top of her, spent and thoroughly taken by my wife.

Reason was left at the door. I could care less that we're sprawled in the center of the living room, windows open and sunlight streaming through in hazing ribbons that set Charlie's hair on fire. We're tangled up, sweaty, and perfect.

"Let's stay like this forever, with you on top of me," she says, scraping her fingers through my hair. "And with me loving you more than I did when the sun met the sky this morning."

I lean up to find her mouth, threading my fingers through her curls and pulling, kissing her with what I hope is a lasting intensity. "I begin and end with you, Charlie. There is no separation from my soul to yours. Even if you wake alone, I am with you," I murmur into her lips. "Don't underestimate the power of my love. It will always fight for you and win."

She hums and runs her nose along mine. "No more fighting. I surrender. Happy and glowing with orgasmic glee, I surrender."

I take in her giggle and roll over. Without prompting, she straddles my hips, hair flowing down in a halo of red. Tickling her was not my intention, but even the slightest touch to her sides has her peeling with laughter. The wiggling, the grinding—Christ, I want her again.

I try to encourage her afternoon snack and nap, she needs them, but my Charlie, she decides there's enough nutritional value right here on our tiny island in the middle of a forest. It's my turn to surrender with my hands held above my head.

Growth comes with adversity. The challenges in life can break you or build you. In this moment, we both feel it, as sure as the energy humming between us; Charlie and Colin are whole, stronger than we ever were before.

TWENTY-SEVEN

Charlie

I CAN'T STOP STARING in the mirror. He asked me to watch. Watch what I look like when he makes me come and he has, over and over again. Now I'm breathless and speechless, and he's lazy on top of me, between my thighs, running his hands over every inch of my skin. I watch it happen in the floor-to-ceiling mirror, leaning against the wall in our room. I like it; I can see parts of him that I can't when I'm on my back, but I still get to feel the delicious pressure, his weight resting against my most sensitive places, the loving caress of his hands along my flushed skin. I can watch his reaction to my nails digging in his rounded ass, and dragging up to his shoulders. It's like our own dirty little movie, a chose-your-own-adventure—lick here if you want Charlie to come; suck here for Colin. So many choices that we explored all day and into the night.

"You're tired," he murmurs into my neck.

I shake my head, but my lids fail me, sinking even when I tell them to remain open. "Can we get this mirror at home? I like it," I say, stifling a yawn. "So much."

Popping up on his elbows with a smile, he nods. "I'll have it delivered before we return. Rest now, love. I'm going to grab dinner and come back."

"You cheated."

"How's that?" He slips off the bed to find his pajama pants, but they're so low I prefer to call them an invitation to get naked—again.

"Chef Rene and the menus; you can't hide from me. There's probably a ten-course meal waiting for us downstairs."

He chuckles, rubbing his chest. "I had to think of the family, baby. I'll get food in that belly one way or another, even if I have to rely on the good chef's pastries. Did you say donut?" Leaning down on one knee, with his hand next to my cheek, he finds my mouth for a dangerously sweet kiss, his finger holding my chin in place. But it's his eyes that get me every time, midnight blue and devious.

"Why do you have to be so tempting?" I cry and push him away. "So far there's a short list of pros and cons to pregnancy: the barfing is a nasty drawback but, God, I'm horny. It's seriously getting ridiculous."

Laughing, he kisses my stomach. "I'll be right back. And don't touch yourself while I'm gone. I want all of your orgasms. They're mine, got it, Wife?"

"They're more fun when you give them to me anyway—just hurry. I can't hold out much longer."

I watch his ass as he goes, mumbling something about setting a timer for every thirty minutes. Funny, but the spark in my nether-region says it might be his best idea to date. A glance at the clock indicates it's eight-thirty but the horse pills and bottle of water beside it catch my eye. Pre-natals, ugh. I force them down one at a time, and then fall back into the sheets.

Snuggling under the blankets, I think I'll just lie here for a minute while he's gone. I won't fall asleep. I won't.

When my lids bounce open the room is broken by shadows, driven in from the hall light that remains on. Colin is wrapped around me, his nose pressed into the crook of my neck. Saliva rushes my mouth—lots of it. He needs to get off. *Move*, I say, but nothing comes out. I pull at the sheets for leverage, the floor tipping as I slip from the bed to my feet and lunge to the bathroom. I barely make it before I heave for what feels like an hour. I can't stop, even when there's nothing to expel and I'm exhausted.

I don't know when he woke up, but Colin has my hair and he wipes my forehead with a damp rag, whispering words I can't comprehend. Darkness comes in an eerie similarity to a night in April, where I count my breath to know if I'm awake or drifting. At some point I'm back in bed, but it happens again, a repeat of the first time. After the third installment I beg for a shower—anything to wash the misery away.

He's so good to me, gentle as he rinses the shampoo from my hair, soaping my body with his gel, massaging my breasts enough to make me curse and kiss his neck. I think the worst moments have passed as we step to the rug. A reprieve cleanses my mind, and I enjoy the stroke of his towel-covered hands on my thighs enough to fist his hair, just for fun and to bring a smile to his worry ravaged face.

"Feeling better, baby?"

"Ye . . . argh." The word becomes a moan as pain stabs low in my belly. I bend under the strain of it, whimpering as Colin's eyes grow wide.

It happens again, so sharp it contorts my frame. As the stinging ache wraps around and squeezes, an unsettling thought won't stop pounding in my head.

Nothing is ever as it seems.

HE CAN'T STOP STARING at the screen. I can't stop staring at Colin and then the monitor and back again in a game of whiplash I'll pay for in an hour. This moment should be recorded, yet my phone is buried under the pile of clothes in the corner. It's priceless stuff one day I would like to reflect upon and say *yes, he's just as adorable as you remember*.

Colin's eyes glass over, and he can't help the triumphant, smug smile from burning a dimple in his cheek. It burns through when the doctor implies he may have over-reacted a tad when he had the military escort his pregnant wife to the hospital—by helicopter. The grin remains when we learn the pain was caused by rapidly elongating ligaments. Colin lights up like the national Christmas tree as the galloping whoosh of a heartbeat sounds over the speakers.

The brilliancy shines through when Doctor Henry Waters explains Baby A is sharing the same sack as Baby B and because of that, we should expect identical twins—*twins* being the keyword. Two babies, Thor *and* Clark, super sperm splitting the egg in two.

My heartbeat hammers out of control, and for a second I'm afraid I may black out. Holy cow. I can't wrap my head around it, even though I see the bugs on the monitor.

"Charlie?"

"Yup, mm-hmm, present," I say, still staring.

Colin laughs. "I'll buy you a sonogram if you would like to see them every day, but for now we have to say goodbye."

"Oh." I tear up as the screen goes blank. *Bye, babies.* Then I touch my stomach, because those bugs are in me. Colin's hand reaches mine and my gaze meets his.

"Don't cry," he says with the same grin.

"I have to," I wail, and bury my head in his neck when he pulls me in. God, he smells too good, soaped up in sandalwood from our shower before all hell broke loose. I'm exhausted from worry and wanting and bugs. "Is it possible to have hormonal fatigue?" I mumble, but Doctor Waters has super hearing and pats my arm.

"Early pregnancy symptoms are intensified with twins and typically ease after the first trimester, around fourteen weeks. Based on what we saw today, I'd say you're just shy of nine. I've placed your due date as December thirtieth, but you should follow up with your obstetrician when you return to D.C. I'll send you home with something to help the nausea, and that should do it for now. I can see you're in good hands." He nods and retreats. "Congratulations, Mr. President, Mrs. McKenna."

My bugs, our bugs, are due on our first anniversary. I smile. It has to mean something. A good omen. The hardest part is behind us—it has to be. As the doctor leaves, I climb out of my fog and Colin's arms to dress. He stands and hovers close by, trying to assist as I remove the hospital gown and fumble with the straps of my bra. If my boobs don't hurt, they throb for his hands, and this is what I mean by hormonal fatigue.

"Please don't touch me."

His eyes flare, but then that damn grin spreads into a dimple. "My hands belong on you. When they're not, I never know quite what to do with them."

I moan and look at the closed door. I can't. I shouldn't—not here when the nurse could walk in at any moment. But, yeah, he's Colin and I'm Charlie, so I don't fight it. "Just a little touch. Make the ache go away."

A low rumble sounds as he comes up behind me, his arms round to my front and his hands lift up to cop a feel, holding the full weight in his palms. Oh, God. I reach for his hair, and his mouth finds my neck to suck a gasp into the silence. He's right—his hands are meant for me, even in the emergency room after finding out we're having twins. *Twins!*

I sigh into the feel of him, tugging on his hair until he growls again. "Bras are overrated painful, torture chambers. I've decided the White House should support a bra-burning ceremony. We could make a statement—change the world."

I hiss when he pinches my nipples and relish the sting zinging in all the right places. "So sensitive, baby, heavy, too. You need me to take care of them and you."

Kissing a path to my ear, he bites the lobe. I cover his hands with mine and squeeze harder, turning my head to find his mouth. He needs to hear a truth that's been burning a hole in my heart. "I don't want to lose this when we go home. I've missed you."

Wrapping me up in what feels like his whole body, he breathes into my hair and whispers, "When we're apart, I'm quite honestly a broken man. Ready yourself for my hands and my mouth and my body, because I don't plan for you to go needy. We shall feed each other with our basic needs and grow new life that will sustain us through eternity."

I smile into my favorite place while the warm and fuzzics tingle across my shoulders. "How do you come up with this stuff? Sweet one minute and downright dirty in the next."

He chuckles. "It's a gift."

"God's gift to women."

"No, only for Charlie."

"I like that."

"I should hope so; eternity would be a very long time if you didn't."

I giggle. "Kiss me then, because I'm so damn hungry."

He starts with my nose, an amused twinkle in his eye. "Whatever you need, it's yours," he says and kisses me, really kisses me.

And after that, I can't remember if my stomach growls, or how to say my name for that matter. Assign Colin a task and he's on the ball. Give him a baby and he's giddy; give him two and he wants to make another.

He's a greedy, greedy man—and I'm the luckiest girl in the world.

THAT DAMN MAN. HE'S so sweet my tears are on a non-stop cycle. Twelve hours after they found two bugs in my belly, we walked the steps of the White House together and we stayed that way, heading up to the residence where I found this in our room.

The ceiling was painted the same color as his eyes, matching the deep blue of the rest of the room. On the wall opposite our bed, the space I watch in silence with the covers pulled to my chin, is a glowing mural, so crisp it's as if we're looking out the window. Light hovers over a horizon line. It streaks into layered lines of pink, orange, and purple, fading out to the constellations perfectly placed throughout the room. I don't know how or who did it, but it glows as if the world was brought inside.

"What have you done?"

He steps behind me, his chest to my back with his chin resting on my shoulder. "I hear you, Charlie. I devour every word you say, and even when you don't speak I listen to the secrets in your heart. The sun is the brightest star in the sky; you said you'd look for it and find me. Your search is over. I'm here, and I brought you the midnight sun. It never sets; it hangs over the horizon and shines through the night. You will never be lost, and we'll always be home. There is no need to be afraid."

I turn and hook my arms around his neck. My fingers stroke into the luxury of his hair, threading through it as I work to slow my galloping heart. It's always his eyes. They give him away; his voice didn't waver, but they shine a reflection of my own emotion. I try hard to hold it in, but my chest hitches as the thoughts form.

"At the Kerrs, every night I prayed so hard but I didn't think anyone heard me. But God did." I kiss his lips, his cheek, and taste his chin as my tears start in earnest. "Because He gave me you."

Feeling gives way to need, and I express how much his thoughtfulness means to me with my mouth and my body. And then it's his turn. There are no words. It's in the way he moves, how his back and shoulders rise up with each thrust, shutting out the light and pitching me into darkness. But I'm not afraid because I have him.

My Colin.

He is at once hard and all-consuming, as if he owns every inch of me, yet delicate for fear I can break. It's in the clench of his fingers through mine, over my head, pushed into the mattress, twined together in a grip so fierce I know he will never let me go, never let me fall apart and be broken. I am his—possessed by him and loved by him. Together, we are unbreakable.

And so the next chapter of our story unwinds.

His sweet turns into a little bit of dirty, and the days slip by. True to his word, we never stray too far apart. When he works late, I lie on the couch in the Oval Office. Colin has Betsy find the softest blanket and a pillow. He keeps them there for when I fall asleep, which is often, because the bugs wear me out. If our schedules merge, I travel with him. If not, I fall asleep to a midnight dream and look forward to his return home.

I love life. Maybe because spring blends to summer and the world is bright. The sun and flowers burst with color, the grass has never been greener, the air clear and fresh—even in D.C. I find my stride, and it's confident, commanding and buoyant.

Not every day is wonderful. I have flashbacks, and doubt knocks on my door, but Colin is always there. So are Ali and Kyle, and my parents, and Gram and Gramps, who visit once a month. Evan is distant—hurt by Ali's rejection. Colin and I push them both, but it seems as we do it's into opposite corners instead of face to face.

Work at the rehab hospital continues. Katherine Hess and her team arrive, and we film for days. Molly is more than happy to take my place in the ring with Cupcake—I mean Caden, who comes back to finish the self-defense portion of the documentary. Hollywood was not as enthusiastic about her participation, but in the end it's for a good cause and he got on board.

We host parties and dine with dignitaries. Attend events. A White House photographer captures the beginning of our marriage and Colin's presidency in vibrant still life. The European tour is rescheduled and I tag along. Colin is right; I fall in love with him all over again. The butterflies in my belly are a testament to that, and as the bugs get bigger it becomes more elephant than insect.

Colin follows Joan Montgomery's court proceedings and mentions updates—the long list of charges and her continued denial of guilt. But he stops after my blood-pressure skyrockets into the no-go zone at her claim Kilpatrick was the mastermind. I want the knife back as she insists her participation was forced because she feared for her life, claiming coercion was to blame. I stay strong through her pre-trial and up to the day I take the stand. In a closed courtroom, I glare at the vile woman and repeat every word she said. I relive everything, including her backhands that I still feel on my cheek, but it's in present day. With Colin waiting in the wings, the truth explodes from my chest and sets me free. I'm strong enough to send this woman to jail for the rest of her life.

A month later, a surprise phone call launches Kyle's world into outer-space. Faith's water breaks two weeks early. The tough exterior falls away to a panicked soon-to-be father who requires an escort to the hospital. Fourteen hours later they have their princess, Ellison Skye. For the second time in a year, Kyle takes time off to be with his girls.

Something changes. I give up on the past to focus on the future. It's unstoppable, and that's exactly how I feel. The sticks-and-stones mantra is finally true. In the political arena, perception is a huge component, but it's made easier when there are no secrets. Smiles become effortless, and supporting my husband is simple because he's worthy of his position. When criticism comes or rumors surface, I brush them off and go on with my day. I change. I'm ready for my fresh start and it comes in cycles like the sun: centered, energized, and fueling new life. I hate the morning sickness that sometimes lasts throughout the day, but growing babies is amazing, and I give myself over to it. My stomach expands faster than I can keep new clothes in the closet. Every night Colin talks to them. Sometimes we listen to music. As time goes on, he plays with their feet or hands or however they reach out to touch him. It's beautiful. I'd thought love lived in his eyes before, but when I catch him looking at me with his bugs growing inside my belly, I *see* it. It's as if the stars shine and burst forth in a hallelujah of fireworks.

He is the best husband. It doesn't matter the time—Colin heads out for food or tums whenever the emergency strikes. I have a serious obsession with fresh fruit, which Chef Rene stocks in abundance, but it's the Reuben's that are harder to come by—sauerkraut and all. Together we attend each pre-natal visit, and I am not the only one crying when the heartbeats gallop or the twins' silhouettes pops on the ultrasound. Yet they remain a mystery, and we don't know if we should decorate in pink or blue.

Before bed, Colin massages my skin with cream, and inevitably we end up rubbing something else. I relish these days. Even with the joy of becoming four, I savor our last minutes as a duet, when Colin makes love to me softly with his chest to my back. Or when we dance, swaying together with my nose pressed into my favorite place, and stay up late to talk about everything and nothing. Sometimes we stroll through the house and find all of its secrets. Bowling becomes a favorite of mine until my belly surges past the size of the ball. The blush burning up my chest whenever movie-time is mentioned is a sure giveaway as to how much I like the family theatre, and what Colin does to me when the lights fall.

The trees lining the Potomac announce autumn before the weather turns cool, their leaves burnt into dark umber. The documentary airs every Monday in September to a primetime audience, and it receives staggering feedback. So much so that we plan a follow-up to begin shooting after Christmas.

Braxton Hicks contractions slow me down and force hydration and more rest. The twins' arrival is scheduled for days after my birthday in November, four weeks before the official due date in December. Weeks before delivery, I find myself dressing for one of the few events I'm still scheduled to attend—Georgetown University Hospital's Halloween fundraising ball. It's a Friday-night party to raise capital for a new pediatric unit, and it's my job to support Ali. A generous donation was not enough—*attendance is required,* she'd said—*it will be fun.*

Trying to corset a double-sized basketball into a gown is a two-person job. Colin is up for the challenge and seems to enjoy himself. I find him in the mirror, the same one from Camp David that arrived hours after we did from our two-week retreat into the mountains. His Phantom to my thirty-three week Christine is plain, not fair. I'm supposed to be the beautiful one, but he glows behind his mask. His eyes shine as if he's thinking of stripping me bare even as he cinches my laces.

This is my life. Perfect until it's not.

TWENTY-EIGHT

Charlie

"IF YOUR HAND, PLASTERED to my ass, is on the front of every newspaper tomorrow, you're going to get it." My nose is pressed to Colin's ear to ensure he hears each word and the bevy of reporters on the red carpet do not.

I catch his smile expanding into a deep dimple as I pull away, yet his fingers clench harder on my backside. "I look forward to it."

To make matters worse, as I look up he stares down and into my eyes. The camera flashes go crazy. Behind the white mask, his lids sink into wicked thoughts as his gaze drops to my lips. He takes smoldering to a whole new level. *There go my panties*. I should know by now to carry a spare pair in my clutch. My husband is dangerous for my lingerie.

"You're terrible."

"And you're glowing. My cock has a way of doing that to you."

I bite my lip to hold back my giggle. Chastising Colin gets me into trouble, and I had enough of it in the back of the limo. It's a miracle my petticoats survived his assault. "I love you, Mr. President."

He brushes his mouth against mine and at the same time a chorus of sighs spreads through the crowd. "And I you, my sweet Charlie. Come," he says, taking my hand and using his other to wave a farewell to the media and guests gathered to watch us walk in. "Let's make our official appearance so I can get you home and back in bed."

My bottom lip pops out. I want that too, but his reason for hoarding together time weighs down my mood. "I'd like to go on your trip, too."

He stops three feet inside the entrance. Our entourage—the theatre administrator who met us when we arrived, Kyle, Fitz, five more agents, and a medical team—halts, too. At Colin's instance, the medics that are never far from his side are now affixed to mine as well. He does not take any chances with me or his children. *Safety first.*

Cupping my cheek, he says, "I know you do, but the doctors have said it's best if you stay home. We've gone over this, baby. Now is not the time to have you flying all over the United States. No more travel before the boys arrive."

"But I feel fine, I am fine. The girls are fine," I tease, and motion over my stomach to the babies who are finally resting after a recent wrestling match had limbs in my ribs. "I don't want to miss you for a week."

I've always been addicted to Colin, but it's neared DEFCON Level One recently. I need him more than ever. Only his presence and touch and reassurance ease the vulnerability that sneaks up on me. I've never been happier, I have it all, and sometimes I worry about Colin, the babies, the delivery, and everything. Mom said it's a symptom of late pregnancy many women experience. For me, I want my people around all the time—Colin especially.

He sighs, pressing his mouth to my forehead. "And that's exactly why I've asked Robyn and Will to join us in Washington."

"Can we at least discuss it . . ." My eyes pop wide. "Wait, what?"

His grin is beautiful. "I don't need to be in Indiana to talk with them about supporting Pearce on his election bid for governor. They'll stay in the Blair House here so we can all visit, together."

"You're staying?" My heart stumbles and he nods.

I grab him by the hair, pulling his mouth to mine. This kiss is not chaste, but big and smacking with laughter, his as it bubbles up. "Charlie . . ."

"God, I love you," I murmur, peppering kisses on his mouth and cheeks. "Love, love, love. Thank God we're married, because if we weren't I'd force you down the aislc."

"Ah, baby, I'll come willingly every time you want me too." Colin waggles his eyebrows and rubs my ass again. Oh, boy. *Time to get this ball started before we get out of hand.*

"Right, let's go. Ali's probably having heart palpitations wondering where we are. She has plans to auction you off for the first dance," I say, twining our fingers together. His good mood changes to a growl. "It's for a worthy cause."

"You better have brought the check book," he mumbles.

A theatre not too far from the hospital donated their space for the fundraiser. It shimmers in gold from floor to ceiling. Nearing a century of celebrating movies and live performances, the structure and the interior's recent renovation restored it to its ornate origins. Everyone is in costume: angels and devils, the Mad Hatter and Alice. You name it and they're here. Five hundred people mingle through the lobby, on the balcony above us, and in the ballroom below concourse level. Although Colin has on a cravat, a cape, and half of his face is covered in white, he's instantly recognized. That and my flaming red hair is hard to miss against the stark white of my flowing gown. A bristling hum follows us as we part the crowd and head down the stairs to a much quieter anteroom.

Tall ceilings and baroque furnishings mirror the space's larger counterpart. Animated conversations of the twenty-or-so guests stop when we enter.

"There you are." Ali drops her notepad on a corner table and turns to rush forward.

My mouth falls open because there is nothing Disney about this Sleeping Beauty. Her blonde hair flows in shining waves down her back, but it's the pink, boned gown that verges on indecent. "Could your fairy godmother not conjure enough fabric to cover your boobs?" I ask in her ear as we hug.

"Pot, meet kettle," she says, while pulling away.

"Yes, but my cups runneth over because of biology. What's your excuse?"

She shrugs and lifts her lips in a devious smirk. "Do I need one?" She bats her lashes, and then kisses Colin's cheek.

"First thing's first—where's the ladies room? I have to plan out emergency visits. These bugs don't give much notice before they bounce on my bladder."

She rubs my belly and starts talking nonsense about how much Auntie Ali loves them.

"Focus up, Sister."

"Oh, alright. Down the hall." She points. "And two turns to the left. Big sign above the door; you can't miss it. By the way, we have about thirty minutes . . ."

Tuning out the entire room, I close my eyes as my lower back twinges. It's not uncommon in itself, but this, this wave of pain is a deeper, longer ache than any I've experienced to date. I hold the babies with one hand and my lumbar with the other, and soon I'm not alone. I moan as Colin's fingers join mine to rub, and I focus on my breathing. Two seconds later, I'm lowered into a chair that was brought to me and Ali has my wrist.

I open to find her checking my pulse. "I'm fine," I pant. "Holy cow, that was some spasm."

Fifteen people huddle around me. Kyle's crisp stare levels me with his worry, his wrist hovers next to his mouth, as if he's already calling for an ambulance via the microphone hidden there. Colin, his face as pale as his mask, rips the plastic shell off as he sinks into a crouch beside me.

"I'm fine."

Taking my hand, he shakes his head. "You don't look fine."

Ali holds her cool fingers to my forehead. "How long has your lower back been hurting?"

"It hasn't."

"How do you feel now?"

"Good, fine. I'm okay." But the ache remains. It's not as bright as the first pang, but aggravating all the same. "When are you selling my husband to the highest bidder?

"Charlie." She stoops down to Colin's level. "Now is not the time to placate us. If something is off, we need to know."

Breathing deep helps, one breath, two, and the ache eases. I look to my sister and then my husband. Both of them have wrinkled brows and flick tense glances between themselves. No two people have loved me more. "I'll tell you if I think something's wrong. Really, I will."

"Everyone okay?" Ali's white knight says from the door. *Evan.*

She groans. "What's he doing here?"

I beam at her, at Colin, and then at Evan as he sneaks past the hovering bodies to peek down at me. "Having those boys early, Mrs. McKenna?" He winks.

He's over-the-top handsome in a tight black sweater, tucked in only by an inch as a planned afterthought right in front to display his belt buckle. He shows off his sleek muscles and cool attitude with sunglasses hanging in the center of his V-neck. I'd say he's making a statement and Ali's definitely listening, or at least looking. And he does the same. Whatever isn't happening between them is going to, soon. The bulging veins in his neck speak of further conversation, or based on the clenching and unclenching of his hand, maybe a spanking.

"I'll deal with you in a minute," he says to her.

Ali turns as pink as her dress. Jumping to her feet, she stands her ground with her arms crossed under her chest. It only amps up her cleavage. "This is an invite-only costume party, and you're not on the guest list."

"Or," he mumbles, "we can do this now." Taking a step forward, he grabs her chin. She tugs away, but he holds her hip and then her neck. "For a long time, I thought I was crazy to want something solid with you, but I've had months to think about this and I've come to the same conclusion every time. I'm fucking insane for you, Ali."

As if to prove his point, Evan crashes his mouth to hers. She relaxes for a second, but then she shoves away and wipes the back of her hand over her lips, growling out her anger.

"We're not done." His smile starts small and stretches into a challenge. "Not by a longshot."

Turning to face us as if that spectacle didn't happen, Evan pulls out his phone and addresses Colin. "This would have been easier had you not directed your calls to voicemail."

He chuckles. "I had a pressing matter to take care of on the way over."

Evan's eyebrow shoots up as he glances at me. "I'm sure you did. But I have news you'll both want to hear."

I wave my husband's concern away and grab his hand as he helps me stand with him. I'm fine but for a manageable pelvic throb. Colin gives a nod to Fitz, who clears the room of strangers. The medics hover just outside; he and Kyle flank the door, leaving the four of us to listen to what Evan has to say.

"Judge Thornton accepted a last-minute deal from Joan Montgomery. Her trial has ended."

My pulse thrums. Colin tucks me into his side with an arm around my waist. We rarely say her name. Not because it causes flashbacks, but because Charlie Carter McKenna lives in the present, and there's no way in hell I'll let Joan Montgomery or that damn family wreak havoc with my life. Not anymore.

All eyes pop to me as Evan relays the details. "The evidence was too overwhelming, so at the eleventh hour she decided to plead out instead of let a jury decide her fate. In exchange for full disclosure, she'll serve concurrent sentences in a minimum-security facility. The possibility of parole occurs when she's ninety."

It's over. My heart erupts in my chest. I lean against Colin as tears rush to my eyes, thankful that this is behind us before the babies come.

"There's more. She submitted the full account at the time of her plea bargain. I have a copy at the office, and it has some interesting tidbits the CIA is investigating. If proven true, they may help us capture a portion of Kilpatrick's cell that still exists overseas. She talked a lot about Abby and Sara, her downward spiral after their death, and how she and Alex fell into an unhealthy alliance." Evan's eyes lose some of the excited luster. "Charlie," he says softly, glancing quickly to Colin and back to me, "take this for what it's worth. Joan claims Alex went insane in part because he's been impotent since he lost Abby."

Ali squeals and throws her hands in the air. A laugh bubbles up and out of my mouth. I hold it in behind my hand and try to think. Of all the things, I had not expected that news. Colin watches me as Evan relays more details about how they framed John, used Ella as a vehicle for their hate, and that the information Joan provided will be vetted to determine its authenticity. My mind swims with the details. This news does little to reinforce what I've known since Camp David. I don't need the tests to prove it, or confirmation from Joan that Alex couldn't rape me. Colin feels the same.

I take Evan's hand and squeeze. "Thank you for rushing here to let us know about Joan. I'm relieved I won't have to testify again, but now I'd like for all of us to close the book on this part of our life. Will you stay and have some fun out of the office?"

"Not tonight," he says, leaning in to kiss my cheek. "Call me if you're having those babies."

He turns for the door. Just before walking out, he looks at Ali. "I'll see you sooner rather than later, Alison Carter."

"Don't count on it," she calls after him, but he's already gone.

And that's it. Chapter closed. As our party of four dissipates, the rest of us move to the ballroom. Colin kisses my cheek and makes his way to the stage where he accepts a flute of Champagne, awaiting his fate as the last man auctioned off for a good cause. Behind the podium, Ali acts as auctioneer. She cites all of Colin's attributes, the list is long, and when complete she accepts the opening bid. Colin dons the expressionless expression, but I can see in the slight strain around his eyes he hates that nameless women offer their next paycheck for a dance with him. One throws in her firstborn child which he declines gracefully, reminding her he has two of his own on the way.

As Ali raises her hand to bring the gavel down on a final bid, I raise my flag. I giggle at the relief easing over Colin's features and state rather firmly that he belongs to me. "One hundred thousand dollars."

Handing his sister-in-law his empty glass, a grin burns across his cheeks. Mine is just as big. I tune out the collective gasp, and this time when Ali slams down her hammer, my husband hops from the stage and stalks toward me. People fall away to make a path for him, and I can see why. He's got the whole dark-and-dangerous Phantom look down pat. I groan when he takes me by the arms, and then when one hand holds my lower back and he barely bends me into a dip, kissing me while he does. His mouth is warm, and sweet like Champagne.

What I don't tell him as he rights us into an embrace is that Ali and I have had this planned for weeks. I'd always intended to donate to the hospital; Lord knows we can afford to help the good cause. I think Colin figures it out when it's our song the house band plays. His arm tightens around me. We cling to each other, my nose pressed to his neck as the lights dim and he slowly twirls us around the cleared dance floor. It's magical, and so is my life.

"Thank you for saving me, my love." His voice is rough with emotion. Somehow I know he's not referring to the auction. Clutching him as close as my ginormous stomach allows, I breathe in sandalwood and Colin.

"In this life and into the next, I am yours," I whisper his wedding vow. Leaning back, I smile as his eyes mist, and fully accept his mouth for one last kiss.

Just as Cinderella runs from her prince, I must, too. Nature calls—frequently. I whisper my plans in his ear. I smile when our gaze connects, but his is muddled and his brow is drawn into three lines.

"I'll go with you," he says, taking my elbow.

"Don't be silly. The pediatric chief of staff is waiting to thank you." I nod over his shoulder. "I've got Kyle, and I feel fine." It's not a lie. My back is achy, but that's not so unusual at this stage of the game.

He shakes his head. Indecision is written all over his face. "Go." I encourage him with a hand to his oblique to twist him in the right direction. "I'll only be a minute."

His features don't ease, but I leave him with the good doctor and race to the restroom Ali pointed out earlier.

"You okay, boss-lady?" Kyle's shoulder is parallel to mine, and although he scouts out the area first, he breaks off his surveillance to look down at me.

"Yeah, I don't get much notice lately before peeing is imperative. I gotta go."

He holds the door open when we get there. Even after my bladder is empty, it seems one wrong move will leave a pool in my panties for all the wrong reasons. Laughing or sneezing is a disaster. I smile in the mirror and at the woman next to me as I wash my hands. My lips are pink, but my skin is pale. White has never been a great color for my complexion, but this is more than that. I look tired. And it's as if seeing the evidence makes it so. The ache in my lower back tunes into a high pitch. I rub it, but kneading doesn't help.

"I'm not liking this, Charlie," Kyle says, as I step into the hall. "I think you should go back to the residence and lie down or better yet, to the hospital to get checked out."

"For once I won't argue . . ."

"Mrs. McKenna!"

I turn and squint at Sandra Burke, *The Post* reporter. The lighting is not bright, yet my eyes burn. Blinking doesn't quite bring her into focus.

"I'm so glad I caught you," she says, fanning herself with a large manila envelope as if she ran to find me.

Kyle takes one long step and stops her before she reaches me. She peeks around his shoulder.

"What can I do for you?" I ask, and press my fingers against the wall to steady myself.

"I wanted to give you this." She hands over the papers, but Kyle takes hold of them. "You've been so kind to me, Mrs. McKenna. I thought it only fair that I give you a heads up about what will run in the paper on Sunday morning."

I break out into a cold sweat, clammy. I'm not sure if it's because of her, or because my body hums with a nervous energy, almost as if it wants me to take some kind of action. Warning bells ring in my brain. "I have to go."

"Mrs. McKenna," she calls as I turn away. "You don't want to ignore this. We have proof. I have proof."

I return to Kyle's side, still cognizant of the few people strolling in the hall. He crowds her in with his chest, inching her in the opposite direction.

"What do you want, Sandra?" I ask.

Kyle turns a steely stare in my direction, watching me as the damn reporter takes back the envelope and rips it open. He lifts his wrist to his mouth and snaps out a muffled order.

"I want you to look at these," Sandra pleads.

She holds up pictures—Colin and Raquel pictures. Hair on my nape bristles to attention. In the first they're at a dinner for two. Candles burn on the table between them. The next one that she so kindly flips to, they're walking side by side. His head is bent close to her mouth in what appears to be an intimate moment. But if you look closely—and for me there is no need, because I trust him, because I know him, I know everything about him—this is not my Colin. The sadness that lived in his eyes when I first met him is there, and the dimple that pops up during our happiest moments is missing. And so are the sideburns he's had since I met him.

I laugh and close my eyes. *Shit.* On cue, a gush pools between my thighs. Holding the babies below my stomach, I take a breath to calm my pulse, and with a second inhale I bite my lip, but I can't hold back my tongue lashing.

"Here's the quote I know you were hoping for. Let's be clear, it will be the last I ever make to you or to *The Post* directly, as you have foolishly failed to vet the material you've referenced. Here it is, ready?" I hiss, and try to straighten through the pain ripping along my lower back. "I trust my husband implicitly. Thank you for your time."

And I do trust him, without a whisper of doubt. Whatever that is evidence of, it is not an affair. I turn to find him even as Colin calls, "Charlie!"

My leg buckles on my first step in his direction, and I glance down to find out why.

All I see is red.

My once white dress is stained with it.

Colin

CHARLIE'S PALE FACE HAUNTS me. Something is wrong. After half listening to the pediatric chief of staff, I apologize and rush in the same direction my wife took moments before. Fitz follows, as does the rest of my detail. I ignore waves and calls for attention and burst out of the ballroom into the damn hall. It's a maze of different directions, and I have no idea where to go.

In a hushed, yet urgent tone, Fitz speaks to Sommerton via radio connection. *Something is happening.*

Ali must have seen my mad dash and is behind me. "This way," she says, possessing that same kind of sixth sense as I do when it comes to her sister.

Twenty yards down, we turn a corner and my chest rips open. "Charlie!"

Sommerton catches her as she falls. Ali dashes to her side barking orders to the medics, already opening boxes and pulling out materials. An ambulance is in wait wherever we go, a standard protocol, and Fitz instructs the team in. It plays in slow-motion as Charlie whimpers and writhes in pain, blood pooling beneath her. I fall to my knees, unable to reach her with so many people caring for her all at once.

Charlie. I say her name in my head and out loud, over and over again. I swallow it down my throat as Fitz tugs me to my feet to make room for the stretcher. She's got an IV in her arm and Ali squeezes the bag, screaming at the top of her lungs. "Move it, people!" She rips a phone out of a medic's hand and dials while they strap Charlie in.

"This is Doctor Carter, I am three minutes out with a Level I trauma, probable placental abruption." Agents hold back the curious gawkers as they get my wife in an elevator and up to ground level. Ali's determined eyes find mine before the doors close.

My whole life leaves without me, gone.

Anger flares. I rip the damn cape and cravat off as Fitz gets me moving, up the steps and into the waiting motorcade. Charlie's ambulance is seconds' ahead, sirens on high alert. Incredulity lives in my mind as the last couple of hours play on repeat. She was fine. Charlie laughed and rode me to completion right here on this seat. I grip my hair and pull a howl out of my lungs, my head thrown back as agony darts through every part of my soul.

My Charlie. My children.

I know of the terror she felt when I was shot. I'd imagined how deeply she was wounded, but I feel the raw slice of it now. It's unbearable. We pull up to the emergency room, a portion of which is cleared by the Service as I storm through the doors. I'm left to pace in silence, with the solemn men in my detail for an interminable amount of time. A hospital administrator comes in to provide updates, but they're useless platitudes. *Our best physicians are working on her, sir. We'll know more soon. Can I offer you anything?*

With my fists by my side and then in my hair, I rage. I rage at him, at the ceiling, and at anyone who will listen as my fear is expelled in bleating bouts of gibberish that have me bent over in pain.

Evan storms in, but I can't look at him. He places his hand on my shoulder. I keep my head down and concentrate on breathing, blocking out any possibility other than fine, okay, and stable. *All three of them.*

I feel the answer coming. Like a tsunami rising in the distance, it crashes in on me as Ali breaks through the double doors, one clutched in each hand. She stands suspended in time.

I can't breathe.

Air is pulled from my lungs. I know by her stricken eyes that life will never be the same again.

*E*PILOUGE

Two years later

Colin

LIFE IS NOT DEFINED by one decision, one act, one tragedy or a miracle. It's the sum of all parts. I once asked Charlie if she was happy. What I thought was a simple question has a complicated answer. Living for the moments when we are most content would mean losing everything in between. And I treasure all of my memories. Each day that comes and then goes is one I thank God for and never take for granted. I know how valuable they are.

I've been blessed with good fortune in many ways. In this simple moment, it's in the sun, and lying in the grass with my boys. Killian's laughter tugs at my heart even as it pulls out my smile. It reminds me of his mother. Holding him up an arm's length away, he fills my vision—dark hair, blue eyes, and a dimple in his cheek and chin.

"Dada, throw," he squeals.

I oblige because I'd give him anything. Up he goes, flying for only a second before he's back in my hands. And when I set him on his feet, he teeters and then plops to his butt, giggling as if it were the funniest thing in the world. It's enough to draw Carter away from his book as he studies his brother. The only differences between the two are the colors of their shirts and their personalities.

But with just a glance, they apparently decide to join forces, and in seconds they're using my stomach as a trampoline. I grunt when a knee digs into my kidney and then pause. I always sense Charlie;

she's everywhere I look and never far from my thoughts. But the energy simmering under my skin is too strong to ignore, and I turn my head in the direction of the trees to find her.

Charlie

THE LAZY DAYS OF summer are winding down, yet the sun remains high and hot in the sky. August in the mountains at Camp David is breathtaking, as are my boys—all three of them. Wrestling in the green grass, Colin throws Killian in the air. Two-feet high he flies, and my stomach falls even though he's already safe and squealing in Daddy's arms. Dizzy when set on his feet, Killian stumbles and plops to his diapered bum. I laugh as they do it again and again, all the while Carter sits to the side watching and contemplating, his favorite book held in his lap.

My twins may be as close to identical in looks as you can get, but their personalities are on opposite ends of the spectrum. Killian's sense of fearlessness and freedom is beautiful and scary at the same time. I have flashes of him sky-diving and hanging from cliffs when he's twenty. On the other hand, my sweet, studious Carter watches his brother and worries about him more than I do. He was the first to race to Killian's side after a daring climb onto the sofa left his brother with a bump on his head. Sometimes, like now, he deems the adventure worthy of a break from reading, and he dives into the fray.

Their giggling burns memories into my heart and brings tears to my eyes. I *love* them. I love this life so much, with all of its flaws and the obstacles within it. I don't regret one thing because it crafted me into this woman, this wife, and this mother, the person who has everything.

Colin turns, his eyes heating when he finds me. I smile and move away from the old maple that had been holding me up. He watches as

I get closer, and with each step he gets hungrier and hungrier. *Naptime is going to be fun, really, really fun.*

"I missed my boys," I say, and sit by his side, grass tickling my bare legs.

My bugs squeal *Mama* and rush into my waiting hug. As soon as they're settled in their favorite spot, curled up, one in each arm, I rock and hum a song I heard on the radio earlier. I press my nose first into Carter's hair and then Killian's, breathing in fresh air and my babies.

"We missed you, too." Colin rolls to his elbow. I meet him halfway as he stretches closer for a kiss, soft at first and then deeper, his tongue sweeping against mine. Baby hands join us, patting our cheeks, and he smiles against my mouth.

"Hmmm." I mourn his lips when he pulls away. "That was a perfect hello."

"Are the cottages ready for the Carter/McKenna invasion?" he asks.

It takes my mind a moment to skip past his fingers tracing the hem of my sundress along my thigh to the explosion of family coming to visit tomorrow. "We're set. Gram is going to love her view, mostly because Agent Winters is assigned to the perimeter of her cabin. I think she called Kyle to ask if he could make that happen."

Colin's grin is fleeting. His brow tugs down into three lines as he studies me. Bright blue eyes, shining from the sun, move over every bit of my face. It's not unusual. He's terrified.

"How are you feeling?" he asks.

My heart sinks. I want him to be as happy as he was when we learned about the boys, and a pang twinges in my chest because the next six months are going to be so hard on him.

"Great." Reaching over, I hold his chin up with my finger so he can see that I am. "No nausea—nothing. This pregnancy is completely different than with these guys." I squeeze them as I say it. "And the delivery will be, too."

He closes his eyes and swallows. I know he's remembering a day I barely connect with. One minute I was dancing, and in the next I woke up in the hospital minus bugs in my belly and with tubes everywhere.

"I don't want you to worry about me every minute of every day."

At the sound of my voice he looks at me, and then at the boys, who share a silent moment. This translates to twin telepathy and a plan to take over the world in two-point-five seconds. As if on cue, they struggle out of my arms and run like mad on their tiny little legs for the plastic coupe for two. That and their toddler push-cars can keep them busy for hours.

I use the momentary childless reprieve to push Colin's shoulder so he falls to his back, and then I straddle his waist. His knees come up behind me as his hands land on my thighs, sneaking under my dress. Relaxed in a white V-neck T-shirt and shorts, he's delicious, and it stirs the familiar pangs in all of my places. I squirm on him in hopes it will pull out his smile, but it's a growl instead as he adjusts me so I'm in the perfect spot to feel just how fun naptime is going to be.

It's hard to look at his heavy-lidded eyes and not get carried away and play, so I shimmy on him once more. He groans. "You and that ass are what got us back in this predicament, you know."

"The odds are in our favor; everything's going to be great," I say, running my hands up his hard chest, the cotton of his shirt hot under my fingers.

"Yeah?"

"Yeah. What does your gut tell you?"

Colin pauses a moment, his fingers sinking into the meat on my ass. And then he smiles. A beautiful, broad grin that stretches into a dimple, the same one I see in the faces of my bugs every day. "That our grandchildren will sit by our feet at the campfire, listening to you play the guitar, while our five children sing their favorite songs."

I choke on a laugh. "Five. You may be pushing your luck, Mr. President."

He sits up so fast I squeal like the kids, and smile into his mouth pressed against mine. "What does your heart tell you?"

I kiss him. With our boys peeling in baby giggles ten-feet away, with our next bug in my belly, and with so much to look forward to my heart explodes with joy, I kiss my Colin.

"That we're living our happily-ever-after," I murmur into his mouth. "Thank you for being my dream come true."

The End

Thank you for reading the McKenna Chronicles. I truly hope you've enjoyed Charlie and Colin's journey! Please consider telling your friends about it or leaving a short review. Word of mouth is an author's best friend and is much appreciated.

Xoxo *–EM*

Also by Elizabeth Miller:
The Midnight Series, McKenna Chronicles
Only Tonight, a McKenna Chronicles companion novella featuring Kyle Sommerton

Recommended reading order:
Midnight
Midnight Sky
Only Tonight
Midnight Sun

ABOUT ELIZABETH MILLER: She wears many hats. Some include wife, mother of two small boys, writer, reader, lover of gummy bears and Henry Cavill. She's a proud Indie author who adores a broken hero, a feisty heroine, and lots and lots of sexy times. In 2013 she decided to flex her writing muscles and began her debut novel: *Midnight*. Published in 2014, she continues writing sweet romantic, okay maybe a little bit erotic, suspenseful adult contemporary novels with characters you're destined to fall in love with. Connect with EM, she loves to chat with readers.

Follow my blog, Addictive Romance, for all things McKenna and news on upcoming projects: emillerauthordotcom.wordpress.com
Facebook: Elizabeth Miller Author
Twitter: @emillermidnight
Email: Emillerauthor@gmail.com

61869698R00153

Made in the USA
Charleston, SC
29 September 2016